W9-BBZ-375

Personal Assets

Personal Assets

EMMA HOLLY

Venus
provocative reading for you

BOOKSPAN

GARDEN CITY • NEW YORK

Published by Venus Book Club of BOOKSPAN
401 Franklin Avenue, Garden City, New York 11530

TO ALICE COUNTRYMAN:
forthright, loyal, friend to man and beast.

May your stories be as true as you are.

*Special thanks to Nita Abrams
and four very beautiful cities.*

Best Friends

THE SHOP SAT on the rue du Faubourg St.-Honoré, nestled—but in no sense leaning—between Givenchy and Hermés. Indeed, if anyone's coattails had passengers, they belonged to Meilleurs Amis. Ever since its opening, this boutique had inspired more *lèche-vitrines*, more window licking, than any of the houses on the venerable Paris street.

Emanating from the bowed Belle Epoque window was a golden glow, almost a scent. Spice and flowers, light sparkling on the Seine, warm bread and melting chocolate: all conveyed a portion of its charm but not the whole. One never knew what one would find behind that curving glass. The perfect velvet gown? The perfect diamond collar? The perfect antique comb and mirror with which to dress one's hair?

Sophie Clouet, who had founded Meilleurs Amis, was not designer but collector. Those with a nose for such things said her daughter Evangeline's taste was even more exquisite. Alas, the latest Clouet daughter expressed little passion for the family trade. Were it not for the widower, the oh-so-delectable Philip Carmichael, the shops might have gone to strangers. But he appeared to have the reins in hand. Brit though he was, he had brought something new to the business: true friendliness.

Now visitors did not merely look; they entered. Most couldn't afford the smallest beaded bag, and those who could didn't need it. But Meilleurs Amis wasn't about need, it was about want. How could one resist when the salesgirls smiled so prettily, when they ignored the scuffs on one's shoes and the less-than-fortunate cut of one's hair? Such forgiveness of one's flaws was unprecedented in the world of haute couture. And the shop itself! Why, it soothed a woman just to step inside. One gazed at the molded ceiling. One marveled at the give of the Persian carpet. One ran one's hand along the rainbow of lingerie that lined the back of every Best Friends boutique.

Most of all, though, when inside the elegant jewel box of a shop, one remembered the stories one had heard. Stories of Sophie's royal Russian affair. Stories of the famous dancer who fucked his Giselle in the dressing room, causing her to scream so loudly with pleasure the clerks from Givenchy came running into the street. And then there were Evangeline's antics: wild parties, wilder lovers, culminating in her marriage to a struggling designer twenty years her junior. What Philip would do now that she was gone—and so dramatically!—no one knew.

Whatever his plans, the shop remained an aphrodisiac. The label alone could make one feel beautiful. Meilleurs Amis, it whispered: Paris, London, Rome, New York, with the magical words bound up in a ribbon of gold. There were other Best Friends, of course. In Moscow, in New Orleans, in Tokyo, in San Francisco. There was even talk of opening a Best Friends in Beijing. These cities did not matter. Paris, London, Rome, New York. That mantra alone conveyed the store's cachet. Style. Self-indulgence. Sensuality. Power.

What self-respecting female could resist?

Paris

One

ＢＥ́ＡＴＲＩＸ ＣＬＯＵＥＴ ＳＴＯＰＰＥＤ at the door to her mother's office, a knot of pain compressing her chest. The man who sat behind the tulipwood desk was almost too lovely to bear. He was more beautiful than Rodin's *Kiss.* More beautiful than the Paris spring that flowered, lush but decorous, down the Champs-Elysées. More beautiful even than the rail-thin models he used to dress. His beauty did not depend on makeup or lighting or good photographers. Like fairy dust, it shone from his pale English skin, from his tamed gold hair, from his hands, from his hips, from his kind gray eyes. Philip Carmichael was beautiful inside as well as out. His smile lit up a room. His generosity could stun.

And she hated him with all her heart.

She could not, however, turn away. What a difference one man's presence made! Six months ago this room had been cold and sleek, an audience chamber for a queen whose hive filled two floors of a skyscraper in La Défense. Unlike the rest of Paris, La Défense was no bastion of cozy, antiquated charm. No, this Manhattan by the Seine was new and steely and tall, the perfect *mise en scène* her mother had claimed, from which to launch into the twenty-first century. The marble floor stretched like ice to the modern desk. The ceiling, an ominous black mirror, intimidated with its height. The furniture was minimalist, metal and wood and glass, all painfully stylish. Even the view, which took in the Eiffel Tower, the Arc de Triomphe, and the soft white domes of Sacré-Coeur, failed to warm. The windows that stretched from floor to ceiling inspired a sense of awe more precarious than pleasant.

None of these things had changed, and yet, with Philip at the helm, the very scent of the room welcomed visitors inside. Clutter had overtaken the conference table: fashion sketches, a haphazard spill of apples, a single tattered running shoe. A huge bouquet of tulips, yellow and red, blocked the vertiginous sweep of glass.

And then there was Philip himself, who could never be frightening, not even in his solemn black suit with his beautiful hair brushed so severely into a tail behind his neck. He'd worn his hair loose once, with jeans and flowing shirts. He'd tossed it when he laughed. In those days, he'd been young and irresponsible. And poor, of course. An irrepressible cocksman who still believed in his dreams. Sleeping his way to the top had been the last thing on his mind.

Now he paged through a portfolio of designs for a charity event, none of which he'd drawn. His lips, sculpted and strong, pursed with concentration. His hands were graceful, their careful manicure disguising the fact that he bit his nails. Poor Philip. He'd been a good designer, not brilliant but sensitive. His clothes had been wearable and flattering. He'd have done well if he hadn't set his heart on conquering the rarified world of haute couture. His first and only show had tanked. *Elle* had called it "pedestrian"; *Women's Wear Daily* "a bore." And those were the print reviews. The society ladies' claws were even sharper.

But pity for Philip was dangerous. Pity threatened the wall Béatrix had wrestled, stone by stone, around her heart. She cleared her throat and braced to meet his splendid eyes. He looked up.

"Hullo, Bea," he said, cocking his head in that hopeful way he had, his smile unsure, his eyes promising to tolerate whatever outrage she was sure to unleash.

"*Allô*, Phil," she responded, knowing the nickname annoyed him.

He winced, just a little, then gestured to a black leather chair. Béatrix lowered herself into its gentle Scandinavian hold. An English tea occupied the corner of Philip's desk. Always the gentleman, he poured her a cup of Darjeeling: her favorite, not his. She accepted a scone, still warm from the corporate kitchen, slathered it with jam and settled back.

She wore a new earth brown suit. The boxy jacket and leggings offered more in the way of comfort than fashion, but Bea was a comfortable kind of gal. She crossed her legs, though she knew her sturdy calves would catch no one's eye, least of all this man's. Curly black hair, freckles, and a figure best described as generous could not impress a man who'd seen the cream of the catwalks in their skivvies. Nor could she claim any particular style. She was presentable, that was all, and she wouldn't be that if she hadn't grown up in Paris. Béatrix Clouet had no illusions about her looks. It was, she thought, one of her few good traits.

"So," she said, plate balanced on her knee. "Why did you call me here? Did someone spot me on the town with my shirt untucked?"

"Bea." His tone was fond and scolding, the ideal *beau-père,* the only problem being that this *beau-père* was barely five years older than his stepdaughter. He spread his fingers over the surface of the desk, their length sending a rebellious sluice of heat between her legs. "You know I've given up on telling you how to dress. I must say, though, that shade of brown you're wearing isn't quite—"

"Phil."

He smiled at her warning, his lips satin smooth and faintly rosy. One long dimple sprang to life in his left cheek. Béatrix curled her nails into her palms. Let me out of here, she thought, before I melt in my chair. This crush had been bad enough when she was fifteen. Now it was intolerable.

Suddenly he frowned. "Bea. Have you lost weight?"

To her disgust, a blush stung her cheeks. "I've been riding my bicycle to work."

"All the way from Montmartre! On the motorways! Are you insane?"

"No." She set her teacup firmly on the desk. "Last time I checked I was twenty-three, an adult, and perfectly capable of deciding how to get from one place to another."

"But, Bea, your mother would want me to keep an eye on you."

"Puh-leeze," she said, stealing the intonation from her best American friend. "Mother didn't give a damn if I screwed up. In fact, she welcomed it."

"What a terrible thing to say. And completely untrue."

"Oh, really? You know what the shop girls called her? The queen of a thousand pinpricks." Actually, they'd left the "pin" out of it, but she wasn't quite rude enough to say so. "She loved when people made mistakes because it gave her a chance to make them feel small."

"Your mother was a visionary."

His defense woke a tide of anger she didn't try to stem. She rose from her chair, parked herself on the corner of his desk, and poked his too-sober navy shirt. "My mother was an occasional visionary. The rest of the time she was an opinionated bitch. People didn't listen to her because she was right; they listened to her because she was Evangeline Clouet, a beautiful, rich woman who, by sheer force of will, managed to consolidate *grand-mère*'s glittering little empire. I know it's hard for you to admit how selfish she could be, how snobbish and how shallow. Admitting that would make you seem like the boy toy everyone said you were. But it's time you faced the truth. Mother married you for your pretty face and your rock-hard, twenty-year-old cock. She married you to make her rivals jealous. The fact that you had a brain in your head was completely beside the point."

Two spots of color stained Philip's chalky face.

"I hadn't realized," he said stiffly, "that your opinion of me was quite so low."

"Don't be an idiot. My opinion of you was ten times higher than *maman's*."

Philip gripped the edge of his desk as if he meant to crush the wood. "By God, I'd hate to hear what you'd say if that weren't the case!"

She didn't know what came over her then: eight years of hiding her feelings, perhaps, eight years of his ludicrous paternal kindness, eight years of smelling him, eight years of pasting his face on every one of her doltish lovers. Whatever the reason, she'd reached her breaking point. She grabbed his lapels, pulled him forward in his chair, and plastered her mouth across his own.

He made a startled sound, a silly English splutter. His lips were as smooth as she'd imagined. She softened her hold and licked their enticing curves. The sound he made then was no less startled, but not silly in the least. No, it was low and throaty. Her neck prickled with awareness. He was aroused. He liked this. He tilted his head. His mouth parted. With both astonishment and delight, she felt his tongue, wet and warm, pressing for access.

His arms slid around her, under her jacket. Béatrix couldn't hold her moan inside. He answered with a moan of his own. His fingers speared her curls. He was dragging his nails along her scalp and the kiss had deepened, slow but hard. He tasted of tea and jam, but it was her he wanted to eat. His tongue swept her molars, tickled her palate. Then it sucked, sweet, fluttering tugs that told her he'd know how to kiss her just as effectively somewhere else.

A wave of fever swept her skin. Her head pounded in time to her pussy. She had to touch him, had to hold him.

She gripped his shoulders. She moved her legs and caught his narrow hips between her thighs. His body stiffened, then rolled forward. He pushed her back on the desk, his groin meeting hers and digging in.

His trousers could not hide his arousal. His cock was thick, as thick as her mother had always bragged. A real *saucisson,* with balls like a pair of plums. His erection lurched as he ground it over her mons. It felt outrageously good. Béatrix dragged her nails down his back and clamped his buttocks hard.

"Good Lord," he said, wrenching free for a gulp of air. He stared at her, eyes shining, searching.

Now he'll stop, she thought. Now he'll tell me I've lost my mind.

But he didn't. He swallowed, cheeks flaming like a young boy's. His head lowered. Their breath rushed together, and he kissed her again, even harder than before. It was a starving kiss. It shifted angles, this way, that way, full of noise and juice. His teeth bruised her lips. His back clenched under her hold. He'd snaked one hand beneath her shirt to reach bare skin. Now he shifted it to her front, pushing his palm up her heaving ribs. Her bra gave way. He cupped the fullness of her breast, pinched her nipple, and shoved his tongue toward her throat.

Pleasure spangled outward from his touch. He wanted her. He was panting for her. Béatrix lost the last of her control. She wrenched his shirt from his trousers. She fumbled with his belt. It clanked and fought her until it fell free. Then *his* hand yanked down his zipper and *his* hand pushed hers inside. They struggled through fine Egyptian cotton, through silk, and then she grasped him, his beautiful, meaty cock. The shock of his heat went through her like lightning. He cried out, short and sharp, and swelled against her palm.

Her laugh seemed to belong to another woman. It gurgled from her throat, rich with triumph. He squeezed her hand, wordlessly encouraging her caress. She did not resist. She wanted to touch him, wanted to feel the silken skin move up and down, the crisp curls at the base, the plump ridge of the head. But he grew impatient with her exploration. He renewed his grip, directing her to a firmer stroke. Closer he forced her hand, and tighter, until she thought she must be hurting him. Down he pushed, until her fist nudged his balls. His glans brushed hot against her inner arm. He dripped with lust. She pulled upward, rubbed the wet curve with the heel of her palm. His kiss turned ragged. He was murmuring against her mouth. She took a moment to decipher the words.

"Fuck me," he was saying. "Fuck me, Bea. Fuck me."

She clutched his cock so hard he gasped.

He pulled back, lips red and slack. His pupils seemed to have swallowed his eyes. Then they cleared. He stared at her. Her shirt was up around her armpits, her bra askew, her breasts bare. His gaze locked on her sharpened nipples.

"Bloody hell," he swore, unable to look away.

And then they both heard it: the clack of heels approaching swiftly down the hall. The door was open. Béatrix had not closed it.

"Down," he hissed. With far more possession than she could claim, he shoved her beneath his desk. Fortunately, the space was large because Béatrix was no wood sprite. She scrambled back as far as she could go. An instant later Philip sat, wheeling his chair into the kneehole to hide his disheveled clothes. He didn't have time to zip before his secretary reached the door.

"Mr. Carmichael?" she said. "I've brought Mr. Renard for his four o'clock."

Philip cleared his throat. "Uh, yes. Hullo, Alain."

Alain, whom Béatrix knew to be the company accountant, walked briskly across the polished floor. She heard him take the selfsame chair she'd occupied minutes earlier. Paper slid across the wood above her head. "I've brought the figures from the New York store. I thought you'd want to go over them together." Alain paused. "Are you all right, Philip? You look flushed."

Béatrix shook with silent amusement. Philip had to feel it because his knees were wedged to either side of her body. He squeezed them in warning. "Uh, I was doing sit-ups. Too much time behind a desk, you know. I'm getting soft."

"That'll be the day," said Alain.

Béatrix was forced to agree. Her eyes had adjusted to the shadows and she had the most graphic evidence possible of Philip's continuing rock-hard state. She bit his thigh to control her urge to laugh. Philip's hand flashed under the desk and cuffed her ear.

"Why don't you read the report to me," he said. "I'll save my questions until you're done."

Béatrix wasn't as familiar with the office staff as Philip, but she'd heard her mother complain many times about Alain's long-winded ways. Who knew how long the accountant would take? And in the meantime, Philip was trapped, his trousers conveniently open, his cock eager to finish what Alain had interrupted. The temptation was too great to resist.

Licking her lips, she trailed her fingers up the back of his calves. Philip shivered. He must have guessed what was coming. His hand, which he'd left resting on his thigh, pinched her ear. Ignoring the little pain, she turned her head and caught his thumb inside her mouth. She sucked it gently, both promise and threat. This is how I'll suck you, she thought. This is how I'll push you to the edge.

His thighs tightened, catching the side of her breasts. "Mm-hm," he said to some comment Alain had made. The tension in his voice was clear.

He'd feel more than tension soon. Releasing his thumb, she leaned closer to his crotch. His cock was quivering with excitement. It, at least, suffered no qualms. The wrinkled foreskin was fully retracted, the head swollen to bursting. The shaft angled so high it nearly strafed the buttons of his shirt. His balls lay atop the waist of his white silk boxers, held up by the sheathed elastic. How utterly masculine he was, how strong and straight! Lost in admiration, she breathed on him, a warm, slow exhalation that washed his throbbing rod. That soft stimulation was enough to excite him. His hips pushed helplessly forward.

Permission granted, she thought, and licked the curve of his scrotum. He squirmed, a sigh catching in his throat. He swallowed it quickly, but she had heard it, as clearly as she heard the restless rustle of his clothes. She licked him again, and again. His buttocks tightened with every stroke. She kept them light, teasing. His hand snuck inward, lifting his sack for a fuller exploration. When even that failed to please, he nudged her closer, his thumb on her jaw, his fingers on his balls, urging the two together until she'd sucked his testes into her mouth, enveloping first one side, then the other. He seemed to like this. His thighs relaxed, and he petted her cheek. Béatrix could almost hear his spine unkinking in his chair.

But he was a fool if he thought she'd let him off so easy. She began to lap him again, like a cat, only rising this time, up his underridge, over his glans. His crown was slick with pre-come and melting smooth. When she teased his little slit, he jerked as if she'd slid a live wire under his skin. His hand moved from her cheek to her curls. He gripped her hair. She thought he would pull her back, but apparently he could not bring himself to do it. He held her immobile instead, while her tongue crossed the inch between them, skating over his slippery dome, around and around, soothing him with the flat, tormenting him with the tip.

She didn't grip his root the way she could have. She wanted to prove this was all it took to slay him. Sure enough, lick by lick his resistance weakened. His grip faltered and fell away. Béatrix took her chance. In one long swoop, she swallowed him whole. Oh, he was rich and hard. Her sex pulsed with the pleasure that filled her mouth. His skin, his heat, his salt-rich flow of need. She sucked him deep, rising until her head touched the bottom of the desk, sinking until her chin bumped his balls. A girl like her, not pretty, not thin, had to have a skill. No doubt about it, this was hers. No one gave better head than she did because she genuinely loved it, loved it better than fucking, most times. This was her personal gift. Philip would fall to it like the rest.

In the distance, she heard Alain droning on and imagined how stiff her victim's face must be, how his jaw would clench like his fists were clenching, like his thighs and his adorable buttocks. Philip coughed and it seemed a groan. Remembering how forcefully he'd wanted her to rub his shaft, she tightened her lips and intensified her pull.

"No," he hissed, his chin tilted down.

The accountant asked some question, obviously confused, but she would not stop what she was doing. She could not. She wanted him to come. She wanted him in her power. In front of Alain. In front of the world. She wrapped one hand around his balls, her longest finger reaching to massage the swollen ridge of his perineum. The pressure must have felt too good for comfort. Philip gripped her hair and pulled, but he did not have the leverage to pull quickly enough. When she reached his glans, her tongue caught the sweet spot under its neck. She rubbed it hard, a quick, repeated strafe. That was the switch she'd sought. His penis leapt. His balls tightened, and suddenly he was pushing her down as urgently as he'd pulled her back. Now, she thought. Now. She heard him curse under his breath, felt his hips jerk upward. She sucked, pulled, squeezed his updrawn balls. His shaft swelled, impossibly it seemed, and then he came, a strong gush, salty-sweet and hot.

Béatrix had never gotten such pleasure from giving pleasure. Every shudder was a joy, every burst of seed a paean to her skill. She could not hold it all. He came until he spilled from her mouth. He came with rigid thighs and clawlike hand. He came until sweat rolled down his belly, until his breath could no longer be held.

Something thunked the desk above her head. His elbow, she thought. Alain said something, alarmed.

"Sorry," Philip gasped, still pulsing against her tongue. "It's this damn . . . this damned migraine. We'll . . . have to finish this later."

The accountant must have left. She didn't hear him go, only Philip's lengthy groan as he collapsed back in his chair. His hands settled in her hair. Weakly, he pulled her closer, milking the last soft twitches of orgasm between her clasping cheeks. Then he really was finished. Limp. Drained. His cock slipped from her mouth to lay against his clothes. Her heart settled into a dull, rhythmic thud. The moment of insanity was over. Everything was over.

He seemed to think so, too. He lifted her head and wheeled his chair backward.

"Bea," he said. "Come out from there."

His voice was its kindest, its most compassionate. Her spirit sank at the sound. Her *beau-père* was back in all his stuffy glory. She tugged her clothes into place and crawled free.

PHILIP SHOVED HIS cock away and set his clothes to rights. Considering what had happened, it seemed silly to turn his back. All the same, he was excessively aware of the cool weight of his stepdaughter's eyes.

He could not think what had come over him. Well, actually, he could, but he didn't want to. There had been a time in his life, before he married Eve, when he couldn't keep his trousers zipped to save his soul. He'd been fair game for every model he met, every seamstress, every half-pretty female with a twinkle in her eye. Marrying Eve had changed that, thank God. She'd taken all he had and more. It was, however, six months since her death, six months since he'd shared his bed with anyone. Nonetheless, to come that close to shagging his own step-daughter was beyond anything he could condone.

A shudder racked him as he remembered the feel of her mouth. Lord, she'd been warm. Just wet enough. Just strong enough. He'd felt his skull tingle every time she sucked. In fact, it tingled now at the memory. He hadn't been able to resist shoving deeper, even when he knew he shouldn't. Instinct had taken over, sheer animal lust. He couldn't remember the last time he'd come like that. Maybe never. Alain's presence across the desk from him, the unknowing witness to his bliss, had made him want the climax all the more. He and Eve hadn't gone in for the kinky stuff; straight fucking and lots of it had been their style, but perhaps now . . .

No, no, no. He dug the heels of his hands into his eyes. He mustn't think that way. This had been an aberration, a temporary loss of sanity. It would never happen again.

Which didn't prevent him from regretting the things he hadn't done when he'd had the chance. Bea had the most amazing skin. He'd always thought so. Like cream with a sprinkling of cinnamon. Soft as a baby's bum. And her breasts . . . Whatever Bea might think of them—not much, he gathered—they were admirably Juno-esque. It killed him to think he'd barely touched them. Disgusted with this train of thought, he moaned and shook his head.

"Pull yourself together," Bea ordered, forcing his eyes to her face. She wore her customary mask, half mocking superiority, half defensive teen.

That look had tugged at him the first time he met her. She needs a friend, he'd thought from the lofty wisdom of his twenty years. Now and then she'd let him be one. More often, though, his overtures had been met with rebuffs. Whatever Bea lacked in confidence, she more than made up for in biting wit.

"This is not going to happen again," he said as firmly as he could with his cock gone heavy from his thoughts.

"I didn't expect it would." Her hips rested against the edge of his desk. She folded her arms beneath her breasts. Beneath her shirt, their tips remained hard, wrinkled like currants. Philip's groin prickled. He looked at his shoes.

"I had something I meant to discuss with you," he said.

"You mean, before you were distracted by my amazing oral prowess?"

"Bea." He sighed. "I'm sorry about that. I—"

"Don't." She lifted one hand, the word vibrating with anger, her eyes sparkling with hurt. The anger he was used to. The hurt surprised him: not its existence, but the fact that she let it show. Jaw tense, she lowered her hand. "Don't apologize. Let's just say I saw one last chance to take a stab at Mother's memory."

He nodded stiffly. No doubt this was precisely why she'd jumped him. She and Eve had always been at sixes and sevens. Too much alike, and too little. Despite this, her dismissive tone made his throat tighten with sorrow.

Don't be a clod, he told himself. She hurt your pride is all. Good Lord, she could hurt anyone's.

"So," she said, quicker to recover than he. "What did you want to discuss?"

But he couldn't face that now. He needed his wits about him or in minutes they'd be rowing.

"Later," he said. "Come home for dinner tonight. I'll make bangers and mash and we'll knock back a bottle of Pouilly-Fumé."

"And pretend nothing happened."

"And pretend nothing happened," he agreed, but he couldn't quite leave it at that.

He cupped her face and swept her broad Irish cheekbone with his thumb. Those bones were her father's. A rolling stone, according to Eve, who'd rolled on before Bea had been more than a sneaking suspicion. From her mother, Bea took only her spirit and her name. Eve had been slim and fair. Bea's eyes were as brown as rain-soaked turf, her mouth as broad as a clown's. Hers was a wonderful face, with its creamy skin and freckles and its brows arched in perpetual surprise. A face formed for sunshine and laughter. Philip wished he knew how to give her those things. She might not believe it, but he loved her very much.

"Oh, don't get maudlin," she snapped, reading the sentiment in his gaze. "Yours isn't the first cock I've conquered, and it certainly won't be the last."

"On that score, I have no doubt," he said. He'd meant only to bolster her self-esteem, but his cheeks fired with memory. She'd been good, outrageously good.

Careful, he thought, with an added mental lash for his twitching cock. This was stickier ground than a man in his position could afford to tread.

Two

ÉATRIX EMERGED FROM the gleaming office tower. The day was lovely, with scarcely a haze to mar the robin's egg blue of the sky. The Seine flowed placidly beneath the arches of the Pont de Neuilly bridge, and on its current rode a *bateau-mouche,* both decks crammed with sightseers, like a wide-hipped matron out for a stately stroll.

She fought an urge to run to the next boarding point. Much as she would have liked to play hooky, especially in view of the traffic she saw crawling toward L'Étoile, she had responsibilities. Her mother had left her a sizable inheritance, and she felt obliged to earn it. Philip put a good face on assuming chairmanship of Meilleurs Amis, but she knew he had a fight on his hands. Everyone—bankers, customers, merchants—wanted to see if Evangeline's stud-muffin had what it took to run the Clouet shops. It didn't matter that he'd been handling more responsibility all along. Eve was gone. Her influence couldn't save him if he put his foot wrong now.

As it happened, Philip was savvier than anyone gave him credit for, and much harder working. He could not, however, do everything. Which was why Béatrix planned to spend the afternoon at the St-Honoré boutique. Of all their far-flung employees, those in Paris were the slowest to adjust to the new regime. They seemed to feel that treating customers with disdain was their sacred duty as Frenchwomen. Béatrix wasn't positive she could whip them into the desired kinder, gentler shape, but the task was beyond Philip. Discipline was not his forte.

With a grimace of determination, she retrieved her bike, squeezed the safety helmet over her curls, and pre-pared to do battle with Paris motorists.

Battle it was, though the distance to the shop was small. After having her thighs brushed twice by heedless cars, she popped between the flowering chestnut trees and onto the sidewalk. There she encountered the inevitable dirty look when the sprawl of café tables forced her into a pedes-trian's path. She made her excuses, but inside she was un-repentant. If motor scooters could treat the sidewalk like an extra lane, why not she? A collision with her pretty blue ten-speed was unlikely to prove fatal.

Humor restored by her triumph over traffic, Béatrix ar-rived at Meilleurs Amis in time to see an exquisitely coifed poodle beginning to squat beside the door. With a hauteur that would have done her mother proud, she snapped her fingers at the chicly dressed woman who was walking it.

"*Non, non, madame.* Not unless you have a bucket and a scrub brush."

The woman sniffed, but she did hustle her little poop factory away.

Better, Béatrix thought, inhaling the mercifully untainted air. She tucked her helmet under her arm and examined the display window. A Second Empire vanity sat in the carpeted space, its black lacquer surface inlaid with mother of pearl. Scattered on top and reflected in the gilded mirror were perfume bottles, newly minted, but clearly objet d'art. A hand-painted scarf, Japanese, draped the back of a spindly chair as if the owner had stepped away in the middle of her toilette. The lighting was perfect, the arrangement inviting, and, of course, each item was on sale inside. None of this surprised Béatrix. Presentation had never been this shop's problem.

But business flew from her head the instant she stepped inside. A woman was leaning like a lazy whippet against the old-fashioned glass of the glove counter. Her chestnut hair spilled past her shoulders in a rippling satin fall. She wore two snug ribbed T-shirts, one white, one scarlet, and a pair of low-riding, well-worn jeans. A rip in the denim bared the muscle of her thigh, and tiny construction boots, brown and scuffed, wrapped her narrow feet. The thick white socks that peeped above their tops were the only undergarment in sight. Despite this low-budget approach to fashion, she looked every bit as good as the silk-draped *vendeuse* behind the counter.

When she caught sight of Béatrix, she tipped down a pair of small black-rimmed glasses.

"Hey, buddy," she said, as if it hadn't been a year since they'd seen each other. "How's it hangin'?"

Béatrix laughed and pulled her into a hug, not caring the least about the shop girls' stares. Her friend was an inch shorter, a good bit thinner, but nearly as strong as she was. When they'd squeezed each other breathless, she pushed back to arm's length. "Lela! What are you doing here?"

"The usual. Working. Playing. Mooching off my latest swain. I'm writing a travel thing for American *Vogue*. And he's on a perfume hunt for his boss."

"A perfume hunt?"

"Long story. I'll tell you over pâté and baguettes."

"But how did you know I'd be here?"

"I didn't. I'm gift hunting." She spread a lilac bra-and-panty set across the glove counter. The lacework was exquisite. "Is this still your size?"

"Lela! You can't buy that for me. It's too expensive."

"Nonsense," she demurred. "I'm planning to mooch off you, too." She twitched Béatrix's jacket aside and squinted at her figure. "I don't know, Bea, you're looking pretty buff. I think I'm gonna have to go smaller."

Béatrix blushed, but her laugh was all pleasure. "I'm still a terrible frump compared to you."

"Nah, you wear your frumpitude with élan. In Kansas you'd be a nonpareil."

"But then I'd be in Kansas."

"True," Lela admitted with her trademark crooked grin. "Guess you'll have to muddle on here."

They beamed at each other, pleased they hadn't lost the rhythm of their wit. At college no one had been able to keep up with them. People had called them the quip sisters, even people they didn't know. They'd been mildly famous on the campus at Columbia, a first for Béatrix, who tended to fade into the background wherever she went. But Lela had called to the courage in her. Amazingly, the other woman had set out to make a friend of her. "The gorgeous French girl," she'd called her, as kind as she was nearsighted. When Béatrix was with Lela, she almost believed she was gorgeous. Together, they'd been prankish and bright, wild women with brains, the despair and delight of their professors. Now, when Béatrix felt lonely, those memories reminded her she had the best friend in the world.

"Give me fifteen minutes," she said. "I want to discuss a few things with the manager. Then we'll grab a taxi and you can see my new apartment."

"Will do," said Lela in her breezy American way.

Béatrix pressed a kiss to her cheek. Lela was here! *Beau-père* be damned. The day was looking up.

FOR THE LAST six months, Béatrix had lived in Montmartre, a *quartier* north of central Paris. Up till then she'd shared the spacious family apartment on the avenue Foch. That changed when Philip's grief over the loss of his wife grew too painful to watch. Her own feelings about her mother, not to mention the circumstances of her death, were too conflicted to commiserate with his.

So she had moved to the avenue Junot. For the first time in her life she lived completely on her own. No roommate, no cook, no maid. She'd expected to hate it. Instead, she blossomed like a flower that finally had room to breathe. The solitude, the quiet, the freedom to answer to no one but herself acted as a tonic to her spirits.

The six large rooms topped a cream-colored house near

the Moulin de la Galette, a seventeenth-century windmill like the one that inspired the Moulin Rouge. On one side, her rooms overlooked the Square Suzanne-Buisson. On the other, Sacré-Coeur, the Basilica of the Sacred Heart, dominated the view like a cross between a wedding cake and a temple of Islam. From these images, she chose the colors of her home: bone white, tree green, and the soft silver-blue of the sky. Her walls were dusky pink, trimmed with white and hung with reproductions of her favorite Impressionists.

Heart thumping with anticipation, she led her friend up the narrow stairs to the fifth floor. For as long as Béatrix had known her, Lela had been on her own. With a friend so fearless, living with her mother had been embarrassing, even if she did have her own suite of rooms. But now Béatrix, too, was independent.

She opened the door with a flourish.

"Ooh," said Lela. "Look at that view!"

Pleased, Béatrix ushered her through the sitting and dining rooms, through the restful kitchen and the amiable guest room. Her bedroom's scheme of yellow and pink inspired a gratifying sigh. Then they climbed the open spiral stairs to her studio. Here the outer door gave way to the rooftop garden. Lela barely glanced at the wild roses. Her attention was caught by the score of canvases stacked against the wall. She pulled her glasses from the top of her head. Béatrix had never seen them before this visit. The dark frames gave her a strange, nerdy glamour. Her retroussé nose seemed to tilt more fetchingly under their weight. Her cheeks seemed leaner, her mouth fuller, her lashes and brows more black. Leave it to Lela, Béatrix thought, to make a pair of glasses an enhancement to her allure.

"Well," Lela said, lifting the nearest painting and turning it toward the light. "I can see you've been busy. But why are these beautiful pictures languishing in your studio? They ought to be in a shop somewhere. They ought to be selling."

Béatrix squirmed in her shoes. "I did have a show."

"Did you?" Lela picked up a second painting, a glowing, sunny portrait of Sacré-Coeur.

"Yes, a little one. On the Left Bank." She pressed her thumbnail between her bottom teeth. "A few critics came. Because I'm a Clouet."

"And . . . ?" Lela was fighting laughter. Béatrix could tell she wasn't going to be sympathetic.

"They said my work was 'pretty.' And 'romantic.' "

"I take it that's supposed to be an insult. But it is pretty and romantic. It's also very good. Look at the light in this picture, Bea. Look at the color. The paint is singing off the canvas. If the tourists could see this, they'd snap it up in a New York minute."

"Tourists." Béatrix made it a dirty word. Lela laughed and punched her shoulder.

"You little snob. You paint what you like. Why shouldn't you sell to people who like what you paint?"

"Lela, they called me a Wyeth wanna-be."

"I like Andrew Wyeth. He did that 'Christine' picture, right?"

"Yes, 'Christina's World.' But—"

"No buts. You're always griping about how Philip took one slap in the face and gave up. Do you want to be like him? Or do you want to say, 'Screw the critics. I'll let the people tell me what they want.' "

"Screw the critics," Béatrix mumbled, and retrieved her

thumbnail from her teeth. She smiled at her friend. "How could I have forgotten how good you are for me?"

"I don't know." Lela's grin tilted her elfin face. "Maybe it's been too long since you called me."

THEY MADE A meal of stale bread, fresh pâté, and brie so gooey it stuck to the roof of their mouths. They washed it down with a sweet Sauterne, growing progressively mellow as the level in the bottle sank. They sat at the chef's island in her kitchen, herbs dangling over their heads, sun slanting gold and warm through the single narrow window. The walls were tiled in sea foam and all the fixtures, even the cabinets, were fronted in silvery, molded zinc, like an old-fashioned café. The effect was a room slightly out of step with time. Lost in her thoughts, Lela swirled her wine around the bottom of her oil-smeared glass. Her glasses sat on top of her head again, glinting in the buttery light.

"I'd buy that one of the girl leaning out the window," she said. "It's worth five hundred at least, but I'd take it for two fifty."

Béatrix knew she couldn't afford either. "You'll take it for nothing," she said, "or you won't take it at all."

Lela's smile was rakish. "You really feel guilty that your mother left you rolling in it."

"Considering that I hated her, yes."

"Come on." Lela sagged onto her forearms, her breasts swelling, brown and round, into the layered scoop of her T-shirts. Her voice, always throaty, slurred slightly with the wine. "You didn't hate her. She was your mother. Maybe you didn't get along, but—"

"Trust me," Béatrix enunciated. "What I felt was more than 'not getting along.' Evangeline Clouet was not a good woman. She was shallow and selfish. Never thought of anyone but herself. She terrorized everyone who worked for her, badmouthed her friends behind their backs, and let the world believe a hardworking English boy—who adored her to pieces, mind you—was little better than a gigolo."

"Be fair. How could your mother control what people thought?"

"If she'd wanted to, she could have changed their opinion. But she didn't want the world to respect her husband. She never wanted anyone to get respect but her."

Lela shifted on her stool. "I don't know. The woman I met didn't seem that neurotic."

"She wanted you to like her," Béatrix said, her ribs tightening around her lungs. "She hoped I'd be hurt if she treated you better than she treated me. And don't shake your head like that. You met her twice. I lived with her. I knew what she was like." Her voice had risen: too high, too sharp. She shouldn't have let herself be drawn into debating this. Lela had never understood her enmity for her mother, perhaps because she'd grown up in a series of foster homes. Any mother seemed better than none at all. And maybe no one could understand Evangeline the way Béatrix did. But Béatrix didn't want to fight, not with Lela, not when their visits were so few and far between. Lela was her best friend, her only close friend. Béatrix could not afford to lose her.

Lela seemed to sense her misery. Her tone grew softer. "Okay. Maybe I'm romanticizing. Still, I saw her fuss over you when you were together. She could be picky and bossy, but she sure didn't act like she hated you."

"I don't know that she did hate me. I only know that I hated her."

Lela drew her glasses from her head and swung them back and forth on the tip of her finger. "At least you had Phil."

"Yes." Béatrix poured the last of the wine into their glasses. "Philip always tried to be kind."

A silence fell. Lela knew about her crush, though they rarely discussed it. Béatrix found the whole situation too humiliating. I ought to be over this by now, she thought, for the ten millionth time. She blushed to remember what she'd done beneath his desk. An ocean of wine could not erase the taste, the feel of his pulsing cock against her tongue. She didn't know how she was going to face him.

Fortunately, Lela's thoughts had taken a different turn. She folded her glasses. "I'm sorry I missed the funeral. Even if you did hate her."

"It's just as well. The press turned it into a circus."

"That was kind of strange, that guy stalking her. You don't expect to see that kind of crime outside America. At least I don't."

A weight settled on Béatrix's shoulders, dark and sad. "I knew him."

"Who? The stalker?"

"Yes." She stared into the past, seeing Julien's dusty *atelier*, his long hands spattered with clay, his eyes glittering with passions no one else could share. "He was a talented sculptor. He had some sort of bipolar disorder, I think. Said he couldn't work when he took his medication. When Mother broke off their relationship—"

"Wait a second." Lela's eyes were huge. "Your mother was cheating on Phil? Phil the Thrill?"

"Yes. Julien fell apart when she broke it off, but she led him on. Twice I saw her do it. She'd call the *gendarme* one day and Julien the next, crying about how sorry she was it had to end that way. The police begged her to stop contacting him." She shrugged with remembered helplessness. She'd begged Eve herself. *Please, maman,* she'd said. *You have to give him a chance to get over this. He's too fragile for your games.* "I think she wanted to push him over the edge. She just didn't expect him to drag her with him."

"But why?"

"Because that was the ultimate ego boost, to have a brilliant young man kill himself over her."

"That's—"

"Crazy? Yes. I know. But maybe it runs in the family. Rumor has it *grand-mère* collaborated with the Nazis."

Now Lela really was shocked. She pushed the wine bottle aside, donned her glasses, and peered into Béatrix's face. "I thought that was just a story."

"I'm not so sure. I found an SS insignia in her jewelry box once, next to the diamond brooch she got from the Russian count."

"Yeesh. Maybe it is better not to know your roots. But at least *you're* not crazy."

Béatrix hung her head. "Sometimes I feel crazy."

"You mean because of Phil?"

Béatrix shrugged one shoulder toward her ear.

As warm as she was pretty, Lela needed no more prodding to be kind. She took Bea's hand and kissed it. As she had many times, Béatrix marveled at Lela's ease. For a woman who'd grown up so rough, she was quicker with a hug than anyone she knew.

"Bea," Lela said now. "Sweetheart. You've got to stop mooning over that man. Get out and gather ye rosebuds."

"I see other men. Lots, actually."

"Do tell." Lela cocked one brow. "Any of them good in bed?"

"There aren't many of those around."

"Well, I've got one you can borrow. Have, actually. I'm pretty much done with him."

Béatrix gaped at her. "You can't just hand off your old boyfriends."

"Why not?" Lela nibbled on her earpiece and grinned. "He keeps trying to fix me up with his boss. Says I'd be just the ticket to unkink his corporate spine."

"He sounds charming."

"He is," Lela insisted. "Except for that." She swept her hair back from her face, her hazel eyes dancing with amusement. "Andrew is very urbane. Good looking. Good humored. Great in bed. Killer accent. You could come to dinner with us tonight and meet him."

Béatrix's stomach dropped at the reminder. "I'm supposed to have dinner with Philip. Actually, I was hoping I could convince you to tag along. I don't want to be alone with him right now."

"That's a first."

Béatrix wrinkled her nose and ignored the question in Lela's eyes.

"All right," Lela surrendered. "Why don't Andrew and I both tag along? You can compare the two studmeisters side by side. See if you want to take mine for a spin."

"I won't," said Béatrix with all her firmness. "Anyway, he wouldn't want me once he'd had you."

"Don't say that until you've met him," Lela said, and laughed as if she knew a joke too good to share.

"NOW THAT'S WHAT I call a woman!" said Andrew Laborteaux.

He met them at the market in rue Lepic. The stalls were not their best this time of day, but they still held fruits and greens and tomatoes as red as blood. Andrew looked at home. He was a lean, tall man with hair the color of straw and a face creased by laughter and sun. He had to be ten years older than Lela, but that was no surprise. Most of her lovers were. And Béatrix couldn't deny he was boyish. His smile, a mile-wide stretch of brilliant American teeth, made her lips twitch with an urge to smile back.

He'd dressed simply, but in a manner that conveyed his means. His pale linen trousers were well cut, his green silk shirt impeccably pressed. His woven Italian loafers suited the cobbled street. From his collar hung a black string tie. Its silver clasp bore a chunk of polished turquoise *Grandmère* Sophie would not have scorned to wear.

Now he took her hands in his own and beamed as if God had never created a more enchanting woman.

She was beginning to see why Lela liked him.

"Stop drooling," Lela warned, rising on tiptoe to kiss his sunbrowned cheek.

Andrew's grin didn't lose a single watt. "She's smilin' back at me, *chère*. I think she likes me."

"*Quel enfant fou!*" Béatrix exclaimed, amused by his foolishness.

"*Non, non,*" Andrew murmured back, his lips nuzzling her ear. "I'm not a foolish boy. I'm from New Orleans. We like our women hot and rich."

Béatrix slapped him away, but it was hard to be angry with such an engaging *bête*. As Lela had promised, his drawl was a killer: a cross between Texas and France. Unfazed by her rebuff, he tucked one of his arms through hers and the other through Lela's. Under guise of protecting her from passing pedestrians, he pulled Béatrix close enough to press her breast against his biceps. A hum of unexpected awareness slid over her skin. Her nipples hardened and a soft pulse jumped to life between her legs. Andrew looked down at her and smiled, promises gleaming in his faded denim eyes.

"You are prettier than a picture," he said in an easy, friendly tone. "And that's not me teasin'."

"You see," said Lela, laughing from the other side. "I told you he'd go for you."

But Béatrix wasn't used to flattery, or to having another woman encourage it. Andrew seemed to sense her embarrassment.

"Are we shoppin'?" he asked, gazing at the colorful stalls. "I purely hate to crash a party empty-handed."

THEY ARRIVED AT eight, laden with bags and bottles and a large bouquet of flowers. Despite steeling herself by every means she knew, despite her new admirer and Lela's staunch support, when Philip appeared at the door, Béatrix flushed so strongly her ears turned hot.

His eyes flew straight to hers, startled but not angry.

"I brought guests," she said, and thrust the huge yellow

mums, which Andrew had bought but forced her to carry, into Philip's hands.

"So I see. Thank you." He turned to the others. "Lela. I almost didn't recognize you with those spectacles."

She made a sound of annoyance and flipped them back atop her head. "This is Andrew Laborteaux, a friend of mine. He's come to Paris hunting perfume. Andrew: Philip Carmichael, chairman of Meilleurs Amis."

After the men shook hands, Philip bent to hug Lela. He wasn't normally a hugger, but he and Lela had hit it off the two times she'd come to visit. Lela hit it off with most men who weren't comatose, but this was more than the effect of her flirtatious nature. She and Philip were easier together than he and Béatrix. Given Lela's willingness to share her playmate, Béatrix tried hard not to mind.

Philip held the door while the others went ahead. She thought he meant to scold her for surprising him with extra guests, but he merely ushered her in, his palm a gentle brand at the small of her back. She wore an outfit Lela had chosen: a red boatneck top with a calf-length black skirt. Both were tighter than she was used to. The shirt, in particular, was no protection against the warmth of Philip's hand. No doubt the movement was accidental, but, as they walked, his palm slipped lower, closer to the curve of her bottom. Béatrix felt herself simmer even as they crossed the diamond-dotted marble floor. He'd touched her before, of course—a pat on the cheek, a squeeze of the arm. Philip's British reserve did not preclude his being an affectionate man. Tonight, however, his touch was flame on a river of oil. She wasn't sure how much of it she could stand.

To her relief, Andrew drew their attention by whistling at the grand salon.

"This is some setup," he said, head craned to take in the ceiling's ornate plasterwork. The chandelier sparkled in agreement, two hundred hand-carved pendants of smoky quartz. Then Andrew lifted his grocery bags. "We brought extra fixin's. If you'll point me toward the kitchen, I'll get to work on 'em."

Philips hand fell away from her back. The offer seemed to fluster him, but his good manners rescued him soon enough.

"Of course," he said. "Why don't we all go to the kitchen?"

The evening took on the air of a party as the wine was opened and the packages unwrapped. On one side of the big kitchen, Andrew and Lela performed brutal acts on a heap of shrimp. On the other, Béatrix was given the task of mashing Philip's potatoes.

"What happened to the cook?" she asked.

"What?" Philip had been staring into space. Actually, he'd been staring at her breasts, though she couldn't imagine that was intentional.

"Madame Daoud. The cook?"

"Oh." He shook himself and turned a sausage in the shiny copper pan. His face was rosy from the heat. "She quit. Those crazy reporters kept trying to interview her. I never got around to hiring another."

"Not surviving on scrambled eggs, I hope."

"Oh, no." He ventured one of his shy, boyish smiles. "Generally, I eat out."

Béatrix had just begun to smile back when Lela asked for a vegetable peeler. With an odd sense of belonging, Béatrix dug one from a drawer. Her cooking skills were no better than Philip's, but she did know her way around.

Philip waited for Lela to leave before he spoke again, in a tone too low to carry. "You weren't afraid to come here by yourself, were you?"

"Of course not." She cursed the blood that flooded her cheeks. "Lela surprised me. I thought you'd be happy to see her."

"I am, but . . ." He set his cooking fork on the edge of the broad, stainless steel stove. "I hope you know I don't hold anything that happened this afternoon against you. It was both our doing. We've been going through a period of adjustment, and, well, I want you to know I'm not angry."

"I'm not angry, either," Béatrix said.

He stared at her as if she'd spoken Swahili. The pink the stove had brought to his cheeks deepened to a claret red. She couldn't imagine what was going through his head, but her statement seemed to shake him.

"Right," he said, recovering with a jerk. He picked up his fork and busied himself over the sausage. "Glad to hear it."

Andrew chose that moment to grab her around the waist and lift her off her feet. "Lela's gonna stir the pot. How 'bout you give me the grand tour?"

When he smiled at her like that, she didn't know how to refuse him. Most likely, no woman did. Veins fizzing from a combination of his attention and Philip's, she led him through the parlors and the halls, pointing out the family treasures that had once been her constant companions. The dining room made him blink. Above the wainscoting, the walls bore murals of romantically pastoral scenes: shepherdesses with belling gowns and golden crooks, shepherds with pan pipes, and sheep like gamboling clouds.

"Very Marie Antoinette," he said. He marveled at their proximity to the Bois de Boulogne's big, wooded park, and he poked his head into every closet they passed.

She thought him the nosiest man she'd ever met until he opened the door to the master bath and immediately pulled her inside. He backed her bodily against the wall.

"Just what we need," he said, "a door with a lock."

He was tall and warm and smelled delightfully of lemons. Somehow his thighs—two lean, hard lengths of muscle—had pressed between hers until his knees hit the powder blue tile. His hands flattened on either side of her head. She was surrounded by him, physically over-whelmed. The anxiety she felt was decidedly pleasant. Andrew seemed to like the position. He was breathing slowly, but with extreme concentration.

"What are you doing?" she said, surely one of the sillier questions she'd ever asked.

He smiled and pressed one of her hands to the center of his chest. His heart was thundering beneath his ribs. The force of it surprised her.

"The question is," he said, "what are you doin' to me?"

She didn't get a chance to answer because his head swooped down and she was caught in a fiery kiss. Her ex-clamation of alarm changed quickly to a mewl of pleasure. His tongue seduced her mouth. His ardor warmed her sex. He was dragging her hand down his silk shirt, press-ing it over his erection as if he couldn't wait to have her touch it.

"That's what you've done to me," he said, forcing her to rub him up and down. "That's what you've been doin' to me since I saw your gorgeous curves." Under the linen, his cock was a long, firm rod. Her fingers tightened before she could wonder if encouraging him was a good idea.

Her body thought it was. It leapt with excitement as soon as his did.

"Oh, yeah," he whispered. "Give me a good squeeze. Squeeze me all over, *chère*. Make my poor lil' pecker cry."

Hardly little, she thought, working down to his balls and back up to his glans. He might not have Philip's size, but he was nothing to sneeze at. And he was getting bigger by the second. She pressed her thumb over the center of his knob and a spot of damp seeped through the lining of his pants. His breathing quickened, echoing against the tile. He liked that, she thought, and she did it again. Then a breeze fluttered between her thighs. He'd been gathering up her skirt. She'd been too engrossed to notice. She tensed at his advance, but when his fingers slipped under her panties and curled up through her lips, her sex released such a gush of welcome he groaned.

"Mm," he hummed, dipping his tongue into her mouth. His fingers probed, stroking her gently. "You're like one of those chocolate *petits pains*, all sweet and melty inside. Good God, sugar, I could eat you all day."

Before she could stop him, he fell to his knees and nuzzled between her thighs. His fingers cleared a path, combing through her curls and pushing her labia aside. His thumbs slid in her cream. He kissed her, mouth puckered and soft, then teased her with a long, slow lick. She gripped his straw-colored hair. He licked her again, more closely. His tongue was gentle and fearless: curious, she would have said, but that wasn't enough of a compliment. Her climax was rising already. When he drew her clit into his mouth, she knew she wouldn't be able to hold it back. Her first orgasm was always like this, a bullet train speeding out of control. It embarrassed her, but there was nothing she could do to stop it, especially with a mouth as skilled as his.

He found her sweet spot with his tongue, the one that was almost too sensitive to bear. She moaned, then whimpered when he flicked it again. He chuckled, guessing her secret. No, he wouldn't have pity, not this man. He kneaded her thighs, spreading them even farther for his assault. Again he teased the crucial bundle of nerves, steadily, mercilessly. He wouldn't let up. He kept at it until her pussy ached with anticipation. Oh, it was good. Her head fell back. Her knees trembled. She was losing it. She couldn't hold on. He pressed harder, drew deeper. The tension rose and shattered . . . and immediately began to gather again.

He replaced his mouth with his hand and smoothly regained his feet. He was smiling, his fingers lazily stroking the flesh he'd just licked. Her hips refused to stay where they were. Her sex was a welter of need. She had to reach for more, but it didn't do her any good. Though Andrew continued to caress her, he did not pull her back to the edge.

"I knew you'd be like this," he said, his drawl turned to smoke. "The minute I saw you, I knew. You want to come again, don't you?"

She knew her face was on fire, but she bit her lower lip and nodded. His fingers slid deeper, then stopped moving. His thumb covered her clit and pressed. She could feel her pulse and his beating in tandem on the little rod. The pressure felt so tormentingly lovely, she didn't want to move.

"I'll give it to you tonight," he whispered. "We'll fuck each other limp. We'll fuck each other until we're sore. And when it's over, I'm gonna lick you from head to foot and have you for breakfast."

She laughed at the image of herself laid out on a plate of toast. He kissed her silent, a kiss that poured all his unassuaged lust into her mouth. She gripped his buttocks, found them flat and hard. He made a sound low in his throat and rubbed his rigid cock against her mound, up and down, as if he were ironing a stubborn wrinkle.

"I'd take you right now," he purred, his lips brushing hers. "But we'd never make it to dinner."

At once, reality came rushing back. Dinner. Philip. This was his bathroom she and Andrew were making out in. Her hands clapped her cheeks. She knew her face would give her away. Muttering imprecations in her native tongue, she made what reparations she could with a sink of icy water and a towel that smelled disturbingly of Philip's cologne.

"You're worryin' 'bout nothin'," Andrew assured her, licking his longest finger like a cat. "Your stepdaddy wants you happy. So does Lela. They're both adults. Nothin' we've done here will shock them."

Béatrix wasn't so sure. In any case, they weren't the ones she was worried about. She'd always controlled her desires. Always. If today's events were any indication, that state of affairs had just come to an alarming end.

Three

ROM THE HEAD of the table Philip watched the others grow merry over the wine. Bea sat in Eve's old seat. Seeing her there was odd. Not that she reminded him of Eve. Every glance shouted how different she was. She'd piled her blue-black curls atop her head, a careless arrangement with tendrils spilling around her face and down her neck. Compared to the powder-wigged maidens on the walls, she seemed a peasant, as healthy and ripe as a peach. Her aura reached him clear across the table, making him aware of his own maleness, of needs one hurried encounter, however stimulating, could not quench.

He would have preferred his thoughts not take that turn, but it was difficult to avoid. Her color was high from laughing at the American's jokes, her lips soft and relaxed.

Andrew was telling the women about his boss: how one secretary had been so frightened of him she peed in her pants when he asked her for coffee, how he worked so hard he hadn't taken a vacation since Reagan was president, how he'd discovered Andrew waiting tables in New Orleans and told him charm like his shouldn't be wasted on the tourists.

"Simon Graves made me a businessman," he said, his eyes sparkling with amusement. "Me, Andrew Laborteaux, whose only conquests up till then involved the fairer sex. Of course, my job still requires an understanding of women."

Lela saluted him with her glass. "To the director of marketing for all of Graves Incorporated."

"And perfume hunter extraordinaire," Bea chimed.

Philip hadn't the faintest what they were toasting. He was apart from them, one glum face in a merry quartet. Unable to join in, his mind turned back to the moment he'd shared with Bea in the kitchen. *I'm not angry,* she'd said: Bea, who'd been angry at the world with far less cause than he'd given her this afternoon. And the way she'd met his eye, so forthright and steady . . . His blood had moved under her regard, thickly, slowly, gathering in his chest and groin, pushing his cock within its skin until the rising pulse rang a warning for him to look away.

She'd changed. In one day, she'd changed. She even looked different, in her tight red shirt and her straight black skirt with her hair tumbling as if she'd just got out of bed.

She looked like an adult.

That wasn't all, though. Something was happening between her and the American. Lela's friend couldn't take his eyes off Bea, as if whatever had mesmerized Philip had Andrew in its spell as well. Granted, Philip had always thought Bea attractive. She might be a stone or so heavier than she ought, but she carried it well. She reminded him of a Maillol sculpture: firm and round and monumental.

Eve had liked to call her daughter a "big girl." Bea hated the phrase. Philip saw that straight off. When he realized Eve knew it, too, he'd asked why she'd knowingly hurt her own child.

"I suppose I'm angry," she'd explained. "Bea's so stubborn about staying the way she is. Never asks for help. Never takes my advice. Sometimes I think she judges me for caring about my appearance."

Philip tended to agree, but he didn't understand why they couldn't both live as they pleased. Why did one of them have to be right?

"Because I am right." His wife had laughed in that captivating way she had, light and bright. He could almost hear her now, filling the air between the murals, as if her ghost were made of sound. She'd thought she was doing what was best. She'd loved her daughter. But her insecurity had led her to hurt Bea instead, and to hurt herself in the end.

Eve, he thought, shaking his head at his plate. Did you even know what you threw away?

"So," he heard Lela say from a distance. "How's the rag trade been treating you?"

Her hand, glittering with silver rings, settled on his forearm. Why, he wondered, did some women's hands set off explosions within one's nerves, while others just offered comfort?

"Philip?" Her voice vibrated with hidden laughter. "You still with us?"

"What? Oh. Business is fine, thank you." Throat tight, he swallowed half his wine. "Except New York."

"New York?" Bea abruptly sat straighter. Andrew was leaning toward her. He'd been about to hand-feed her a shrimp. Those two had only met today, but Bea didn't act as if the intimacy bothered her. She set her heavy silver fork across her plate. "What's wrong with the store in New York?"

Lord, had he said that? He hadn't meant to. But the cat was out of the bag. Maybe he ought to broach the subject now. At least in front of guests Bea wouldn't cause a scene.

"They've been operating at a loss," he admitted. "Last quarter they almost canceled out the profits from San Francisco."

A line appeared between her brows. "Didn't I hear somewhere that their manager requested a leave of absence?"

Philip willed his blood not to rush to his face. He knew precisely where she'd heard the news: from Alain, while she crouched under his desk with his prick in her mouth. He couldn't look at her for fear he'd see her remember, too.

"Yes," he said. "She's going on maternity leave. More or less a whisker before she gets fired. I was thinking— hoping, really—that you might want to take over."

"Me?"

"Yes," he said. She looked genuinely surprised. He wondered just how boggy the ground was that he'd stepped onto. One could never tell with Bea. "You've been spending a lot of time in the shops lately. I thought you might fancy an official position."

"In New York?" Her face had paled.

An answering wash of cold swept his cheeks. Bloody hell, he thought. She doesn't know I've been meaning to ask this for weeks. She thinks I'm trying to banish her because she made a play for me. She thinks I don't want her around.

"No," he said, hands tight on his fork and knife. He looked like Henry VIII, but he couldn't make his grip relax. "I didn't mean it that way. The opening happened to be in New York. If you want a position here . . . Your stake in the company is as important as mine. Naturally, whatever contribution you choose to make, I'd welcome."

"I don't want to make any." She sounded dazed. "Apart from helping out the way I am now."

"Of course. That's fine, too. Whatever you like. Very helpful, I'm sure." He swallowed and fought the urge to gnaw his ragged nails. He knew he was babbling. He was breathing too hard as well, the air not wanting to fill his lungs.

Lela patted his arm the way one would a senile old man's. "Bea can't take a full-time job. She needs time to paint."

"To paint. Well. I knew you'd had a show, but I thought . . ." Bea wasn't looking at him. Her thumbs rubbed the edge of her plate. How many times had he seen that expression on her face while her mother belittled something she'd done? Stubborn. Sullen. Refusing to betray her pain. And now he was the one who'd caused it. "Of course, you should be painting," he said, striving for a hearty tone but managing only to sound idiotic. Sweat popped out on his brow. Bloody hell, why couldn't he shut up?

Bea muttered a curse under her breath.

"I'll do it," Lela said.

"Do what?" he said, grateful for the interruption but thoroughly confused.

Lela's smile was as bright as a new penny.

"I," she said, hand over heart, "will take over the New York store."

"IT'S ALL ABOUT brandin'," Andrew declared as they climbed the crooked stairs to her apartment. Once again he'd taken the middle of the trio, though it was hard to say who was supporting whom. They were all drunk, Andrew most of all. "Target has a brand. Saks Fifth has a brand. But who knows what to expect from Graves Department Stores?"

"I certainly don't," Béatrix muttered, squinting to get her key into the lock.

"Exactly!" Andrew said as they stumbled inside. "We may not be Saks, but we're much nicer than Target. We have to communicate our identity to the consumer. We have to get our brand across."

His fist punched the air, throwing him off balance. Laughing gently, Lela led him to the fat flowered sofa that dominated the sitting room. He collapsed across it as if his bones were made of rubber.

"The coffee shops were a start," he said as Lela slipped off his loafers. "The coffee shops were classy. Kept the women in the store. Made 'em shop a little longer." He tapped his chest. "Was my idea to buy them. Simon said I was a genius."

"You are a genius," Lela assured him, pressing a kiss to his furrowed brow. "And the perfume you find will be just as wonderful."

"Better be." His eyes closed, gold lashes fanning across his cheeks. "Gotta stay the fair-haired boy."

"Speaking of coffee," Béatrix said. "I think I'd better make some."

To her relief, Lela stayed with Andrew. She needed a moment away from her friend. Lela's offer to manage the New York boutique had caught her unawares. She doubted Lela had held any job more than a few months— apart from her freelance magazine work, which didn't require punching in at an office and could hardly be called regular. Lela was a dedicated good-time girl. The thought of her assuming responsibility for an entire store for more than ten minutes was laughable.

But she really seemed to want to.

"Why not?" she'd said when Béatrix choked on her spicy shrimp. "I've worked retail before. I know fashion. I know women. I'm young and energetic. I'm charming. And I've probably spent more time shopping than anyone in this room."

Naturally, Philip was doubtful. He liked Lela, but when it came to business, he was no patsy. Then Lela offered the kicker.

"Send me in as a salesclerk for a month," she said. "I'll scope out the situation, get a feel for personnel, and at the end of the month I'll send you a business plan laying out what I think needs to be done to turn the store around. If you like it, you hire me. If you don't, no hard feelings."

"It'll take at least a month to interview candidates," Andrew put in.

"Which you can do while I'm in place." Lela flattened her hands beside her plate. "I'm not asking for the job on a platter. I'm asking for a chance."

"Can't ask fairer than that," said Andrew, and Philip weakened before her eyes.

"One month," he said. "With another month's probation when and if you take over."

Lela had jumped and squealed even as Béatrix's heart sank to her stomach. She didn't want the job herself, but she didn't want Lela to have it either. Not because she feared her friend would fail. Because she feared she would succeed.

I'm a horrible person, she thought as she scooped coffee into the shiny Italian espresso pot. I am a horrible, jealous person who ought to be happy for her friend. Her best friend. Who would never, never begrudge her a chance for success.

Lela had never begrudged her anything.

But that's because Lela's always had more than you, said a nasty inner voice. More looks, more charm, more men, and now, most likely, more respect.

Béatrix gritted her teeth and set the coffee on the stove. She would be big about this. Lela would never guess she wasn't thrilled for her. Lela would never know how small her best friend could be.

ANDREW WAS TOO drunk even to be poured into a taxi and returned to the Hotel Meurice. Béatrix left him snoring where he was while she and Lela had coffee by themselves.

They talked quietly, but without their usual verve. Lela seemed as preoccupied as Béatrix. When she stifled a yawn behind her hand, Béatrix led her to the guest room.

They hugged outside the door.

"It's so good to see you," Lela said.

"Yes," Béatrix agreed. "It's the best."

Then she was alone, or almost alone. Her apartment contained two more bodies than usual. She lay on her back under the sheets, hands folded over her belly. Two people who cared about her, at least a little, slept beneath her roof. All in all, that was not a bad feeling. She closed her eyes and drifted off, dreaming of colors the way she sometimes did: the green of spring grass, the brown of a rolling river. A picture began to form: a country girl dabbling her feet in the current. Blue dress. Pink legs. Big sister, she thought, and two younger children appeared by her side.

She didn't know how much time had passed, or even if she'd slept. Warmth lapped her body, her feet first, then her thighs. The warmth changed to weight and settled close to her chest. It was comforting, arousing. She shifted her legs and heard the covers rustle. Lips pressed the curve of her cheek.

"You didn't think I'd forgotten my promise," he whispered.

"Mm," she said, and tried to stretch. Her arms were caught by Andrew's. He was lying on top of her, stark naked. He'd showered and shaved and brushed his teeth. The only sign he might still be drunk was the sleepy blink of his eyes. Béatrix arched her back, unable to stop herself. "I thought I was dreaming."

His lips drifted down her neck. "I hope it was a pleasant dream."

"It was . . . warm."

"I'm feelin' a bit warm myself. Maybe we should dispense with these covers." He kissed her as he pulled the sheets from between them. When he settled back, his cock was hard and hot against her thigh, the bare, pulsing skin a pleasant shock. He licked the hollow where her collarbones met, then squeezed her breast through the man's silk pajama top she wore. "Could be you're overdressed as well."

Button by button, as if it were a very important task, Andrew removed her shirt. Béatrix didn't stop him. Being caught half-asleep had shorted out her usual self-consciousness. She hated undressing for a new man, baring her many flaws, wondering if his disappointment would show on his face. But it was dark in her room, and resisting Andrew's will seemed as pointless as telling molasses not to drip. He wanted his way and he'd have it: politely, charmingly, but he would.

When she was naked, he rolled her onto her side and into his embrace. His mouth settled over hers. Groaning, his hands dragged up and down her flesh, squeezing her close as he pressed his planes into her curves. His kiss reached deeper, grew wetter. She stroked down his side, over his hip. He was so lean his muscles were almost flat, almost as hard as his bones. He held her too tightly to explore as she wished so she pushed out with her knee to make a space between them.

"Somethin' wrong?" he asked.

She silenced him by catching his cock in her hand. He

jerked, then sighed. His tip throbbed in the cup of her palm. He was circumcised, his shape clean but vulnerable. She rubbed him gently, up and down, not knowing what he liked but hoping she could please him. Apparently, she could.

"Oh, sugar," he groaned and rolled her onto her back. He arched lower, nuzzling her chest until he found her nipple. His mouth clamped onto it. He hummed with pleasure, sucking with a greed she found endearing. He was careful not to hurt her, though the sounds he made were quite enthusiastic. He cupped her closer with his hands, dampening her skin with the heat of his breath. His cock he rubbed against her calf, just enough to keep it eager.

Bea smiled in spite of her nerves. Obviously, she had what Andrew liked. Happy she could satisfy this primal preference, she stroked the flowing muscles of his back. Most men would have relaxed into the suckling, but Andrew grew more and more avid until finally he wrenched free and reached for the bedside lamp. "I've got to see you. Just got to."

She caught his wrist before he could pull the chain. "Please don't spoil this."

"Oh, sugar, no." His voice dripped sweetness and compassion. "A little light won't spoil anythin'. You're so pretty. You're just the kind of woman I like."

"Please," she persisted. "I was enjoying it as it was."

"She's shy," said a voice from the door. "She doesn't know how gorgeous she is."

Béatrix caught her breath in shock. Andrew stiffened and turned. Even he, knowing Lela's easy ways, seemed to consider this an awkward moment. Regardless of whether she'd given her blessing to his latest conquest, he obviously hadn't intended her to witness him in action.

"Lela—" he said, with a hint of guilty spouse.

She stepped inside, her feet whispering over the carpet. "Don't worry. I've only come to help."

"Help?" Béatrix said, a strangled cry. She pulled what bedcovers she could reach back over her chest.

Lela ignored her alarm. She set something on the night table and struck a match. In its flickering light, Béatrix identified a bottle of brandy and *Grand-mère* Sophie's prized Louis XIV candelabra. Three brass nymphs supported the curving branches, and crystal pendants swung from the metal leaves, one of them cracked by age. With an air of ceremony, Lela lit the long white tapers, then poured an inch of brandy into a snifter.

When she offered it to Andrew, he shook his head. "I've had enough for one night."

But Béatrix suspected she'd need all the Dutch courage she could get. She took the glass and downed it in three swallows. Andrew rubbed her back when she coughed. They both waited for Lela to enlighten them. She set the bottle and glass on the floor.

"Now," she said, "let's see if we can't turn this girl's self-image around."

"Ah," said Andrew, nodding in understanding.

Oh, great, thought Bea. Now I'm a community-improvement project.

She was certain she wasn't up for this, but Andrew didn't care. He tugged the covers from her stubborn hands and backed out of the bed. For a moment, Béatrix forgot her self-consciousness. He was stunning by candlelight, his body slim and rangy, his cock thrust outward from his golden thatch. Lela stood beside him. Without blocking Béatrix's view, she flattened her hand over Andrew's belly, fingers spread, and pulled his skin upward over his rippling abs. His cock lifted higher, the underside beginning to show. One vein twisted up the ridge, a vigorous river of blue.

"See what you do to him," she said, "just by sitting there."

Béatrix shook her head. "You can't sell me that bridge. He's a *coureur de jupon*. He'd screw anything in skirts."

"You wound me!" Andrew cried. "And you are very, very wrong. I am a connoisseur among skirt chasers, and you are a goddess. Come." He beckoned with his fingers. "Let me show you how I see you."

It seemed childish to refuse. She climbed naked from the bed, blushing furiously, feeling heavy and horrid and wishing Lela most heartily to hell. *She* wore her bra and panties, delicate scraps of orange silk that hugged her lean boyish hips and her perfect peachy breasts. Those were the sort of breasts a Frenchwoman was supposed to have, like upside-down champagne glasses. Evangeline had had them. Grandma Sophie had had them. And both had delighted in calling Bea the Irish heifer. Lela, in contrast, could not have been less cowlike. She had the limbs of a ballerina. Even her feet were feminine. Feeling ten times uglier than she had before, Béatrix wrapped her arms around her waist.

Andrew coaxed them away. "No, no, sugar. You have nothing to hide. These are a woman's curves. And these are a woman's breasts." He teased her nipples with his thumbs until they tingled. His palms warmed her, then slid down her back to grip her buttocks. "These are a woman's muscles. They make you firm beneath your curves. They make you good to hold on to, good to squeeze."

He showed her what he meant, compressing her flesh between his fingers until her bottom tingled as pleasantly as her breasts. His actions pushed his erection into her belly. At this graphic proof of admiration, something rose inside her, something too strong to contain.

"I'm fat," she gasped. As often as she'd berated herself with the words, she'd never said them aloud, not to her mother, not to her friends. Letting them out broke a restraint she had not known was there. Tears rolled down her cheeks, but they were almost tears of pleasure.

Immediately Andrew drew her to him and tucked her face into the crook of his shoulder.

"You're sexy," he corrected. "The sexiest woman I ever met. And that's saying somethin'."

She chuckled through her tears, and he kissed her. As soon as his mouth touched hers, her need for him returned. She became aware of his warmth, of the softness of his lips and the tension in the muscles of his arms. The brandy she'd drunk caught fire in her veins. She could not recall having been so aroused with a man. She felt light and powerful. When Lela's hands smoothed down her spine, she merely laughed. Let Lela touch her. Let the world touch her! She was the gorgeous French girl. She could do no wrong.

Lela lifted her hair to kiss her nape.

"You are beautiful," she murmured, close to the skin. "As beautiful as anyone I know."

Her body pressed Béatrix's back. Lela was naked, her limbs silken hot. Her groin spooned the hands with which Andrew cupped Bea's bottom.

"Yes," he purred. "That's the way to help."

They rubbed up against her like cats, the pair of them, kissing and stroking until Béatrix felt as drunk from that as from the brandy. Andrew lifted her, carried her to the queen-size bed. She did not have to do anything. They moved her as they wished, touched her as they wished. Andrew cuffed her wrists above her head and pinned them with a single hand. Lela combed the curls between her legs.

"Don't touch her there," Andrew said. "That little firecracker is mine."

Lela did not argue. Instead, she trailed her hands up Béatrix's arms. Andrew sank his teeth into the roundness of her hip. Lela massaged her scalp. Andrew licked her breast. Their hands met at her knee and stroked her quivering thigh. They did everything but get her off. No one had ever tried to make her wait. Men always wanted her to come quickly so they could get theirs. Now Béatrix shook with need, her body rolling with frustration, her nerves jangling like unanswered phones. Andrew murmured praise for her groans. He enjoyed tormenting her. His breath came hard, almost as hard as hers.

"Tell him what you want," said Lela, her voice husky. "Make him do what you want."

"I want to ride him," Béatrix said, all inhibitions lost. "I want him laid out on the bed for me to take."

Her ferocity made Lela laugh. She nodded at Andrew. "You heard the lady. Are you going to be a gentleman or not?"

"Always," he said, the hitch in the word barely audible. He released her wrists and rolled onto his back among the rumpled covers. Lela scooted to the headboard above him, out of Béatrix's way.

"You hold his wrists," Béatrix instructed. "He's not to move until I say."

Lela obeyed. Béatrix looked at her prisoner, a living statue in the candlelight. All but his eyes and his throbbing cock were still. She pulled his thighs apart and watched his scrotum roll between. She massaged the tendons that stretched from his thigh to his groin. His diaphragm lurched.

Too tempted to resist, she bent to taste his cock. His skin was smooth and hot. She turned her head sideways, sucking hard wet kisses up the raphe. He twitched when she reached the top. Then she swallowed him, crown to base. His moan was music to her ears. Twice she sucked his length, her lips tight, her tongue soft. When she released him, his hips tried to follow her mouth.

"No moving," she scolded, and stretched up his body until her breasts brushed his chest, until she could reach the night-table drawer and the precious accessories it contained. She grabbed three boxes, then sat back to study them with pretended nonchalance. "Let's see. Ribbed, mint-flavored, or extra thin."

"Mint!" laughed Lela. "Ooh la la."

"Am I allowed a vote?" Andrew asked.

"No," chorused the women.

The sense of shared mischief reminded Béatrix of a college prank, though they'd never pulled one like this! She could barely contain her giggle.

"This," she decided, and removed a single packet. She covered it with her hand before Andrew could read the label. With the condom cupped under her palm, she drew a circle around his nipple. The tiny bump beaded tighter. She moved to the other, treated it to a slow caress, then slithered the packet toward his navel. His skin quivered.

"If you guess which one I picked," she said. "I'll put it on you with my mouth."

Andrew smiled, an unexpected fondness in his eyes. "I know which one you picked. The one you thought would please me most."

She inclined her head to hide her smile. It was the perfect answer, the right answer. She ripped the corner of the extra thin and extracted the rubber. She pushed the tip backward and let a little drop of spit fall from her tongue. That broadened his grin. He must have known the lubrication would increase his sensitivity. With two fingers, she balanced the furled latex ring on the head of his cock.

"Cheater!" Lela exclaimed. "You're supposed to use your teeth."

Béatrix stuck out her tongue, then bent closer to Andrew's cock. He shivered at the wash of her breath, goose bumps prickling across his groin. She drew a deep breath and pushed the rubber down with her lips. His shaft seemed to thicken as she went, as if it knew the end of its wait was near.

Near enough, she thought, and drew back. Andrew watched her, his hands clenched in Lela's hold. Béatrix swung her knees outside his hips. More daring than she'd ever been, she drew one hand down her cleavage and cupped her mons. Andrew licked his lips.

"Do it," Lela whispered, all hint of teasing gone. "Fuck him."

Her excitement was catching. Béatrix felt her sex close in and heat, felt her pulse race ahead. She lowered herself until the ball of his glans pressed between her folds. Andrew grunted and bit his lips. She grasped him between finger and thumb and slid him back and forth. His neck arched. His eyelids drooped. Béatrix glanced at Lela. Like Andrew, her cheeks were flooded with color, her pupils huge. Her breasts shook with the beat of her heart. Her thumbs drew circles on Andrew's wrists, a compulsive motion Béatrix doubted she knew she made.

"Take him," Lela urged in that same eager hiss.

No one could doubt she was enjoying this.

Willing to please, Béatrix took him, sinking by degrees until her inner thighs met the rise of his hips. He filled her well, a hint of stretch to the invasion, a hint of more than enough. She bent forward to kiss him, a quick tender peck, then eased back to ride. He was breathing through parted lips, his eyes glittering with excitement.

"Sugar, you are hotter than my mama's gumbo."

Béatrix laughed as she rose and sank, slowly at first, teasing herself, teasing him.

"You're cruel," he accused. "Cruel!"

Her pulse skipped at his squirms, at the way his cock flexed inside her, as if trying to reach deeper by itself. Finally, she leaned down. "You want it faster?"

"Yes," he said. "And harder. I want you to be sore tomorrow. I want you to know my cock was there."

Where did people learn to talk this way, and why did it make it impossible for her to wait? She had to come. Her sex was a throbbing, hungry ache, and his cock was the perfect tool to soothe it.

She planted her hands beneath his arms. "I'll give you fast."

They were eye to eye now, breath to breath. His body jarred as she rode him, as hard as he'd asked, as fast as he'd asked. Sweat rolled down his face, some of it hers. Her responses spun out of control. They had played with her too long and too well before she'd grabbed the reins. She came before she'd thrust a dozen times, the spasms tightening her around his shaft.

"Oh, yeah," he said, feeling her go. "Beautiful girl!"

Then she rode him, not for release, but for the pleasure of driving his solid, heated rod inside her sex, for the pleasure of his groans, for the pleasure of watching his beautiful body glowing with desire.

"Let him go," she said to Lela. "Let him touch me."

With a hum of gratitude, he slid his hands around her buttocks.

"Curves," he said, his eloquence reduced by passion, "'s good."

It was good. Her hips were well-oiled hinges, her pussy a clinging, juicy cushion. He swelled inside her. His face tightened.

"He's going to come," Lela whispered, hands stroking his laboring chest. "He can't last much longer now."

He didn't deny it, but he tried to draw the moment out. He began to breathe deep and slow, to thrust upward at her downstroke. Yes, slower, Béatrix thought, her crest drawing nearer as his did. It was pleasant to hover, pleasant to feel her enjoyment stretch. His thumbs reached round to meet at her clit. He rubbed her as she rode, side to side, one pad squashing the tip of the little rod, the other the base. Then he worked his thumbs in opposition. The sensations were intense, twining deliciously with the friction inside her cunt. Béatrix closed her eyes, lengthening her thrusts, making each inch of push and pull count.

"Yes," Andrew whispered. "Yes."

The three of them were breathing together, the same

dreamlike rhythm to which she rode Andrew's cock. She heard the pillows rustle as Lela moved forward, heard the wet, moaning slurp of Andrew's mouth. He was eating Lela out. She couldn't look. She couldn't. But the sounds excited her, wound her tighter than she'd ever been wound before. Lela must need this by now, really need it. Lips nuzzled her breasts, softer than Andrew's, smaller than Andrew's. Béatrix clutched a pair of narrow, satiny shoulders. Fingers pinched her nipple, thumbs pressed her clit. Sensations raced up her nerves like bottled lightning.

The final flash was exquisite. The pleasure stuttered through her in staccato bursts, again, again. She couldn't stop the waves. Andrew thrust faster, jackrabbit fast. Lela panted in her ear. Her hips were jarred by a second set of shudders. Andrew's cries were muffled by Lela's flesh, but he came as violently as she had. A second later, Lela wailed, her body arching strongly in release.

And then it was over, except for the heavy breathing. Béatrix couldn't open her eyes, couldn't move. Embarrassment rushed in as pleasure rushed out. Lela had kissed her breast. Lela had pinched her nipple. Lela had come while Béatrix held her in her arms.

Now Lela stroked her curls and kissed her gently on the cheek.

"It's all right," she said, feeling Béatrix's stiffness. "It's all right."

But it wasn't all right. It would never be all right again.

"It's nothing," Lela insisted, cupping her face until she had to look up. "It's a shared pleasure. Like a bottle of wine. It doesn't mean it's going to happen again. It doesn't mean I want it to. It's just . . . sometimes words aren't enough to show how much I love you. That's all it means, Bea, that's all."

Béatrix swallowed. "I love you, too." But the words didn't come out happy.

"Well," said Andrew, forgotten in the crisis. "I hope someone loves me enough to get up."

He stayed with her when Lela left, cuddling her against him and drawing circles on her back. When Béatrix suggested Lela might need his company, he kissed her temple and drew her closer.

"Didn't invite her in the first place," he said. "Mind you, I enjoyed myself, but if she put her foot in it, she's got no one to blame but herself."

Was Béatrix's discomfort Lela's fault? Would her night with Andrew have been as enjoyable if Lela hadn't joined them? There was no way of knowing now.

But maybe that was the biggest problem. Lela had helped too much. Béatrix would never know if those moments of courage were real. She'd never be sure she could have attracted Andrew on her own. Lela had given her a gift.

And a gift wasn't what she needed at all.

Four

PHILIP STOOD BESIDE the front window, sipping a dark German beer. The hundred-year-old draperies held a musk they would never lose: women's perfume, stinky French cigarettes, three generations worth of dust. Their color was indescribable—not cream, not silver, not rose, but a shading of the three. They made him want to paw through bolts of fabric to find a match, to drag out his dressmaker's dummy and pins.

The longing was a tiny pain, a manageable pain. He weighed it in his mind as he watched the desultory midnight traffic on the avenue Foch. The city glittered, fairy-like, beyond the thick old glass. Come and play, it called. Don't you remember how much fun you used to have?

Philip was tempted. He hated this apartment at night.

He didn't much like it in the daytime, but night was worse. Then even pleasant memories were tainted by the knowledge of how they'd ended. Every sordid detail had come out in the papers. The reporters had raked up his failed career as a designer, his suspiciously advantageous marriage, the difference in his and Eve's ages.

And they'd interviewed her lovers.

Philip tilted his bottle for another swig. He'd known her lovers existed, in a vague, unpleasant way. He'd known since the second or third year. Eve denied them at first, then said she couldn't help herself, and, finally, asked why he complained when she always came back to him.

He'd taken a few lovers himself, out of spite, but the affairs left him feeling tired and in need of a wash. Eve was still the most exciting woman he knew, infuriating, but exciting—and the best mentor a man could want. Lela's friend claimed Simon Graves had made him a businessman. Well, Eve had made Philip one.

She liked to tease him whenever he broke it off with one of his partners. "*Maman* does it best, doesn't she?" she'd croon and trail her long red nails down his chest. Sometimes she'd be rough with him in bed, but he took that as a sign he'd truly hurt her, a sign she truly cared. He had too much to prove to give up on their marriage. If he left her, people would say he couldn't have loved her; he must have been out for what he could get.

He hadn't been, but he was beginning to think Eve had. He rested the side of his face against the window, the glass cooling his heated skin. What had Bea said? *She married you for your pretty face and your rock-hard, twenty-year-old cock.*

I've been kidding myself, he thought. That his stepdaughter knew, and had known from the start, was more humiliating than anything he'd read in the tabloids.

His hand suddenly stiff, he set his beer on the sill. The brand was a far cry from what he'd drunk as a lad, and even further from what he'd drunk with Eve. Champagne had been her style, with labels he still couldn't pronounce, for all his fluency in French.

He'd got too high in the instep. If he had a particle of sense, he'd ring a few mates, get roaring drunk, and try his luck tupping French girls. Unfortunately, he hadn't seen his mates in years. They hadn't mixed with Eve's friends. Of course, Philip hadn't mixed with them, either, except in the most superficial way.

Sod it, he thought, the side of his thumb pressed hard between his teeth. He'd go by himself. He deserved a night on the town. He deserved a good shagging he didn't have to apologize for. After all, chances were his stepdaughter wasn't sleeping alone.

HE FOUND HIS partner outside the Moulin Rouge. She was tall and busty and stood by the back-stage door, away from the tourist buses and the glare of the red neon windmill. She was smoking, one shoeless foot propped storklike on her knee. A teetering red heel supported her other foot, obviously the source of her fatigue. Though a trench coat covered her from neck to knee, her glittery makeup marked her a showgirl.

"Finished for the night?" he said in English.

She squinted through the mist at him, through the smoke of her cigarette. He wore his old pub-crawling togs—a loose white cotton shirt and snug jeans. He'd kept in shape. They fit as well as ever. One old girlfriend had called him a threat to public safety. Hoping he still was, he ventured his most harmless and charming smile.

"Yes, I'm finished," she said, wary but not alarmed. "I don't do the third show." She kneaded the ball of her foot. "How'd you know I spoke English?"

He stepped closer. "None of the girls who dance here are French. The Parisians have forgotten how to cancan."

"Damn straight." The woman grinned back at him. She was American, maybe a real Vegas showgirl, come for a taste of gay Paris. She looked him over, head to toe, clearly pleased she'd attracted him and willing to telegraph her interest. She took one last drag on her cigarette before flicking it into the alley. Then, both hands free, she massaged her arch as if it were a sexual organ. Philip was interested to see she wore no tights. Her legs were bare beneath the trench coat, bare and muscled and pale.

"I could do that for you," he said. Not waiting for permission, he captured her naked foot. It was cold but he would warm it. He knew about women's feet, how tender and abused they could be, how sensitive. This woman's foot had crooked toes and calluses, but they were obviously connected to her good spots. She whimpered as he worked her flesh between expert hands, her eyes glazing with sensual enjoyment. The expression sent another surge of interest to his groin.

"That ought to be against the law," she gasped.

Instinct told him to incline his head. Her foot slipped free as he kissed her, a polite seduction with a minimum of tongue. Her mouth answered in kind. He put his hands on her shoulders, warmth rather than pressure. Her weight shifted toward him. She was sturdy from her work.

Her hair smelled of smoke and Emeraude. Still kissing him, she flattened her hand on the center of his chest. Thinking she was telling him to stop, he released her. He was mistaken. Her hand dragged down his torso, turned until the fingers pointed down, then curled in unmistakable invitation around his balls. Her palm was warm. His cock swelled up against it, straining the faded jeans.

"Don't waste time, do you?" she said in a sexy smoker's rasp.

"Not when I'm this hard up."

She liked that answer but hid her smile behind a pursing of her lips. She squeezed him between her fingers and the heel of her hand, rubbing and pressing until he'd hardened to his limit, until his hips rolled forward in longing for a cozier home. She watched him change shape, lips curving, fake eyelashes shielding her dark brown eyes. Finally satisfied, she trailed one finger up his bulging zip. "Want to walk me home?"

"Happen I would," he said.

They walked arm in arm and hip to hip through the narrow back streets, away from the tourists and the all-night jazz clubs. Their hands made promises to each other, fingers sliding and twining in the universal language of desire. They didn't chat. They were both in that state of arousal when the body speaks more readily than the mouth. The streets were wet from the mist and the earlier evening rain. Their shoes made soft, gritty sounds on the cobbles. When they reached the rue Lepic, he knew they were close to Bea's home.

The coincidence unnerved him, though he didn't care to examine why. Abruptly impatient, he pulled the woman into an alley between a *boulangerie* and a greengrocer's. The air was heavy with the smell of bread and fruit. He pressed her firmly into the crumbling wall.

"I want you here," he said. "I want you now."

Her brows rose. Something about their shape, about their arch of surprise made him feel as if he would burst where he stood. His cock ached with arousal. He kissed her, this time without restraint, commanding her mouth until her spine sagged in reaction.

Not wanting her to fall, he used his weight to press her tighter to the building. His hands burrowed under her trench coat, finding not the costume he expected, but a dancer's wrap skirt and bodysuit. Beneath the skirt, the crotch of the bodysuit was damp.

She groaned as he pressed the stretchy cloth between her folds. Her head turned back and forth against the age-weathered stone. "Someone might see."

A tingle of excitement streaked down his tailbone.

"Yes," he agreed. "Someone might."

He took one step back from her and pulled his shirttails from his jeans. Her mouth fell open. He could almost read her thoughts. Was he going to bare himself? Did he dare? Her gaze darted to the nearest street lamp, then returned to his hands. He pushed the metal button through its hole, craving this exposure more than he could remember craving anything.

"You're crazy," she said, but his craziness clearly aroused her. Her hand drifted to her throat and stroked its milky skin.

He lowered his zip and eased out his erection. Her hand stilled. His cock was heavy but so stiffly engorged it curved above the horizontal. The cool night air could not discourage its raging lift. The threat of discovery merely

made it pound harder. His foreskin had pulled back behind the rosy, swollen head, withdrawing as vehemently as
the rest thrust forward. He wanted her to see it. He knew
Americans were fascinated by men who weren't cut, even
when they swore the idea disgusted them.

Smiling, he fisted the base of his shaft and pushed forward, slowly, stretching the wrinkled hood until it covered his crown. He secured the skin with thumb and forefinger, wanking just the head with it, twisting back and
forth, rubbing up and down. The friction was sweet and
soft and the knowledge that she watched made the blood
roar in his veins. A fat drop of pre-come rolled from his
slit, slicking the stimulation even more.

"Oh," she said, watching him darken and stretch. "Oh,
my." Her flush was visible beneath her stage makeup. She
fanned her face. "I hope you've got something for that
handsome fellow to wear."

He did, of course. He dug the necessary from his back
pocket and made a little show of rolling it on. When he'd
finished, the woman's hand fluttered out to touch.

"Oh," she said, fingers skating down his bobbing
length. "Aren't you something? Aren't you just?"

"Want it?" he said. She nodded, still playing with him.
He untied her trench coat and parted it around her torso.
Her breasts were large and full, her waist hour-glass small.
Her hips made him want to test their softness. His gaze
drifted back up her body. Her eyes were dark, surrounded
by silver paint and long, spidery lashes. They glittered
with arousal. She was breathing rapidly through her
mouth. Her breasts rose and fell, hardened nipples strafing
his chest with every inhalation. Good, he thought. She
was ready. He could plunge straight in and ride. He gath-

ered up her silky skirt and popped the two snaps at her crotch. She wore panties beneath, sopping white cotton through which her curls clearly showed.

"Tell me you want it," he said, his voice hard and unfamiliar. "Tell me."

Her head tossed. "You bet I want it."

He ripped her panties at the seam. Her gasp held a laugh. She grabbed her skirt and held it up herself.

"Now," she ordered. "Give me everything you've got."

He took her in a single thrust, inspiring a different sort of gasp, one that changed to a groan as he pounded in and out. He couldn't have waited if she'd begged. He was crazed for this, out of his head. His cock heated quickly at the pumping drive, a white-hot rod of flesh, a machine of selfish pleasure.

Fortunately, his partner shared his need for forceful sex. Her arms hugged his neck, her legs squeezed his waist.

"Yes," she cried, urging him on. "Give me that big, bad thing." She was a moaner, a squealer, a scratcher of backs. If anyone walked by they'd know at once what was going on. Philip didn't care. He loved every heart-thumping second. Coins clanked in the pockets of her trench coat. Cream squelched in her pussy. Cries caught in her throat like a tortured cat. The sounds drove him wilder than he could bear. He took a tighter grip on her bottom, working harder, deeper.

But he didn't forget for an instant where he was.

He was fucking a stranger against a public wall, in a public street, his churning arse bared to the air. He was a stone's throw from Bea's flat, a breath from discovery. His lungs labored. His cock burned. His balls ached as if they'd been filled with a hose. Sparks of feeling raced down his nerves. His orgasm was rising like fury, like fear. Faster. He had to go faster or they'd be caught.

"Yes," said the woman, her eyes screwed shut, her strong thighs gripping his waist. Her pussy was just as tight and twice as hot. If she hadn't been so wet, their frenzied motions would have hurt. The muscles of her bottom worked under his hands, striving to meet him thrust for thrust. Suddenly, she switched angles, smashing her clit against his root. His cock bumped something deep inside her. His balls tightened as if she had them in her fist.

Now, he thought, the pressure blindingly sweet. Let go.

He shouted in triumph as his climax broke, a hot rush, a honeyed spasm of flesh and seed. Dimly, he heard the woman go over, too, felt her pussy clamp on his last convulsion of bliss. They sagged together against the wall, two sweaty, panting strangers who'd just had the ride of a lifetime.

The woman stroked the back of his neck, beneath his ponytail, while he tried to pull himself together. Her nails were incongruously cool, as was her drawling voice.

"Not that I mind," she said. "Given your performance. But who the hell is Bea?"

Oh, Lord, thought Philip, and covered his eyes with his arm.

BÉATRIX WAS ALONE in her bed.

And someone was frying bacon.

A square of sunlight warmed her face, setting the pink and yellow chintz of her bedclothes ablaze. She rubbed her nose and shut her eyes. She could still see the river from her dream. No, not a river, a canal, with a rutted towpath and deep green woods behind. Grasses grew thick along the banks. Wildflowers. Dragonflies. She coaxed her mind to drift. Above the sluggish water lay a green-gold haze, part dust, part sunshine, part essence of summer.

I need my sketchbook, she thought. I need my pastels. She rolled out of bed, eyes still gummy with sleep. She fumbled in her night table and found a stick of charcoal but not a pad. She carried the stub into the bathroom, emerging clear-eyed, but still muzzy-headed. The picture was in her head. She had to get it down. She mustn't let other thoughts intrude.

She wandered past the kitchen, ignoring Lela's hail. Where was that sketchbook? She found it, with her pastels, in the old-fashioned pantry beside her never-used roasting pan. She didn't know how it had gotten here, but since the light in the pantry was good—a bare, bright bulb *and* a window—she plunked on the floor to work.

Just the outlines, she told herself, and a few color notes, but for long minutes she was lost. The composition grew to the clanking of plates and the sizzle of bacon. She could almost see the girl's simple, threadbare dress. Blue. She knew it was blue with white pointelle flowers. The time would be just after World War II. She made a mental note to visit the Musée de la Mode to study the period's clothes. Death would shadow the girl's eyes, would thin her milk-pale cheeks. She'd be too young to have seen such violence and too old to forget. She'd smile at her little brother, though, and you'd know how strong she was. You'd know her little family would survive.

She scribbled furiously, the charcoal making ghost shapes on the page, the pastels smearing together until something like the colors in her head sprang to life among the mix. She couldn't get the expression she wanted for the youngest boy. Maybe she'd haunt the Tuileries today and watch the toddlers play in the garden.

She flipped the page to give the boy's face one last try, then realized her burst of inspiration had passed. The floor was hard and her legs were cramped and she was being very rude to her guests, even if Lela was used to her disappearing acts. Now that she'd recovered from her fugue, their voices drifted in from the kitchen. They were eating, wise souls, but they obviously didn't know how near she was.

"Those two are hot for each other," Andrew said around a mouthful of food. "If she and Philip had blushed any harder, I was gonna look for a fire hose."

"That's old news." Lela sighed. "At least on her part. I don't know what's up with him. Horny widower syndrome, I guess. Before he married, he was quite the womanizer."

"*Non,*" said Andrew, the French odd but right in his American mouth. "If that were all it was, he would have looked at you that way, too. He wants that girl. He wants to burn up the sheets with her."

"Mm," said Lela, her doubt clear.

"I'm not wrong, *chère.* I know a man in heat when I smell him."

"You and your nose." Glass clinked as Lela poured a drink. "If you're right, though, it could mean trouble."

"But why? I know he's her stepdaddy, but the difference in age is so small. And this is France."

"It may be France, but the haute couture rumor mill grinds very fine. Everyone knows he was Eve's boy toy. If he took up with her daughter, with her owning half the stock, he'd lose what credibility he has. I'm not sure the business would survive it."

Her words were stones on Béatrix's chest. She hugged the sketch pad and closed her eyes. She knew this. She'd always known it. Anyway, Lela's worries were moot. Philip hadn't blushed because he wanted her; he'd blushed because her behavior had outraged every sensibility he had.

Phil the Thrill want her? That would be the day.

SHE ATE A belated breakfast while Lela lingered over coffee. Andrew had washed up before Béatrix could stop him, then disappeared to dress. He reappeared long enough to say good-bye, doing his tie as he bent to kiss Lela's cheek.

"It breaks my heart to say this, ladies, but I must catch the train to Provence."

Lela straightened his knot. "For your perfume hunt?"

"*Oui, mademoiselle.* Today, I smell the latest samples from the perfumer, tromp through the lavender fields, and stick my head in the factory's vats."

"Don't fall in," she teased.

"Never," he assured her, then rounded the table to take his leave of Béatrix.

"Thank you for everything," she said, his regard making her shy.

He cupped her face between his hands. "Thank you, Béatrix. I'm glad to have met you and would be very happy to see you again when I return."

His eyes twinkled in his handsome, sun-lined face. *Mon Dieu*, what a sexy man. She could hardly believe he meant it.

"I'd like to see you, too," she murmured. He grinned and kissed her, pressing his tongue into her mouth and drawing deeply, intimately, until the fire that seared her cheeks ran all the way down her body. After what seemed like ages, he pulled back.

"*Au revoir*," he said, clearly pleased to have kissed her speechless.

Béatrix pressed her fingers to her lips and watched him go.

Then she and Lela were alone.

"So." Lela lifted her cup in both hands.

So, thought Béatrix, wishing she could avoid this confrontation. She couldn't though, and it was no time to turn coward. She pushed her plate aside and filled her own cup. She poured a thin stream of cream over her spoon, then stirred.

"You've done that before, haven't you?" she said. "Been with women, I mean."

"Once or twice." Lela's expression was wry. "Oh, don't look so grim. One night won't make you a lesbian."

"Are you?"

"Am I a lesbian? Bea. How many men have you seen me with?"

"Are you bisexual then?"

Lela raked her hair off her face. "You know I've never liked being labeled."

"Fine." Béatrix set down her spoon. "It's none of my business."

"You're right," said Lela. "It's not."

Béatrix had heard that cool tone before, but never directed toward herself. She squirmed with embarrassment. No doubt Lela thought she was being hypocritical. And maybe she was. She couldn't pretend she'd hated what they'd done, so how could she judge Lela for sleeping with however many women she wanted? Of course, the fact that she'd never mentioned the experiences, that she'd kept them secret, made Béatrix think she didn't know her friend at all.

"Look." Lela reached across the table to rub her shoulder. "It was a once-in-a-lifetime thing. Let's chalk it up to experience and put it behind us."

The best Béatrix could manage was a nod, but that was good enough for Lela. She gave her arm a bracing punch.

"Good," she said. "Now tell me everything you know about running a swank boutique."

This particular change of topic did not cheer Béatrix in the least.

Five

THOUGH ANDREW HAD said he wanted to see her again, Béatrix didn't expect him to call so soon. When she heard his voice, her heart jumped—not like it jumped when she heard Philip's, but the skip was noticeable all the same.

They arranged to meet at a café near the Jardins du Trocadéro. Since Béatrix arrived first, she nabbed a table on the pavement and ordered coffee. The spot couldn't have been nicer. She had an excellent view of the Eiffel Tower, and, while she couldn't see the great water cannons through the trees, she could certainly hear the famous Trocadéro fountain.

All in all, she was pleased with herself. She'd spent the morning sketching costumes at the Musée de la Mode. Her only regret was that she hadn't worn comfortable shoes. Dressing up for Andrew was foolish. Andrew wasn't going to be her boyfriend. Andrew was a flirt whose zipper needed a speed bump. Nonetheless, she knew he'd notice the care she'd taken. With that in mind, she'd donned a pretty lilac flowered dress. Its matching shrug ended inches below her arms. The abbreviated sweater was probably too delicate for a girl like her, but she loved the way it made her feel. She'd bought it through Meilleurs Amis the day it came in stock. The hand-sewn beading was exquisite: leafy swirls that curled along the edges like a vine. Best Friends had an arrangement with the supplier, guaranteeing no two models would be alike. No one in the world owned this sweater but her.

With a rueful smile, she stroked the tiny beads at the end of the sleeve. The exclusivity appealed to her. Perhaps she was her mother's daughter, after all.

A familiar blond head ducked under the umbrella that shaded her table.

"Hello, hello," Andrew said, radiating bonhomie. He kissed her quickly on both cheeks, then lingeringly on her mouth. He folded his long body into the chair opposite hers. "You look beautiful! Am I late?"

"Not at all," she said, though he was a little. She patted her traveling sketchbook. "I finished earlier than I expected."

His eyes widened with exaggerated curiosity. "Tell you what. You show me yours and I'll show you mine."

"You have the perfume?"

"I have samples." He dug them from his briefcase. "Here. Give me your wrist. I want to test this on a real woman's skin."

"They only had fake women in Provence?"

He paused to shake his finger at her joke, then misted her inner arm. A sweet scent filled the air, citrus and cinnamon and a hint of vanilla.

"Yum," she said. "It smells like you could eat it."

Andrew beamed at her. "It's my favorite. I'm taking three other scents back to my employer, but I wanted to smell that one on you." He lifted her arm and leaned forward, dragging his nose along her skin. A pleasant shiver slid down her spine. He really was a sexy man. As if to prove it, he drifted back to her wrist and pressed a pulse-quickening kiss into her palm.

"Alas," he said. "Your other kissable places will have to wait. I have meetings this afternoon."

Béatrix wouldn't put it past him to be having meetings with other women, meetings of the carnal variety. She smiled to herself and carried his hand to her mouth. She kissed the first knuckle of each finger, then slid the tip of the last between her lips. As she licked it, his breath hitched, then resumed a little faster than before.

"I don't mind waiting," she said. "As long as you're worth waiting for."

He groaned and scooted to the edge of his chair. His knees bumped hers. "Sugar, right about now I could bench-press that tower on my cock. You bet I'll make it worth your while."

But Béatrix wasn't going to take his word for it. She slid her hand under the table to check.

PHILIP FROZE ON the sidewalk, every drop of warmth draining from his face. He'd been about to wave to Bea, to ask her to share his lunch hour. Two days had passed since his disturbing debauch with the showgirl, and he still hadn't shaken its effects. With an eye toward restoring his nerves, he'd taken the morning off to visit his favorite museum. The display of Balenciaga designs had indeed soothed him, so much so that he was genuinely happy to see his stepdaughter. He hadn't experienced the slightest urge to duck and run.

Until he noticed she wasn't alone.

Until he noticed she and the American were sharing a good deal more than coffee.

Under the flimsy cover of the table, she was wanking him through his trousers. His zip was open and her thumb and pinkie had disappeared into the gap, clearly stimulating the goodies that hid inside. Philip couldn't see actual genitalia but the motion of her wrist and the deep flush on the American's face left little to doubt. Squirming with pleasure, the American cupped her cheek and whispered in her ear. Bea lowered her head. She laughed. The laugh was purely hers, low and throaty and victorious. It was a soft laugh, one you had to lean closer to hear. Philip had heard it once before, the once before that had started this trouble. And now she was laughing that way for another man!

Fury flared like a bonfire in his chest. Bea shouldn't have been touching the man. She shouldn't have been touching anyone.

He was striding forward to yank her away when her partner grabbed for a napkin. Philip tensed. The American was about to come. Bea showed no mercy. Her hand moved faster as he shoved the cloth under his waistband.

Their heads leaned together, nose to nose, like lovers sharing a secret. Bea was smiling. The man bit his lip. She whispered something, something sexy apparently. The man gasped and shuddered into the curve of her neck.

The waiter returned in time to catch his deep orgasmic sigh.

Bea seemed entirely unflustered.

"*L'addition, s'il vous plait,*" she said, not missing a beat.

The waiter left to retrieve their bill, but it was sheer luck that he, and everyone else in the crowded café, had seen nothing more compromising. Philip could not tolerate such reckless disregard for propriety. A memory of his own behavior threatened to puncture his outrage, but, no, this was broad daylight! And Philip was an adult. Bea must have lost her mind. He shouldered through the tables, ignoring the American to glare straight in his stepdaughter's eyes.

"Don't you think," he said in his iciest British tone, "that this family has seen enough scandal?"

True to form, Bea refused to buckle. She licked the pad of her thumb, the same thumb she'd had on that bastard's cock, then rested her chin on her folded hand. Philip felt his cheeks flame.

"The only scandal," she said, "is the one you're about to cause."

PHILIP WAS SPLUTTERING, positively spluttering. If Béatrix hadn't been so angry, she would have laughed.

" 'You—you—you're impossible,' " she mimicked.

"*Chérie,*" said Andrew, gently chiding. He rose, buttoning his suit jacket over his open fly. "I can see you have private matters to discuss, so I'll take my leave." He bent to kiss her cheek. "I'll call you tonight."

"You will not," Philip averred, still seething.

Suave as ever, Andrew smiled blandly and tipped an invisible hat. She watched his compact derriere disappear around the corner, then turned to her self-appointed protector.

"Well," she said, "don't just stand there glaring. Sit down and get that righteous fury off your chest."

"I am not going to discuss this in public."

"*Eh, bien.* I'd rather not discuss it at all."

"Oh, we're going to discuss it." The skin around his mouth was white. "If I have to drag you out of here kicking and screaming to do it."

Béatrix had seen him get stuffy before but never like this. His face was red, and he'd folded his arms across his chest. She half believed he would drag her off. Of course, she more than half wanted him to. With a sigh for her own stupidity, she threw down a handful of francs and stood.

"Your place is closer," she said. "We'll go there."

He took her arm. "It's not my place," he huffed. "It's your family home."

Mon Dieu, she thought, amazed and touched. No matter how angry Philip was, he could still say something kind.

At the curb, she spotted a cab with its white roof light on. On the grounds that empty taxis were rarer than pearls, she flagged it down. They climbed into the back. Philip was so eager to scold her, he started in before the door slammed shut.

"You touched that man," he said, giving his cuffs an indignant tug. "You touched that man where everyone could see."

It was hard to take him seriously when he used that prissy tone. She lounged back in the seat and crossed her legs. "Jealous?"

To her amazement, his flush deepened. "Of course, I'm not."

But he couldn't meet her eye. He turned toward the window where the colonnaded arc of the Chaillot Palace was rolling by. Intrigued by this reaction, her gaze slid to his trousers. Though he'd propped one foot on his knee, his erection was impossible to miss. It distended the summer wool like the bend of a sink pipe. Obviously, what he'd seen her doing had aroused him.

Maybe Andrew was right about him having the hots for her.

"You are jealous," she said, the knowledge shooting to her head like champagne. She grabbed his ankle and pushed it down, baring his bulge in its entirety. "You wish you were the one I'd touched where everyone could see."

He shoved her hands away. "Don't be daft. I'd be mad to want any such thing."

Which wasn't precisely a denial. Even if she wasn't the sort of woman he went for, at the very least the thought of public sex pushed his private buttons. She checked the progress of the cab. They'd reached the avenue Foch, mere blocks from Philip's home. If they got out there, Philip would take control of himself and she'd lose this unprecedented and rather delicious upper hand. She considered the straining cloth across his crotch. Substantial was the only word for his erection. Her pussy quivered. To hell with fair play, she thought. It would be a crime to waste that blatantly virile display. She knocked on the glass between the seats.

"We've changed our minds," she told the driver. "Please take us to Versailles."

"Versailles?" Philip's query was weak. Versailles was no five-minute ride. Versailles was far enough for seduction.

With a smile that would have done her foremothers proud, Béatrix swung her leg across his lap and sat on his thighs. His muscles shifted beneath her, with nervousness and arousal. His groin radiated heat, and she hadn't even touched it. She smoothed both hands down the front of his jacket. Philip glanced over her shoulder at the driver. He was a young man, ill-shaven but clean. From the twinkle in his eye, Philip suspected he was looking forward to having a story to tell his friends. This attitude did not put Philip at ease. Already his face glowed with perspiration. When Bea rolled her hips to snug her mons against his cock, the sheen began to glitter.

"Versailles," she confirmed, murmuring it like a lover's promise. "I have an urge to see what's growing in Louis's gardens."

"I'm expected at work," he said, his voice breaking as her hands slid inside his jacket to stroke his shirt. Beneath the cloth, his nipples were diamond points. "The traffic—"

"Yes," she soothed, rubbing back and forth. "The traffic might slow us down."

"The people in the other cars . . ."

She licked the warm column of his neck, pausing just under his ear to count the racing of his pulse. He shuddered and gripped her waist, but he didn't push her away.

"Please, Bea," he begged. "Don't do this. People will see."

But she could feel how much he wanted it. Her silky dress had pooled around her knees, and his cock was pounding through the crotch of her panties, practically burrowing through the cotton to find a home. His eyes, normally a sweet, placid gray, were stormy. His fingers dug like pincers into her waist.

"People *might* see," she said, and thrilled to the sudden expansion of his pupils. "But I'll make sure they don't."

"Bea." He buried his face in her neck, breathing as if he'd just run up the steps to Sacré-Coeur. His heart thrummed against both their rib cages. "Bea, please."

That's when she knew he was helpless to resist what she was offering. This situation appealed so strongly to his secret kink, he was incapable of saying no. He was counting on her to say it for him. Silly man. Béatrix wouldn't say no for the world.

She undid the first button beneath his tie. His breath sighed from him: surrender, excitement. She released another button, and another, and spread the gap to bare his skin. Her hands widened the opening, sliding under the fine Egyptian cotton find his nipples. She flicked them with her thumbs until he uttered a low, tormented sound. He nuzzled the bend of her shoulder, then bit down through her beaded sweater.

"Put your hands under my dress," she whispered.

His hands shook as he slid them under her hem, cupping her thighs, then her buttocks. His fingers found the dampening crotch of her panties.

"Oh, God," he said, eyes screwed shut. "Oh, fuck."

"Yes." She licked the shell of his ear. "That's just what I intend to do."

The edge of his nails tickled her through the cloth, finding and then circling the little bulge of her clit. The thrill of his touch, there, so intimate, so tremulous, was inexpressible.

"Bea," he moaned, and his mouth turned to hers.

They kissed as if they were drunk, slow and open-mouthed, pausing for breath, for a change in angle, for a new dip and draw of tongues. His lips were soft. His hands roamed her body under the loose dress, up her back, down her bottom, and, finally around her ribs to cup her breasts. Her fullness seemed to excite him. He broke free of the kiss. He pulled down her bra and pushed one breast toward his mouth, sucking its tip through the thin, flowered silk. His tongue was liquid fire, strafing her nipples by turns, coaxing them tighter, making them ache.

After a moment's eager fumbling, his other hand wriggled into her panties. He searched her folds and found her liquid core. His body tensed at the evidence of her arousal. Two long fingers slid up her sheath. His thumb pressed the slippery hood of her clit. His fingers moved. Bea swallowed back a moan. Sweet sensations rolled through her sex. Her head fell back. His touch was surer than she'd expected, stronger. She felt herself grow wetter, felt her pussy soften like ripened fruit.

He felt it, too, around his probing fingers. He bit his lip and breathed through his nose, as quiet as a boy whacking off in the bed he shared with his brother. His struggle for silence was as thrilling as a thousand anguished groans. Béatrix melted as much from that as from the skill of his caress.

"Touch me," he said, breathing the words into her bosom. "Open my trousers and pet my cock."

It was what she'd done to Andrew, obviously what he'd wanted ever since. She pulled him out with both hands. He was big, his skin fevered and damp. She held his shaft between their bodies, in the open, pulling the skin up and down his rigid core. He lowered his head to watch, lips parted, cheeks flushed.

"Good?" she whispered, thumbs sliding side by side up his raphe.

He nodded dumbly, then shuddered when she pushed his foreskin back over his glans. Within the circle of pink, his little slit wept opalescent tears. Philip's gaze slid sideways toward the window, toward the traffic on A13. A black Mercedes rolled past them to the right. A well-dressed matron sat in back, complete with pillbox hat and veil. Béatrix thought of her mother's friends, the fashion dragons. What would happen if one of them saw Philip now? If that elegant hat turned to reveal a familiar face? Philip couldn't seem to look away. His tongue curled over his upper lip. His cock throbbed violently in her hand. Was he thinking the same thing? Was fear part of his erotic charge?

She knew she should stop now, but the power was too heady to relinquish. For once, he was weaker than she was. For once, he was the desperate one.

"I could hide you," she purred. "I could hide you inside me. I could cover us with my dress. No one would know what we were doing unless I moved."

He closed his eyes. His hand tightened on her breast.

"I don't have anything with me," he gasped, as if it hurt him, physically, to admit. "I couldn't protect you."

She took the flare of his glans between her finger and thumb, then stretched his cock from his groin. Tendons stood out beneath the skin. What a marvel was a horny cock. Her antics didn't seem to hurt him at all.

"Do you have anything I need to be protected from?" she asked. "Because I am on the pill."

She could see she'd shocked him. His hips squirmed from side to side.

"Bea," he said, practically panting her name. "You shouldn't ask a question like that when you've . . . when you've got a prick in your fist and a hand up your knickers. Under those conditions, any man would have to be a saint to tell the truth."

"But I'm not asking any man. I'm asking you." Smiling, she released the tension on his cock, then pulled again. "So tell me, Phil, when was the last time you made love without a condom?"

He gulped for air as she stretched him even farther than before. "Never."

"That makes two of us then."

She could sense his awareness of her shifting. He knew she was sexually active, of course, but now she'd laid the knowledge bare. His eyes searched hers, doubts racing visibly behind them. She was offering an intimacy she'd never shared with anyone, a kind of virginity. And she was asking the same of him. He wet his lips. She knew he wanted to accept. She knew he thought it wasn't proper. Not with her. Not in a taxi. Not with the ghost of her mother hovering behind them both.

"Bea . . ." he cautioned.

She kissed him to silence, until his mouth softened and reached.

"Bea," he said, in an entirely different tone.

"Skin to skin," she whispered. "Wet to wet. Think of it, Philip. Think how good riding bareback would feel."

He shivered, putty in her hands. The fingers that probed her cunt slipped free. He tugged at the waist of her panties. "You have to move. I want these off."

He'd decided then. He'd decided he couldn't resist. She rose enough for him to slide the panties down her legs, then resumed her straddle. The vinyl seat was warm beneath her shins. She lifted her skirt and let it flutter over his rudely bobbing cock, over his reaching hands. He gripped her buttocks, tilting her to the proper angle. His palms were hot and damp. She braced on his shoulders and lowered her weight.

"Don't rush," he whispered, a drop of sweat rolling down his temple. "I want to feel every inch go in."

He couldn't have made a more provocative request. Béatrix slowed her descent, tensing her thighs, heat building between them as their bodies came together.

They both jumped when his sex met hers. His tip slipped easily between her folds, warmth meeting warmth, velvet oiling satin. When he breached the mouth, she sighed, an involuntary exhalation of pleasure. Gently, he pressed her downward, the bulb stretching her, the shaft filling her. His eyes slid shut. She sank, grateful for the strength of her leg muscles, grateful for the give of her sheath. He was almost too big. The penetration seemed to go on and on, deeper, fuller, until her hips finally rested on his.

A double pulse beat hard inside her sex.

"Ah," he sighed, his face transformed by bliss. He released her hips and hugged her. His chest was hard against hers, his hair silken on her cheek. He rubbed her back under her dress as if he couldn't get enough of her skin. The moment was sweet.

But neither of them could remain that way long.

Philip's hips were the first to roll, his cock flexing with the small, urgent lift. She laughed at his eagerness.

"I won't come inside you," he promised. "I'll pull out right before."

"You don't have to do that."

"Yes." He rocked a little harder, the crown pressing deep. "Just in case. Just to be safe."

She shook her head at him. For all the good it would do, withdrawal was hardly worth the trouble. But she didn't want to argue, not with that sleek, hard pole inside her, not with the throb of pleasure rising between her legs. She wanted only to have him, to watch him unravel piece by piece while she lived out her oldest dream.

PHILIP COULDN'T THINK straight. Bea's scent surrounded him, vanilla and spice, like something warm from the bakery. Though they barely moved, his cock screamed with the pleasure of each carefully rationed thrust. He could feel everything, as if his nerves had been turned inside out, not only in his penis, but all over his body. Her flesh was heaven under his hands, her breasts, her hips, the sensual curve of her belly. Her lushness made him greedy. He kissed her neck, sucked her skin against his teeth. He shouldn't leave marks, not where people could see, but how could he get enough of her? She was so rich, so sweet. When her body squirmed around his cock, he wanted to cry.

He kept his eyes shut, not wanting to see the cabbie's gaze in the rearview mirror, not wanting to see the knowing smile. His blindness made him feel her all the more. Her excitement rose as he rocked her, an inch forward, an inch back. She was breathing faster. She was pushing more urgently. He hoped this was enough for her, this bridled back and forth. Lord knew, it was almost too much for him.

She came so quickly it startled him. Her pussy grew wetter and tighter, and then she quivered hard around him. It was an orgasm an idiot couldn't have missed.

"Sorry," she gasped. "Couldn't wait."

He had to laugh.

And he had to feel her come again. If it killed him, he had to. He slid his hands under her thighs, urging her higher so he could thrust upward from the seat. Two inches wouldn't hurt. Two inches weren't so much more stimulating than one. But his neck began to wobble at the increase in sensation. She was soft inside, the friction half comfort, half fire streaking down his cock.

This was so good, better than anything he'd ever felt. Her skin touching his, her wetness, the intimacy of fucking without a single barrier between them. He could feel the texture of her cunt, each fold seeming to kiss his sensitized skin. This was closeness. This was the sex of the Garden. Had the apple tasted this good to Adam? Had he thought: who'd go back if they could? He wished they were alone with long, lazy weeks of lovemaking before them. He wished they were strangers, without names or pasts. He would let his impossible tenderness out, the lonely ache that eased, just a little, when he held her in his arms.

She, too, seemed to sense the moment of union. She cradled his head and stroked his neck. His sadness ebbed, drowned by the pleasure of plunge and pull, by the scent of her skin and the gentle brush of her fingers in his hair. The rumble of the taxi was nothing to that, the eyes of strangers, the risk of discovery. Holding her was sweeter than all the rest. Her breath hitched as he rocked deeper still. Her tension was rising. She was going to come.

She tightened around him, adding a swivel to her rock. His cock hiccupped in delight. He gritted his teeth. If he wasn't careful, she'd pull him over with her.

The hand that had stroked his neck dug in, pricking him with its nails.

Yes, he thought, fighting his own climax. Yes, sweetheart, hurry.

He pressed his cheek to hers, willing back the fire that licked his spine. He ought to pull out. He was too bloody close. His nerves were clanging in warning. His cock had turned to iron. His balls were so tight they hurt. You promised, he told himself. You promised. But, oh, he wanted to feel her shake. He'd pay attention this time. He'd memorize every sigh.

Or he would if his head stopped trying to explode.

"Philip," she gasped, and suddenly it was happening. The delicious little spasms were quivering down his prick. Her hips juddered back and forth and she pulled, pulled at his cock as if she had a fist inside her pussy. Every drop of sexual fluid he possessed struggled madly to obey her call.

He hissed in reaction, didn't even have breath for a curse. An urge took hold of him, a primitive compulsion to possess. He wanted to grab her and thrust and blast his spunk to her brains. He wanted it more than breath. With a strangled cry, he yanked free and shoved against her thigh. Furiously, he rubbed, already shooting. His release exploded in white and gold. He spurted, copious bursts of sticky fire. Her skin was warm, his orgasm hard, and for a brief space of time release overwhelmed disappointment.

When he finished, he felt as if he'd won a grueling race.

His need to come inside her scared him. He'd wanted to mark her where she couldn't scrub it off, where his essence could bind with hers and change her smell, her taste . . . her soul. He pressed his palm to his forehead, but the only fever he found was fading lust. What was wrong with him? This was Bea, the young woman whose care had been left in his hands. Churlish Bea. Stubborn Bea. Who had "issues," as the Americans said, that sleeping with her mother's husband would not cure. He opened his mouth to apologize.

"No," she said, stroking his hair with both hands. It had fallen free of its clip, and she spread it across his shoulders. "No regrets, Philip. And no swearing this will never happen again."

"But it can't happen again. It shouldn't have happened today."

She sighed and climbed off him, leaving him chilled with drying sweat. He knew he was right. They couldn't keep doing this. It wasn't healthy. It wasn't right.

But it had felt right. In spite of everything, when he'd held her, when they'd shared that pleasure and warmth, it had felt more right than anything he'd known.

New York

L ELA SIPPED HER white wine and rested her head on the gently humming window. The first class seats were roomy, but not quite roomy enough to keep her seatmate from getting on her nerves.

Andrew bubbled with admiration for her friend: how clever Bea was and how pretty, how daring she'd been at that little café. He couldn't thank Lela enough for introducing them. He only wished he'd had more time to explore her untapped sensuality.

"She's a volcano," he said, unconsciously licking his lips. "Quiet on top and molten underneath. Hot-hot, as they say back home."

Yes, indeed, Lela thought. Glad you liked her, and I'm sure you're very welcome.

But Andrew was merely warming to the topic.

She slouched in her seat and pretended to read the in-flight magazine. Did Andrew think she wasn't human? That somehow it didn't prick her pride to hear her old lover praise his new one, even if she had pushed him into her arms?

"She has the most gorgeous breasts," he said, nudging her shoulder as if expecting her to agree.

As it happened, Lela did agree. That was part of the problem. To her mind, she had one true talent: charming whomever she wanted into bed. In Bea's case, she'd been a little too good at it. She could blame it on being drunk, she supposed, or on the pulse-pounding thrill of watching her friend pop Andrew's cork. The truth was, though, she'd wanted to sleep with Bea for some time.

Lela had never been one to keep her feelings in neat compartments. Sex was the best way she knew to get close, sometimes the only way. When two people were skin to skin, their vulnerabilities exposed, the connection was like nothing else.

But she should have known Bea wouldn't be comfortable sharing that closeness with her. Bea simply couldn't take it lightly. While she could be casual about sex, she was never casual about love. Lela could hardly say the same. She knew something was wrong with her. Other people got close without hopping into bed. Other people fell in love, made commitments. Other people knew how to jump to one side of the sexual fence.

Understandably, Andrew and Bea's admiration for each other inspired a nice double stab of envy.

She flipped to the next page of the magazine, seeing Bea's face as Andrew worked her to orgasm, imagining his as Bea jacked him off at the Paris café. *Are you bisexual?* Bea had asked that morning in her kitchen. Who the hell knew? Who the hell cared? What mattered was she'd fucked up. Again.

She knew the fault lay in her stupid childhood, but knowing didn't seem to help. All those homes, all those foster parents. She hadn't been a troublemaker, not at first. She'd tried to fit in. She'd tried to be lovable, but she hadn't known how, and, in the end, none of them really gave a damn. The minute she proved inconvenient, she was out on her ass, the few friends she'd managed to make left behind. Lost.

She'd learned to make new ones. She was good at that. She just didn't make close friends. Why get attached if you couldn't stick around? But Bea had been irresistible. Bea was a queen who'd mistaken herself for a peasant. She treated Lela like a hero just for pointing out the truth. Lela's flaws were virtues to Bea, and Lela's virtues, well, Mother Teresa had nothing on them! Nor had anything shaken Bea's opinion. When she made a friend, she made a friend for life. Lela blessed the day she'd met her. She was, when you came right down to it, the only family Lela had.

If Lela lost her, she might as well slit her throat.

"Hey," said Andrew. "Where'd you go?"

She shook her head and blinked hard. "Sorry. What did you say?"

He smiled and nudged her glasses up her nose. "I was just wonderin' if you wanted to have dinner with me and Simon when we get back."

Oh, God, she thought. Not that again. You'd think she was a party favor the way he kept trying to pass her around. True, Lela had passed Andrew around first but, frankly, she doubted Simon Graves would be the prize Bea was. How much fun could a man be who did nothing but work?

"Andrew," she said in her sweetest, most insincere tone. "If your boss needs a good fuck, I'm afraid you'll have to do it yourself."

Andrew blushed to the roots of his sun-bleached hair.

Which made her suspect that might be what he wanted.

"YOUR FOUR O'CLOCK is here, Mr. Graves."

Mrs. Winters' quavery voice came through the speaker on his desk. Simon smiled. No matter how many four o'clocks Mrs. Winters announced, they still flustered her conservative soul.

With a mischief few suspected he possessed, he let his secretary stew, though his cock had begun to thicken the moment she buzzed—like Pavlov's dog perking up for a daily treat. He straightened the photo of his adoptive parents, the only photo on his gleaming, mile-wide desk. They beamed arm in arm on the deck of the *QE2,* garish in their Hawaiian vacation clothes, looking more like tourists than people who could have, thanks to Simon, bought their own cruise line. Their pleasure brought him pleasure. Shoulders relaxing, he smoothed his brown silk tie and spun his contoured leather chair toward the picture window.

The Graves Tower stood forty floors high, a sleek, five-year-old needle of polished red granite. Outside, the steel and glass of midtown Manhattan glittered in the sun. The

East River rolled blue beneath the sky, and the subaudible rumble that was the city's pulse vibrated through his bones.

By this time, Simon's well-trained cock was hard enough to alarm his waiting guest. He reached behind him to depress the intercom's talk button.

"Send her in, Mrs. Winters."

Diane swept in on a cloud of Cristalle. He wasn't particularly fond of the scent, but his ability to identify it pleased him. Who said you couldn't teach an old dog new tricks? Expression composed, he turned the chair to face her.

"Simon," she said, with a regal nod.

He took in her deep-red power suit, the skirt precariously short, her legs impossibly long. Her hair, chin length and discreetly blond, was combed behind her ears. Her makeup was impeccable. She'd come a long way from the ragged college student he'd stunned at a campus coffee shop with an offer to pay tuition in return for five pleasant hours of work a week.

And they were pleasant hours, for both of them, or Simon wouldn't have continued the arrangement. When it came to sex, he was a practical man. To him, lust was a healthy urge that ought to be satisfied whenever convenient, without shame or regret. But he had no desire to turn nice young women into whores. Mistresses, yes. Whores, no.

He liked women, of course. He simply wished to avoid the emotional entanglements contingent upon having "girlfriends." He hated falling short of expectations, whether they be for romance or marriage. Better not to inspire any hopes in the first place. His glance fell on the smiling picture of his parents. His jaw firmed. Some debts could never be repaid. Some debts had to come first. Diane understood his priorities and shared them. He had no doubt she'd go far in her chosen field.

"You look very nice," he said.

His compliment seemed to startle her. He frowned. Was he truly so miserly with his praise? He didn't like that idea. Every valued employee deserved positive feedback.

"You always look nice," he ventured. "I appreciate the care you take."

She smiled as if he'd amused her, so perhaps that wasn't right either. She swung her elegant arm toward the door of his private suite.

"Shall we?" she said. Her eyes slid down his body, halting at the thrust of his erection. "I can see you're ready to get down to business."

He was, indeed. More than ready. And yet her quip bothered him, just a little. *Was* their relationship strictly business? He'd thought they were fond of each other.

Foolishness, he thought, forcing his mind to the task at hand. He followed her into the adjoining room. No windows broke the dark paneled walls. No phone sat on the table beside the bed. The thick navy carpet muffled their footsteps. The recessed lighting illuminated the blood rising to the surface of their skin.

"Drink?" Simon offered, nodding at the small tiled bar.

Diane shook her head. "I'm almost embarrassed to admit it, but I can hardly wait to get my hands on you. That's quite a pistol you're packing."

Simon's laugh was a startled snort, but he acceded to her

wishes and began to undress. Diane did as well. No help
was exchanged. They'd discovered early on that each liked
watching the other disrobe.

"Ooh," she said when he was down to his cotton boxers. "I've got to kiss it."

Still dressed in her lacy bra and thong, she knelt before
him, pushed the vent of his boxers down his shaft, and
drew his crown into her mouth. She cupped his balls
through the cloth, humming with admiration as he
swelled even further at her attentions.

He stroked her hair and closed his eyes, relaxing into
the pleasure and not the least bit worried that it would
cause him to lose control. Simon had the happy knack of
coming precisely when he wished, an ability he'd practiced—on his own—for three full months before taking
his first lover at the age of seventeen. He had not been the
girl's first partner, and, as he recalled, she'd been gratify-
ingly impressed by his staying power. Other techniques
had required more training, but he'd been an assiduous
pupil. No one could accuse Simon Graves of giving less
than his best.

Now he lifted his mistress and kissed her gently on the
mouth. "Shall I return the favor or would you like me inside you?"

Her head fell back as he kissed the swanlike length of
her neck. Her fingers kneaded his hair.

"Mm," she said. "Inside first. The other later. I just can't
wait to have you today."

Even as he slipped her delicate bra straps down her
shoulders, even as his cock pulsed with excitement at her
words, Simon calculated how much time he could spend

on each activity. He kissed her lovely young breasts, fingers caressing the rounded, silken globes. He had a dinner meeting at six. He'd need a half hour to shower and shave and change. Kneeling, he slid her panties down her endless legs and nuzzled her brown curls. That left twenty minutes to fuck her, twenty minutes to suck her and perhaps another forty for a second round. He could fit in a third if he managed to recover in time. Simon liked going to meetings well fucked. The release improved his concentration and helped him restrain his sometimes fiery temper.

"Simon," Diane sighed as he teased her clitoris with the tip of his tongue. His fingers slipped through the folds of her sex, their passage slicked by her arousal. When he filled her vagina with his thumb, her thighs began to quiver.

He judged it time to take her.

The condom was a moment's work, quickly opened, quickly donned. Ready to proceed, he laid her back on the low, firm bed, her hips at its edge, her thighs spread. Cock bobbing with eagerness, he knelt and eased inside her. Her eyes slitted. Her back arched like a cat. Diane liked a slow entry. Advancing by increments, he slid his palms up her arms and locked their fingers together. She crossed her feet in the small of his back. His knees dug into the carpet. His cock hilted.

This was his favorite moment, when he was seated deep, surrounded by warmth, tempted by possibilities. Anything might happen now. Anything at all.

"Fuck me," she said, the words drawn out and hushed. "Fuck me hard, Simon. I want to wobble when I stand up."

The request surprised him, but he was happy to comply. Perhaps they'd fit four rounds in today. The thought of such indulgence aroused him. He drew back for the first thrust, then paused. "Tell me if this hurts."

Apparently, it did not, because in minutes she was urging him to even greater force.

"More," she groaned, hands fisted behind his shoulders, heels digging into his buttocks. She threw her hips at his and thrashed her head from side to side. He'd never seen her like this. He didn't know what had gotten into her. Intellectually, he was alarmed. Physically, his body gathered to meet her demands. As Andrew would have said, his prick was a happy camper. The friction was delicious, the heat sublime. He needed all his powers of concentration to hold on until she came, especially since she wouldn't let him use his hand to help her along.

"Your cock," she said, blonde hair clinging to her face. "I want your big, hard cock to make me come."

His big, hard cock felt like an overheated block of lead, but he worked it with all his skill, jamming it high and deep, aiming for her sweetest spots. She began to stiffen, then to moan, and then she hugged him so tightly his ribs creaked.

"Ah," she said, shuddering in orgasm. "Ah, yes!"

He came a second later, unable to hold on now that the need to had passed. The spasm was brief but intense. He collapsed beside her on the bed, panting hard. "Whew," was all he could think to say.

Diane giggled and played her hand down the center of his torso. When she reached his thoroughly exhausted cock, she rolled it into her palm. He let her fondle him long enough to catch his breath, then pulled free and straddled her long, glowing body.

"I don't think so, Ms. Kingston. For one thing, an old man like me needs more time than that to recover. For another, I believe my lips have an appointment with your pussy."

She squirmed and sighed as he kissed his way down her belly. "You're not old. You're perfect."

It was nice to hear her say so, but he was thirty-six to her nineteen. If that wasn't old, he didn't know what was. He stroked the smooth muscle of her thighs, then smiled when they fell obediently apart. The folds of her sex were flushed from fucking and glistened with arousal. He pushed back the hood of her clitoris to admire its rosy engorgement.

"I'm pretty, aren't I?" she said, fingers combing her own curls.

He laughed. "Very pretty. And very verbal. You make me wonder what's gotten into you today."

Her cheeks colored, and she bit her lips. "You got into me. You and that massive prick."

He wasn't sure he believed her, but the praise was inspiring. Despite its recent exercise, his cock began to twitch.

"Swing around," she said, her gaze hot and sleepy. "I want to suck you while you're still small enough to fit."

He swung around and they sixty-nined, another first for them, and very pleasant. It wasn't long before he'd recovered sufficiently to overfill her mouth. They lay on their side and thrust in easy rhythm, waves lapping a delightfully libidinous shore. They hit an agreeable pitch of arousal and coasted, neither struggling to rise, each enjoying the ride.

"You are so fucking sexy," Diane said, on a rest pause.

She rubbed her face up and down his cock while her hands roved his buttocks. "I could suck you all day. I could just fucking eat you up."

He had no idea what to say to that, so he hummed and trilled his tongue against her clit.

"Oh, Simon," she sighed. "You're the limit."

It seemed his cue to turn and fuck her. This time he knelt on the mattress and swung her legs over his shoulders. He steadied her little bottom with his hands. He took her in one quick stroke. She curled her fingers through his chest hair and held tight. It hurt, but it was kind of sexy, too.

"Simon," she said. "I'm going to miss you so much."

Before he could ask what she meant, the door to his sanctum opened.

Diane squeaked and pulled out half the hair she'd been clutching.

"Shit," said Andrew.

"Ditto," said Simon. Rubbing his injured chest, he turned to lift his brows at his head of marketing. He did not, however, withdraw from Diane's body. "You're not due for an hour and a half, Andrew."

Andrew's perpetual golden tan turned the color of a brick. "I'm sorry. I must have set my watch wrong when I landed." He waved his thumb behind him at the door. "I'll just, uh, leave you two . . . Wow." His gaze stalled on Simon's butt. "What a great birthmark. It looks like a horseshoe."

Despite his annoyance, Simon laughed. His lucky birthmark hadn't done him any good today. Then he noticed Diane wriggling frantically beneath him. Her cheeks were even redder than Andrew's.

"Oh, please," she said. "Let me up."

Clearly, the mood was broken. With a sigh of regret, Simon drew his cock from its nice warm home. Diane immediately tugged the covers around her. She looked adorable, all tousled and flushed. He sighed again and turned to Andrew, only to find his associate's gaze had dropped a good bit lower than expected. The sight of his erection, still on the raging side of hard, appeared to have put his underling in a trance. Andrew swallowed hard and straightened his flashy, butter yellow tie.

"Don't mind me," Simon said, amused by his reaction. "Get a good, long look."

Andrew's eyes flew back to his face. "Sorry. I'll just, uh, go wait in your office."

The poor man was so flustered he crashed into the door frame on the way.

DIANE HAD LOCKED her mortified self in the bathroom, so Simon's ablutions had to wait. He pulled his rumpled dress shirt and trousers back on, then padded barefoot to his office. The shirt clung to him, but if Andrew was offended by the smell of sexual exertion, he could damn well take himself elsewhere.

The embarrassed director was perched on the corner of Simon's desk. He held a leather portfolio like a shield across his thighs.

"Sorry about that," he said, his color normal again, though he still didn't seem at ease.

Simon waved the apology away and sat back in his chair. Crossing his bare, hairy ankles on the blotter, he linked his hands over his stomach. "I presume you have news that couldn't wait."

Andrew stared absently at Simon's feet. "News I was excited about."

"Not half as excited as I was." Simon surprised himself by chuckling. Andrew really had been gawking like a fish. "No, no. No more apologies. It was an honest mistake. I'm sure you won't do it again."

"I would have buzzed, but Mrs. Winters had stepped away from her desk."

"Mrs. Winters often steps away when my four o'clock arrives."

Andrew looked up, marveling. "You do this every day?"

Simon did not want to discuss the means by which he met his basic needs. He picked up a fat black fountain pen and turned it between his fingers. Andrew colored as the silence drew out.

"Right. None of my business." He fiddled with the portfolio's fastener. "But surely that woman doesn't work here?"

Simon shook his head, more in disbelief at Andrew's persistence than in denial. How stupid did Andrew think he was? He would never have an affair with a business associate. Nothing jeopardized work relations more.

"Your news?" he reminded.

Andrew raked back his hair and returned to the matter at hand. "I believe I've found a perfume for the Graves label. From the family firm in Grasse. I'm still concerned about their ability to produce large, consistent batches—"

"Assuming demand is high."

"Yes, assumin' that. I have the finance boys lookin' into the possibility of us fundin' an expansion of the factory. The quality of their scents was much higher than anythin' the big firms showed me. Stakin' them might be a worthwhile investment. But . . ." He drew a deep breath and grinned.

Simon knew the real news was coming now. "Yes?" he said, letting Andrew have his fun.

"I think I've found the acquisition we were talkin' about earlier. The one we hoped would give Graves Department Stores the media pop they need."

Simon swung his feet down and propped his forearms on the desk. Andrew's eyes sparkled like midnight at Mardi Gras. A shiver of excitement fluttered down Simon's neck. Andrew drew so close Simon could smell the lemony tang of his aftershave.

"Are you familiar with Meilleurs Amis?" he asked.

"They're an exclusive chain of boutiques, family-owned, founded after the war when the fashion houses re-opened. I believe they have a shop on Fifth near Cartier."

Andrew nodded. "That's right. I've discovered they may be vulnerable to takeover. Evangeline Clouet, the daughter of the founder, died recently." He rolled his eyes. "Big scandal there. Her husband, her much-younger husband, has taken over."

"Is he doing a bad job?"

"I wouldn't say bad, but he's only twenty-eight. A guppy in a pool of sharks. I had words with the local bankers. They just opened a shop in Beijing. He may have overextended his credit."

Simon tapped the end of the fountain pen against his lips. Meilleurs Amis wasn't a household name like Chanel, but it was almost as venerable. For the last year, Simon had been wanting to establish a designer salon in his stores, something to differentiate them once and for all from the Penneys and the Sears, something with a stronger cachet than the Graves name had on its own. He did not, however, want to place them at the mercy of a Tommy Hilfiger. He wanted a label they could own, and control, and slap on everything from sunglasses to bed linens, without kissing some prima donna's butt.

"I see the possibilities," he said, then refocused on Andrew. "What about the rest of the Clouets? Anyone who could catch the widower if he falls?"

"There's a daughter. She might have the makin's of a shark. For sure, she's got her mother's brass. Not her social skills, though, and she doesn't seem to want to run the store. Wants to paint."

Andrew's pursed half smile led Simon to think he'd gotten more than a glimpse of the brassy daughter. Perhaps she was the source of his inside information.

"All right," he said, shoving back in decision. "Have the money boys look into it. See what weak spots we might be able to exploit. I'll take a preliminary report next week."

"Will do." Andrew handed him the leather portfolio. "Here are the perfume samples. And my report on the trip." He cocked his head. "You know, you might want to visit the New York store yourself. I hear it's one of their weak spots." His grin quirked rightward, as if he were enjoying a private joke. "Believe me, boss, you'll thank me."

Simon had no idea what he was getting at, but he nodded and shooed him toward the door.

"Good work," he remembered to say as his subordinate turned the handle.

Andrew flattened his hand across his heart.

"Your praise is what I live for," he said in his extravagant southern way.

Simon could only shake his head. He'd never understand the man, but he certainly was good at his job.

THE DOOR HADN'T been shut five minutes when Diane rushed out, hair wet, clothes crooked. Her head was down, her eyes evasive. She slapped a white envelope on his desk.

"Here," she said. "It's been fun."

Before he could do more than blink, she was gone.

With a sense of unreality, he slit the letter open.

Dear Simon,

I don't care what anyone says. You're a prince among men. The problem is I'm engaged now and I don't think I should see you anymore.

I'm enclosing a check for the unused portion of this month's payment. Thanks for everything.

Love,

Diane

P.S. I hope someday you find a girl you <u>don't</u> want to pay to do it.

She'd underlined "don't" twice and dotted her name with a heart. Clearly, she'd need to work on her memo style before she found a job.

But what did she mean she didn't care what anyone

said? People didn't dislike Simon. Maybe he wasn't universally loved. Maybe he didn't suffer fools gladly. But he was a generous employer and a decent human being.

"Damn," he said, scowling at the letter. Diane had been the most trouble-free mistress he'd ever had.

He did not look forward to replacing her.

Seven

LELA LIVED IN Brooklyn, across the East River from Manhattan, in a converted warehouse loft. It wasn't the greatest neighborhood, but she had plenty of space and she could easily walk to the pretty, quiet brownstones of Brooklyn Heights. Plus, if she leaned as far as she could out her bathroom fire escape, she could see the Statue of Liberty. An old boyfriend had rigged her an expensive security system. Once her door was shut and triple-bolted, she felt as safe as anyone in New York.

As far as Lela was concerned, that was safe enough.

This Monday morning, the first morning of her new job, the sun woke her at dawn by pouring in shades of silver-pearl through the big, lead-wired windows. She dressed carefully, changing three times—four if you counted waffling over shoes. She settled on a short-sleeved, fifties-style turtleneck with a narrow gray skirt, a vintage rhinestone necklace, and a pair of strappy Manolo Blahnik heels. Her feet would die, but the outfit sent the right message. So long as she didn't topple over, she'd dance the fine line between casual confidence and outright snobbery.

You're just a salesclerk, she told her reflection in the age-warped bedroom mirror. You're there to observe, not to take charge.

Despite the assurance, the hands she swept down her skirt were damp. She wanted to succeed at this crazy plan, wanted it so badly she wasn't sure she could bear to fail. She didn't know why she'd decided—suddenly, passionately—that it was time to make something of herself, but she had.

Or maybe she did know why. She laid a calming hand over her belly and stared at her thin white face. Seeing Bea's beautiful paintings had jump-started this ambition. Apart from her freelance fashion writing—chancy work at best—Lela had no marketable skills. True, some might consider her bed skills marketable, but those gifts did not compare to Bea's.

Lela wrinkled her nose. She couldn't keep flitting from job to job forever, relying on charm to squeak by, paying every bill just a little bit late. Nor was money her only concern. She wanted to be more than her latest boyfriend's most memorable lay. She wanted respect.

With a moan of anxiety, she turned from the mirror. She curled her hands into fists and pressed them to her forehead. She could do this. She'd convinced Philip to give her a chance, hadn't she? Sweet as he was, he wouldn't have let her try if he believed she'd just screw up. He must have thought she could pull this off.

"I can," she said, to hear the steady timbre of her voice. She glanced at her watch and chewed her lower lip. Twenty minutes remained until she had to leave to catch the subway. Maybe a piece of toast would settle her nervous stomach. One thing was sure: if she went to work in this state, she wouldn't last an hour.

THE MANHATTAN BRANCH of Meilleurs Amis sat on Fifth beside Versace. The elegant Beaux Arts facade was sooty but not ashamed. And why should it be? Grime was the proud patina of New York's older buildings, like the sepia tint on an antique photo. The stone beneath the smut was a mellow, sandy cream. The sidewalk, though cracked by the passage of many feet, had been swept. The big display window sparkled from a recent washing. Lela's heart picked up a beat at the sight of the familiar gold logo.

This could be mine, she thought. My responsibility.

Squaring her shoulders, she pushed through the wide double doors. The store's biggest problem was immediately obvious, at least to her. Here, the opulence of the Paris boutique had given way to minimalism, no doubt in an effort to seem more elite. But this was the era of cocooning and comfort food, the nervous kickoff of the new millennium. Snobs or no, customers craved an abundance of luxury, if only to be reassured that the beautiful objects of the world, and their right to own them, could never be exhausted.

Besides which, the salesgirls were really lame.

They stared at Lela like paralyzed fish, not a thought in

their pretty heads, nor—apparently—any impulse to see if she needed help. Whether she resembled their usual well-heeled customer or not, she deserved, at the very least, a welcoming smile.

They'll shape up, she decided, or they'll be out on their keisters. On second thought, though, she'd hate to lose the Latina. Her stunning looks sent a potent subliminal message, as if by shopping at Meilleurs Amis, a customer could buy that glossy beauty for herself. The message wasn't rational, but it would open wallets. As a result, Lela was pleased when the brown-eyed belle recovered first.

The woman elbowed her plainer blond companion.

"Hey," she said. "It must be the new girl."

Lela smiled—brilliantly, she knew—and walked forward with her hand held out to shake. She might never advance past clerk, but she'd be damned if she'd act like one.

SIMON HAD NO lunch meeting on Tuesday. Faced with the prospect of eating alone at Lutèce, he decided to buy Diane a good-bye gift instead. Nothing too personal, but nothing too impersonal, either. All weekend he'd debated tearing up her check, then concluded even nineteen-year-olds had their pride. Plus, tearing up a check didn't say "no hard feelings" the way a gift did. He might be annoyed by the inconvenience of Diane's departure, but he wished her all the best.

As he crossed the marble lobby toward 49th Street, the desk guard waved. "Nice day for a walk, Mr. G."

Simon nodded and rubbed the crease between his

brows. See, he thought, remembering Diane's note. People liked him. The guard didn't have to speak to him. The guard could have nodded . . . just like Simon had.

Damn, he thought, and ground his molars together. He pushed through the revolving door. Next time he'd say hello. Next time he'd be friendly.

Outside the traffic was bumper to bumper: cars, cabs, pedestrians shouldering each other aside in their haste to return to their personal grindstones. Only the tourists stopped to ogle the soaring buildings. Office workers flowed around them like water around a stone.

Simon swung along with the rest, smiling to himself. The energy of the crowd crackled pleasantly over his skin. This was his city, and that was his tower they were craning their necks to find the top of. His mood was nearly cheerful by the time he turned right at Saks. The windows did not impress him; Graves had done a much better job this month. Feeling even better, he continued briskly on. He did turn to look at St. Pat's spires, their Gothic grace dwarfed by the tall black plinth of the Olympic Tower. When had he last attended church? Too long ago to remember. His mother would scold if she knew.

The display at Versace stopped him. Maybe Diane would like a nice silk scarf, the sort she could wear on job interviews. He tapped his lips, then continued to Meilleurs Amis. Their window was worth a second glance. A spotlight illuminated a velvet-draped pedestal that rose from a sea of tulle. A single pair of shoes perched on its top. They looked like something Marie Antoinette would have worn. Embroidered and bejewelled, their shape differed from modern shoes. Their two-inch heels nipped in like a woman's waist.

Dramatic, he thought, gazing at the arrangement. But perhaps a bit stingy. Suppose their window shoppers weren't in the mood for shoes? Or were women always in the mood for shoes? Ironically, what women wanted wasn't his foremost area of expertise. He left that question to employees like Andrew. Shrugging, he gripped the brass handle of the door. As long as he was here, he'd see the chain his marketing director was proposing he buy out.

Once inside, the boutique was almost as empty as the window, more like an art gallery than a shop. His gaze swept the polished parquet floors, the gleaming cases, the stark white walls. No wonder they weren't making money. They'd put nothing out to sell. If all their boutiques were like this, he didn't see what he'd gain by acquiring them. Graves Department Stores had a certain snob appeal, but they catered more to the sybarite than the ascetic.

Still—he stopped to brush his hand down a red cheongsam-style gown—what stock they had was exquisite.

"Do you like it?" asked a soft, throaty voice.

Simon turned to encounter a vision. In an instant, every molecule of air rushed from his lungs. A girl stood before him, a lithe, feminine form, her face elfin, her blue eyes flecked with gold. Her brows were darker than her shining chestnut hair, and her mouth was invitingly soft. Her body was perfect from head to toe. Even her arms were shapely. She wore no bra beneath her smooth, eggshell-colored top; an undershirt, perhaps, but the slightly hardened press of her nipples was visible through the cloth.

Smiling, she tipped a pair of small, dark-framed glasses onto her nose. Simon's insides jolted once again, like a boulder teetering off a cliff. The lenses performed a strange alchemy on her fey, sex-siren face. Suddenly she seemed vulnerable, and oddly brainy—an illusion, no doubt, but his body didn't care. His mouth dried, his cock filled, and his heart thudded erratically in his chest.

He was going to have this girl. He was going to take her to bed if it killed him.

"Do you like it?" she asked, and he was dimly aware she was repeating herself. He could not, however, remember what she meant. Then a smooth, slender hand stroked the silk knot that fastened the dress's collar.

Oh. Did he like the dress?

He swallowed. "I like it very much."

She turned over the size tag. Simon watched her eyes. Behind the slight magnification of the lenses, her lashes were fans of black, straight but thick.

"It's a three," she said. "If you need another size, we keep a range in the back. Or we could special order what you need. You're shopping for a gift, I presume."

Simon's brain lurched in an attempt to catch up. He could not give this dress to Diane. It wasn't remotely appropriate for a woman who'd just gotten engaged to someone else. On the other hand, how could he let this wet dream walk away?

"Uh, I'm not sure of the size," he heard himself say.

Was the stall too obvious? Was he too obvious? He shoved his hands in his pockets. His prick was so hard, so insanely heavy and thick, he wasn't sure his suit jacket could hide it.

The girl smiled in encouragement, obviously used to obtuse males. "Is your friend about my size? Or more like Fran or Nita?"

He pretended to consider the two salesgirls, both shorter than Diane, and skinnier.

"More like you," he said, though she was the worst match of all.

She winked, a friendly gesture that made sweat prickle under his collar. "Fine." She lifted the dress off the display. "I'll model it for you."

For the first time, he noticed she held an object in her other hand, a framed painting and a tack hammer.

"Oh. I've interrupted you," he said. "You were going to hang that."

"No worry." She smiled with what looked like fondness at the picture. "The nail's up already. Anyway, customers come first."

"Give it to me then. I'll hang it while you change."

He was pleased that his mouth had managed to connect with his brain, but the offer seemed to amuse her. Nonetheless, she handed the painting over. As she disappeared, the salesgirl Nita led him to the nail.

"She's trying to spruce up the joint," she whispered as he lifted the wire over the hook. The confidence barely registered. He was too busy looking at what he'd hung.

If possible, Simon knew even less about art than he did about women. It struck him, however, that this was a very nice picture. The subject was a plump young female leaning out a Mediterranean-style window, her face to the sun, her eyes flashing enjoyment. If she hadn't been wearing modern dress, he would have said it was an old painting. The style reminded him of that fellow Manet, the one who didn't paint the water lilies.

I could buy this for Diane, he thought, pleased with the

tidy solution. The painting might be more expensive than was proper, but if it happened to be valuable, Diane could sell it in a tight spot.

"I'll buy this," he announced when the first salesgirl reappeared at his elbow. He was so caught up in his decision, he didn't turn around.

"It's not for sale," she said. "It's part of the decor."

"Of course, it's for sale. Just name the price." He turned, reaching for his checkbook, and promptly forgot what he was doing. His chest felt like someone had kicked it. He knew he was staring, but he couldn't stop. The red cheongsam poured over her figure like a second skin. The embroidered yellow dragon hugged her breasts. The hem kissed her knees. His gaze drifted lower. Her calves were curved to fit perfectly into a palm: his palm. She looked like sex incarnate, the sporty version.

"The picture belongs to me," she said, confoundedly calm in a world that had just turned inside out. "A friend of mine painted it. If you like, I'll give you her card and you can get in touch with her. She lives in Paris, but she doesn't charge half what she's worth. I know you'd get a good deal."

This was far too complicated for Simon's addled brain. "Are you free for lunch?" he said.

The girl's smile faded. If she'd been a cat, her fur would have bristled. Suddenly, Simon saw how his actions must appear. Insisting he could buy her painting like some cigar-chomping fat cat. Asking her to lunch while shopping for another woman. These were not the actions of an honorable man.

"I'm sorry," he said, his mind racing to recover. "I

meant no offense. I'll take the dress. Just charge it and send it to my office."

He gave her his business card and his platinum Am Ex. She slapped both facedown on the cashier's counter.

"Nita will ring you up," she said, cool as frosted steel. He cursed his social ineptitude. He was no good at this pick-up thing, no good whatsoever. Damn Diane for getting engaged. Of course, if she hadn't gotten engaged, he wouldn't have met this heart-squeezing, cock-stretching paragon of feminine allure. His palms were sweating as he watched her stalk away. Her rear view was as inspiring as her front, especially her ass. He had to have her, absolutely had to. He hadn't felt so determined since *Fortune* magazine predicted he'd run his father's company into the ground. This woman was a challenge from which he could not turn away. For the time being, though, retreat was his only option.

On Wednesday, Lela peeked out from the dressing room. Mr. I Can Buy Anyone had come back to try his luck again. She'd known he would. She'd seen that besotted look on too many faces to doubt it.

The question was, did she want to reel him in?

He was pawing through the lingerie, waiting for her to appear. Bored by a slow morning, she'd been polishing mirrors when he arrived. Therese, the pregnant manager, had commended her initiative. Poor woman. She thought her newest salesgirl was a prize. Last night, when Lela expressed an interest in helping her balance the daily accounts, Therese had slid them over without a qualm.

"God bless you," she'd said, hands rubbing her bulging belly. "Dr. Sam will have my butt if I miss Lamaze."

It wasn't nice to covet a pregnant woman's job, but when Lela was manager, she wouldn't let just anyone touch the books. Of course, she also wouldn't let salesgirls hide in the dressing rooms.

Ordinarily, she wouldn't have deigned to hide from any man. This man, however, was far from ordinary. He had a striking, almost sinister face: hard mouth, hard jaw, eyes so dark they looked black. His brows slashed upward at the ends, enhancing his devilish air. His skin was slightly rough, as if he'd battled acne in his youth, but for some reason this just made him sexier. His hair was straight and short, coal black with blue highlights. It stood brushlike around the front of his hairline. She doubted he styled it that way; it was simply too thick to lie flat.

It was the sort of hair a woman would pay to run her fingers through. Even worse, his heavy beard shadow made her wonder what he did with all that testosterone.

Slut, Lela thought, and took a tighter grip on the door frame. He was just a man: two arms, two legs, one cock. But the rest of him was as imposing as his face. He wasn't terribly tall—six foot, maybe less—but his demeanor overwhelmed. He strode through the boutique as if he meant to conquer it, shoulders back, hands fisted, feet planting firmly with every step. His expensive suit was cut full, so it was hard to tell, but he looked as if a solid base of muscle backed up his arrogant stance.

This man called to every mischief-making instinct she possessed: an automatic panty wetter. Annoyed, Lela pressed her knees together and frowned. Without a doubt, he was the last thing she needed. She'd barely caught her breath from cutting Andrew loose. She had one short month to discover what made this shop tick. On top of which, she was trying to remake herself, to be less a good-time girl and more a woman the world could count on.

But however she remade herself, she couldn't be a coward.

Courage, she thought, picturing Bea on her bike in Paris traffic. Facing one arrogant fat cat wasn't as dangerous as that. Loins girded, she ducked under the fringed velvet curtain that separated the dressing room from the shop.

She'd give the man credit. He didn't pretend he hadn't been waiting for her.

"Hello," he said, hands dropping from the silky nothings. His voice was raspy, a seductive, midnight sound that had her fighting shivers. Determined to hide the reaction, she stroked the apricot basque he'd been holding.

"Still shopping for your friend?"

He shook his head, eyes stubbornly holding hers. His expression defied her to find fault with him, as if he were a big, shambling bear who despaired of finding words to charm her honey from its hive.

"Dress won't fit her," he said. "She's engaged. I wanted to buy her the painting."

Lela was sure these statements were logically connected somehow. She found herself smiling, in spite of her vow to stay professional. "I can still give you my friend's card."

"Yes," he said. "I should have taken it before. You made me nervous."

He admitted this as if he were blaming her for his flaws. Lela's smile broadened. This was a game she couldn't resist.

"Did I?" she said in her gentlest croon. "It wasn't my intention to make you nervous."

He snorted and lifted the basque from the rod. "Maybe not yesterday." He slanted a look from the lingerie to her. "I suppose you'd bite my head off if I asked you to try this on."

"It wouldn't be appropriate."

"And I probably shouldn't offer you compensation, either."

"No." She folded her hands at her waist, amused beyond words by this glum Casanova. "Meilleurs Amis isn't a peep show."

The big man sighed. Goodness, he was cute. She hadn't expected that, and she didn't know how to fight it. A harried pulse was knocking at her secret door, urging her to hand this man the key. What a pleasure surprising his glumness away would be, what a naughty thrill. She looked around the shop. The man was their only customer. Therese had left for her usual two-hour lunch. According to Nita, their boss spent most of that time with her psychiatrist, a man she'd been seeing, in more ways than one, for the last eight years. Lela had asked if the shrink was also the father of her child. "No," Nita had grinned. "*El bambino* is a revenge baby, conceived when Therese got tired of Dr. Sam sleeping around."

She and Fran had their heads together now, no doubt lost in similar gossip. Not that they posed much danger. Lela already knew too many of their foibles to fear exposure at their hands.

If she wanted, if she dared, she could spin this adventure out.

She touched the man's wrist as he returned the lingerie to the rod.

"I might," she said, "be able to make an exception for a friend."

His posture changed, grouchy boy making way for wary businessman. "A 'friend'? Just how do you define friendship?"

His hands hung by his sides. Lela brushed the cuffs on both his sleeves. His fingers twitched. Good, she thought. He's sensitive.

"A friend," she said, "would treat my friends with respect. A friend would take my friend's card and request a collection of slides. A friend might or might not buy a painting, but a friend would certainly consider it."

"I would have done that anyway." His eyes narrowed. "But I suppose you don't know that."

"No. Because I don't know you." Heart racing, she stepped closer and gathered the tips of his fingers onto her own. The contact was surprisingly electric. His skin was warm and callused. This man did more than sit at a desk. She had to tilt her head back to meet his gaze. She blinked. His eyes weren't black at all, but a very dark shade of blue. I'll be darned, she thought. Navy eyes. For some reason, the revelation made her shiver. With an effort, she steadied her nerves.

"Any friendship," she said, "requires an initial leap of faith."

He nodded, the motion brusque. His fingers slid farther down hers, brushing the slope of her palm. Lela's hand tingled. When he spoke, his voice was so husky her own throat tightened in reaction.

"I'll want to see the outfit modeled privately," he said.

"Of course," she agreed. "I wouldn't have it any other way."

Her pussy was plumping like a peach, sure signal that this dalliance could get out of hand. It won't, she promised, steeling herself. I won't let it. The thrill that slithered through her was delicious. She was going to play now. She was going to have fun.

She knew his eyes were on her ass as she led him toward the back.

SHE HELD HIS hand as if he were a boy who might get lost. In truth, he felt like a boy as he followed her down the hall. The carpeting hushed their steps, but he was barely aware of his surroundings. She wore a cashmere sweater dress in pale mint green. The motion of her legs was a pleasure to behold. Her ankles made his chest hurt. Her buttocks made him sweat. They reached a tall mahogany door. She turned and plastered her back to the wood, as if she meant to bar his entry. Her gold-flecked eyes told a different story.

"This is our private dressing room," she said, her fingers caressing the wood. "Every Meilleurs Amis has one. We reserve it for our most valued customers. No one interrupts them here. They can change without seeing a soul."

He cleared his throat. "Very considerate."

"Would you like to come in?"

A hot flash swept his chest. "You know I would."

She smiled, one corner of her delectable mouth lifting higher than the other. His fingers tightened on the hanger that held the basque. He knew she intended to make a fool of him. He wasn't at all sure he could stop her, or even if he wanted to. Lashes dipping, she lifted a key from a chain around her neck.

His breath came faster as she slid it into the lock and opened the door. At her gesture, he stepped ahead of her. The room was octagonal, paneled with dark, satiny wood and hung all around with mirrors. A second door faced the first. A back way out, he supposed. Two low, built-in benches provided seating on either side. Their cushions were upholstered in moss-green velvet, not blatantly seductive, but inviting. Simon tested one with his hand before he sat. The door closed with a tiny click.

"I suppose you'd like to watch me undress," she said. Her voice was plum-rich, honey-sweet. His blood seemed to thicken at the sound.

"Yes," he said, "but only if you're comfortable with that."

She liked his answer. This time her smile invited him to join. She smoothed her hands down the front of her dress. "You could make me more comfortable."

"You've only to tell me how."

"Take off your jacket," she said, and backed to the opposite bench.

He set down the basque and did as she asked. Her eyes never left his face as his arms tugged free of the sleeves.

"Your tie," she added.

He removed that, too, laid it atop the jacket, and undid the top button of his shirt. Her breasts began to rise and fall, her nipples forming points beneath the dress. As the day before, he'd have sworn she wore no bra.

"Now," she said. "If you'd spread your legs, I'll be completely happy."

Simon flushed. Clearly, she wanted to see if he had an erection. Feeling faintly ridiculous, but incredibly aroused, he moved his feet apart and sprawled his knees. His bulge was bared now to her view. Its head lodged beneath his belt, pulsing madly in its quest for freedom. He looked down at it, then at her. She was staring at his crotch, eyes traveling inch by inch over his cock, heating the swollen ridge like some magic sexual ray gun. She moistened her lips. A tingle of pure lust crawled down his spine.

"Big," she said. "My favorite kind."

He laughed but couldn't answer. His brain had turned to mush. She began gathering her dress up her thighs.

She was wearing stockings beneath the green cashmere, real silk stockings. His heart stuttered when her garters came into view. Ivory lace, fine as spiderwebs, strutted a matching ivory panty. Her hips were the color of slivered almonds, her belly smooth and gently rounded. Her ribs were too prominent, but that just made him want to stroke them with his hands. He would soften their edge with his caress. He would— Her breasts appeared, high and shapely, their cinnamon areolae tightening to rosy tips. His mouth watered. The dress cleared her head. She was lovely. She stood, shoulders back, arms at her sides, displaying herself but not preening. Her hair was tousled as if she'd just rolled out of bed, her cheeks and mouth redder than they'd been before. He needed no further evidence that this game was turning her on.

Which did not change the fact that she remained in charge.

"I'd like to see your cock," she said, quiet but breathy. "Please open your pants."

He dried his palms on the knees of his trousers. His

hands fumbled with his belt, trembled over his zipper. His
boxers were a tangle of pounding flesh and twisted linen.
"All of it," she said. "Balls, too."

Simon rarely worried what women thought of his
cock. It was big enough, he knew, to satisfy all but the
most committed size queens. As for small women, well, he
knew how to make himself welcome. Perhaps it wasn't
pretty, but whose cock was? To him, a penis was a body
part whose function far outweighed its form. Appearance
simply didn't matter. But today he saw his cock through
her eyes: the angry color, the thick, gnarled veins, the dark
pelt of hair around its base. His was a peasant's cock, a bastard's cock, a cock for whom sex was a crude, animal act.
His cock betrayed his roots in a way nothing else about
him could.

"I'm sorry," he said, surprised to find he meant it.

She laughed, then tossed her hair. "Don't be sorry.
You've got a great prick. Very manly. Very intense."

His blood heated. "I want to touch you."

She'd stepped forward to watch him open his trousers
but now she retreated. The back of her knees hit the
bench behind her. She climbed onto it and sat on her
shins. She removed her glasses.

"No," she said firmly. "No touching."

Imprisoned by her will, he watched as her hand slid
down her belly and under her panties. Farther it reached,
stretching the lace until she cupped her mons. Sweat
prickled his scalp.

"Watch," she said, rising to her knees. "I'm going to
show you how I do this for myself."

She showed him without posing, without moaning,
without the affectations of a pornographic film. This, he

knew, was true private behavior. Her knuckles worked under the cloth, squeezing her lips, drawing circles on her clit. Her second hand cupped her breast. She did not pinch her nipple; she simply squeezed the rounded flesh as if she needed something to hold on to. He could not see her sex. Her cupping hand obscured its shape. Instead, he watched expressions play across her face: the faint grimace as she climbed, the subtle shifts in her breathing, the tensing of the muscles of her forearms and thighs. The closer she drew to climax, the more her hips moved, their action shallower than that of fucking. He could see her back in the mirror. What pleasure did she get from that restless clench and release of buttocks? Did the motion rub the walls of her pussy together? Did she wish she had a cock inside her now?

He could not ask. He was afraid to break the spell. She'd closed her eyes, turned inward on her pleasure, letting him watch but intent on herself alone. Her hand moved faster. He couldn't believe how quiet she was. The rustle of lace was louder than her breathing. Her flesh made a clicking sound, wet finger meeting wet cunt. His cock dripped in sympathy, aching for her to come, aching to shove inside her when she did. Her breasts trembled. She gulped for air. And then she went over, hips shuddering, face tensed and red.

The convulsion was brief. She sighed and sagged back against the mirror. Her face relaxed. Her eyes opened. She smiled.

"Now you," she said.

His hand moved, but he couldn't do it, couldn't even touch the throbbing shaft. She'd bared herself for him, more perhaps than any woman ever had. He owed her the same courtesy. He certainly needed release. But he couldn't strip himself the way she had. He didn't have it in him.

"I can't," he said.

She must have read the misery in his face because her tone was gentle.

"All right," she said. "You've been a good audience."

Despite the lack of anger in her words, he knew he'd failed her test. Cursing himself, he straightened his clothes and zipped up. As he did, she turned away to pull her dress back over her head. Her spine was both knobby and graceful. He couldn't bear the thought that he'd never measure its length beneath his hand. When she finished dressing, she faced him, her face composed in a pleasant, dismissive smile.

Dismissal was not something Simon could accept.

"I want to see you again," he said.

She folded her arms. "I'm not sure what you have to offer me."

"I'm a powerful man. I could do things for you."

He knew it was wrong to say this. He knew it even before she shook her head and expelled a weary sigh. "I know lots of powerful men."

"Then consider me a challenge. You wanted to teach me something I couldn't learn."

One brow lifted above the frame of her glasses. "So you think I should try again, eh?"

"Yes." That was all he could say. The promise that next time he'd do what she wished was beyond him. He didn't know whether he would. He looked at his feet, then at her. He offered his hand and willed her to take it. "My name is Simon."

She pursed her lips, amused, but she laid her palm in his.

"Lela," she said. Her handshake was firm, her fingers warmed by her little game. Her hold lingered a moment longer than it had to, or perhaps he hadn't let her go. Perhaps his hope was wishful thinking. Whether it was or not, his pulse began to calm.

He pulled a business card from his wallet. "Please call me, Lela."

She looked at it, her doubt obvious.

"You don't know me," she said. "All you know is what we did and what you hope we'll do next."

He wasn't sure what she was accusing him of. He answered by sheer instinct, the way he did when a delicate negotiation threatened to slide off course. "It doesn't matter what I know or don't know. I'm leaving the choice up to you. You decide if you're interested."

"Don't hold your breath," she warned.

But he thought he probably would.

Eight

HE HAD THE most masculine cock she'd ever seen.

Lela sagged against the door and shut her eyes, the image of his sex seared into her brain. Its thrust had been aggressive, its thickness almost frightening. The bush of black curls around its base inspired contrary urges to tug or snip.

Snip, she decided, hands fisted on her thighs. Maybe she'd even shave him. A trickle of warmth slid from her sex. She'd bare his glory to view if she got the chance.

If she took the chance.

She knew she shouldn't. He called so strongly to the rebel in her, to the girl who'd escaped the pitfalls of foster care by the skin of her teeth. In a system where half the kids didn't finish high school, Lela had graduated college.

She wasn't on drugs or in jail or an unwed mother. If she played her cards right, she could turn herself into a stable, tax-paying member of society.

But she couldn't afford risks like messing around with customers. On the premises, no less.

Through the door behind her, she heard a latch snick shut. Simon must have taken the back way out. Something inside her sighed with disappointment. She'd hoped he'd get himself off after she left. She'd hoped she'd hear it. Apparently, the man was a marvel of self-control. Her shoulders hunched as if to shelter from a threat. Simon oozed power the way his prick had oozed seed. His eyes had glittered with desire, and yet he'd remained in place, unmoving, as if she'd cemented him to the bench.

Lela had never had a more inspiring audience.

"There you are," said Nita, halfway down the back hall. "Fran can't leave for lunch until you come out front."

Lela shook herself, hoping her guilt didn't show on her face. "On my way."

Nita peered at her. "What's the matter? You're all flushed."

"I was vacuuming the back room. In case anyone important comes in."

Nita clucked at her. "I worry about you, *chica.* You work too hard."

"Don't say that." She caught Nita by the arm. "A little too hard is just right. You never know where this job could lead. You never know which customer could be your boss tomorrow."

Nita rolled her eyes.

"It's true," Lela insisted. She thought back to her last social worker, Miss Thompson, the one who'd bullied her into going to college, the one who'd actually listened when she talked. "You're building your tomorrows today. I know it sounds stupid now. You figure you'll hang out, have fun, do the bare minimum until something real comes along. The thing is, something real has a lot better chance of coming along if you start laying the foundation early. You don't want to wake up at thirty and still be waiting for your career to start."

Nita stared at her as if she'd lost her mind. With long, glitter-sparkled nails, she threaded her straight dark hair behind her ears.

"Girlfriend," she said, "you need to get out more."

Lela sighed in resignation as she followed Nita to the front. She'd thought the same thing about Miss Thompson. Back in foster care, especially in the group homes, being good just got you ignored. She shook her head. How was she going to manage a store if she couldn't drum the least sense of responsibility into her employees? It didn't seem like a skill she could learn in a month. Her own life experience had prepared her for getting lectures, not giving them.

Damn, she thought. If only there were some crash course she could take that would teach her how to be a boss. Her steps faltered as she remembered the business card she'd clutched in her sweaty palm. Who better to teach her than a man whose every breath radiated authority?

She looked at the wilted ivory square. SIMON GRAVES, it said. CEO, GRAVES INCORPORATED.

Wait a second. Simon Graves. Wasn't that Andrew's boss? The man whose spine she was, supposedly, uniquely qualified to unkink? When Lela had refused to meet him, Andrew must have taken matters into his own hands.

"Bastard," she muttered, but she was grinning as she stepped onto the sales floor.

She ignored the dull clang of warning in her head, the one that said Simon was just as dangerous as he'd been before she knew who he was. This was fate. She needed a mentor, and a mentor had appeared.

She'd be an idiot not to give Simon a call.

SHE DIDN'T CALL. Simon sweated through the afternoon. He knew it was foolish to expect her to get in touch so soon. She was still at work for one thing, and she was not the sort of woman to jump through hoops. The problem was, the card he'd given her had only his business number. If she didn't call before six, he'd be out of luck all night.

And now he was stuck in this meeting with Andrew and the money boys.

The drone from the Finance VP washed over his head. He didn't even try to concentrate. Ignoring Andrew's lifted brows, he grabbed the conference room phone and buzzed Mrs. Winters. He broke into her greeting before she got halfway through.

"Has anyone called me?" he demanded.

"No, sir," she said, beginning to quaver.

Damn, he hated that. He wasn't an ogre.

"Well, if a call from Miss . . ." His brain stalled. He didn't know Lela's last name. He'd never bothered to get it. "Fuck," he said.

"Miss . . . Fuck?" asked Mrs. Winters, caught between hesitance and horror.

Simon covered his forehead, too frustrated to laugh. He

forced himself to breathe evenly. "Forgive me, Mrs. Winters. If a young woman named Lela calls, please put her through to Conference Room A."

"Yes, sir. Absolutely, sir."

Simon could only hope his outburst hadn't caused another accident. It wasn't his fault his secretary had a tricky bladder, but Andrew would never let him live it down if she peed her pants again.

"Well?" he snapped at Andrew's look of amused inquiry. "I'm listening now. Get on with it."

"I was just sayin'," he drawled, "and Roger here agrees, that the mortgages appear to be their weak point."

Roger nodded, his Adam's apple bobbing with nervousness. "Yes, Mr. Graves. If anything were to make the bankers antsy about their ability to make payments, we could snap up those mortgages at a discount, especially the European stores. One bank holds all the paper on them. If we decide to move forward—"

"Yes. If." Simon drummed the edge of the conference table around which the five men gathered. At the opposite end of the room, his father's portrait hung from the walnut paneling. Howard Graves stood before his old desk, chest puffed, smile genial. A gold watch hung from his waistcoat, the same watch he'd given Simon the day he retired.

"I have no fears," he'd said. "I know I'm leaving my baby in good hands."

It had been the proudest day of Simon's life. He'd have to call his father to talk this acquisition over. Tess said his speech was recovering since the stroke. Happily, his mind was as sharp as ever.

He looked back at his companions, calmer now.

"No dirty tricks," he said. "If we do move forward on this takeover, I don't want the press catching wind of anything dicey."

"No, sir," his employees murmured, a soft chorus of assurances.

Their biddability annoyed him, so he shooed them out. Only Andrew lingered.

"So," he said, swishing his notepad back and forth on the polished table. "You've met Lela."

Simon sat back in his chair. "Don't tell me she's why you were so eager for me to visit Meilleurs Amis."

Andrew shrugged, his mouth curled in a cookie-jar grin. "I thought you'd hit it off. You do have a lot in common. Plus, she's a firecracker, if you know what I mean."

"You dated her? Damn it, Andrew, I do not need your castoffs."

"I know that, but, to be fair, she cast me off."

"Fuck." Simon slammed both hands on the table. Andrew jumped, but he didn't care. It bothered him more than he could say that Andrew had slept with her. First, he thought, with an irrational flare of annoyance. Andrew had slept with Lela first.

"Be sensible," Andrew said, his voice conciliatory. "She wasn't expectin' to meet you. You weren't expectin' to meet her. If you struck sparks off each other, that's your doin', not mine. All I did was give fate a nudge."

"Fate!" Simon did not like that word in Andrew's mouth. Fate had nothing to do with him and Lela. But just in case it did, he didn't want Andrew taking credit. He stood and dug his index finger into the other man's chest. "From now on, you stay out of it."

Andrew bared both palms. "Yes, sir. Wouldn't dream of doin' anythin' else."

"Don't call me 'sir,' " Simon grumbled. Everyone called him "sir." He was sick of it. Besides, Andrew said it only out of mockery.

He pretended he didn't hear the younger man chuckling as he left the room.

THE PHONE RANG at six-thirty. Simon grabbed it, then held it for a moment against his chest.

Calm down, he ordered. You aren't sixteen.

He answered briskly, then flushed when he heard her voice. The sound of it was strangely soothing: rich, full of laughter. She agreed to have dinner with him, but she didn't want to eat at Lutèce or the Palm, or anyplace in Little Italy.

"I'll cook for you," she said.

His eyes stung with unexpected pleasure. She wanted to cook for him!

"That would be very nice," he said.

"Nice-schmice. I want our little negotiation to take place on my turf."

"So we are negotiating."

She laughed and gave him her address. "Be there at eight, big guy. And leave the suit at home."

SIMON WAS NO innocent, but Lela's neighborhood shocked him. Weeds grew from the sidewalk, condoms and crack vials caught among their leaves. Her building was decidedly seedy, a large hulk of stained brown brick, an old warehouse from the looks of it. Once upon a time, someone had cared for it. Cast-iron detailing graced the windows: faux Corinthian columns, oak leaves over the arches. But the city's fetish for gentrification had yet to reach this block. Graffiti smeared the crumbling entrance steps, local youth marking their territory. The security camera that peered at him from the shadow above the door had a Y-shaped crack in its lens.

I've got to get her away from here, he thought, then wondered if she'd let him. He was getting ahead of himself. They'd yet to survive their first date. In fact, he wasn't sure this was a date. She'd called it a negotiation. Sighing, he wiped his hands down the casual khaki trousers he wasn't sure he should have worn. He studied the names beside the buzzers. He'd have felt more comfortable if they'd met at a nice restaurant. Which, of course, was why she hadn't wanted to.

To his relief, she answered when he pressed the button for L. Turner.

Their exchange was brief and businesslike, but at least he'd discovered her last name. Inside and past the vestibule, an old-fashioned freight elevator took him to her floor. Leveling the unfamiliar mechanism took some doing, but he managed. When he wrestled the grille aside and stepped out, she was waiting. A cotton tank dress in brilliant turquoise covered her from cleavage to ankle. It wouldn't have been sexy except for the fact that she was in it. Interestingly enough, the spatula and oven mitt she carried didn't dull his interest, either. He went from semi-hard to hard in a flash. He pretended to shake his trousers straight. Now wasn't the time to let her know how badly he wanted her. He risked a glance at her face. Her seductive little glasses were nowhere in sight. Given their effect on him, he supposed he should be thankful.

"Sorry about the elevator," she said. "I should have warned you." She nodded at the bouquet of baby yellow roses he held. "Hang on to those. I'll get you a vase."

He followed her into a big, airy apartment. The space was almost entirely open. Cast-iron columns, each a soft dove gray, supported a cavernous ceiling. The cement floor was scattered with threadbare but lovely rugs. She didn't have much furniture. A couch, a few chairs and tables, an eccentric collection of lamps, a platform bed in the loft. Her plank-and-cinder-block shelves overflowed with spy novels and travel books, many of them coffee-table size, their tattered covers suggesting she'd bought them secondhand. The largest book, a real monster, featured pictures from the Louvre. A gift, he thought, since it looked pristine. Turning, he took in the colors of the room. They were subtle but warm: peach and gold, mahogany and cream. They blended well with the scent of frying garlic.

"I'm making spaghetti," she said, disappearing around a wall that hid what had to be the kitchen. "I usually make lasagna when I want to impress a man, but we'd be eating at midnight."

He wasn't sure he should follow, so he stayed where he was.

"Spaghetti is fine," he said. "I like spaghetti."

A stack of Paris *Vogue*s fanned across her coffee table. Could she speak French? Would she speak French to him? The possibility sent a thick pulse of feeling to his groin. He turned, seeking distraction. A plastic head with an anatomic cross-section of a brain sat atop her television. Perhaps it was a reminder not to watch, or a gift from a medically inclined beau. If that was the case, Simon didn't want to know. He never wanted to know about his lovers' former partners, beyond the necessary, of course.

He frowned at the color-coded brain. Apathy didn't explain his reluctance to hear about Lela's past. He was feeling possessive. He was wanting her too much. If he wasn't careful, all his good business sense would go flying out the window. Be passionate, his father always said, but keep a cool head. That's how you get one up on the other guy.

With a rueful grimace, Simon drifted toward a wall of black-and-white photos. Most were of the same plump, curly-haired woman. She had a face like a Renaissance angel. Cheekbones like trowels. "Who's this in the pictures?"

Lela poked her head out from the kitchen. "That's Bea, the painter, my fake sister from Paris."

"Who took them?"

"A boyfriend in college."

Simon wrinkled his nose. That was a road down which he didn't want to go. He waited until water finished ploshing in a pot. "Do you have a real sister?"

"What?"

"You said Bea was your fake sister. I wondered if you had a real one."

Silence was his only answer. He knew she hadn't gone deaf, so he followed his nose to the stove. Lela was stirring tomato sauce into a skillet of meat.

"There's a vase under the sink," she said.

He crouched to open the door. Apparently, Lela was no stranger to the FTD man. She had quite a collection here. He filled one of the simpler vases with water from the creaky tap and plopped his bouquet inside. He tried not to resent her failure to thank him. Perhaps flowers were inappropriate for whatever this evening was supposed to be.

At a loss for conversation, he leaned against the counter to watch her work. Her motions were practiced. Simon could open cans in the kitchen, but that was about it. He lived in a luxury suite in an apartment hotel. All his meals came from room service. He tried to remember if he'd watched any woman besides his mother cook. He didn't think so. He would have remembered how arousing it could be.

"So." He bit the end off a carrot he found on the counter. "Do you have pictures of your family?"

Her stirring arm paused. "No."

The answer was terser than it should have been. His neck shivered with a sense of déjà vu. Hadn't Simon used just that discouraging tone when people asked him why he didn't look like his folks? No, he thought. She can't be an orphan. Life wasn't that coincidental. Probably she was estranged from her family, or maybe embarrassed. He opened his mouth to probe deeper, but she grabbed a head of lettuce and thumped it on the cutting board in front of him.

"Here," she said. "Make yourself useful and rip this up."

He could feel her willing him to let the matter drop. Complying was harder than he'd expected. He wanted to know everything about her, but could not see how following that urge would strengthen his position.

LELA LIT THE candles and covered her rickety table with a clean white cloth. Simon's roses made a pretty centerpiece. They even matched the good, barely chipped china. Pleased with her efforts, she plied him with wine and spaghetti and toasted garlic bread. Her college stories made him laugh, especially the ones about Bea. The harsh planes of his face began to soften. He unbent enough to undo the top button of his blue Ralph Lauren polo.

Despite all this, the man still made her nervous.

Simon's power had nothing to do with suits and everything to do with him, his essence, his impressive physical presence. She could see his muscle now, densely packed and smooth. His hands were beautiful, big but well shaped. More than once she caught herself watching them play over the silverware. The color of his shirt brought out his extraordinary navy eyes. His lips were as red from slurping pasta as if he'd been kissed. Every time he blotted them with his napkin, she had to fight not to squirm.

He was an incredibly tidy eater. He chewed every bite, seemed to savor every mouthful. She couldn't help wondering if he'd be as meticulous in bed. Her skin grew fevered.

"Well," she said, suddenly wanting this over with. "Shall we cut to the chase?"

He set down his wineglass, smiling and alert. Had she made a mistake by letting him get comfortable? Should she have kept him on edge? But there was no point second-guessing herself. She had to make the most of the situation as it stood.

"You've decided to tutor me," he said.

"Oh, please." She swept her hair back from her forehead. "You don't give a damn whether I teach you to loosen up. You just want to get in my pants."

He tilted his head to examine her, his gaze drifting to her breasts and back. "I don't think I'm the only one who's interested in that."

To Lela's disgust, she felt her cheeks warm. "Yeah, well, I'm always up for a good fuck. I could, however, live without it."

It wasn't a nice thing to say, but Simon did not take offense. "You didn't invite me here to tell me that. You want something from me. I'd like to hear what it is."

"It isn't what you think. What I want isn't in your wallet, it's in your head."

He propped his chin on his hand. "I'm listening."

Damn his smug self, she thought, but she pushed her anger down. She wanted this. She wanted him. She wasn't going to screw it up.

"I want to manage that store I'm working at, and I need to learn to do it in a month."

The words came out in a rush. At first she thought he hadn't understood. Then he blinked. "A month?"

"Are you saying you can't do it?"

He shook his head, but not in negation. "I don't know."

Lela leaned forward. He was close to saying yes. If she gave him the right push . . . "I know a lot already. About fashion. About women who like to shop. What I don't know are the nuts and bolts. Finances. Accounts. The money end. And—" she pleated the tablecloth "—I could use advice on how to manage people."

His laugh was soft. "I suspect you're a natural at that."

"People I'm not sleeping with," she snapped. "Look, you don't have to do it all yourself. Give me books. I'll read them. Send me to shadow your best employees. They won't even know I'm there. I might not have been born with a silver spoon in my mouth, but I'm smart. Probably as smart as most of the people you know."

"I don't doubt that," he said, which was good, because she wasn't as sure as she sounded. People always told her she was smart, but who knew? Use your brains or they'll use you, one of the staff counselors used to say. Lela had thought he was all right until he tried to grope her one day in the laundry room.

But that wasn't a thing to think of now. She had to keep her mind on Simon. He swirled the wine in his glass.

"You know," he said. "I wasn't born with a silver spoon in my mouth. My father made me work my way up from the bottom, just like he did. Never mind the difference in our situations. They might not be as big as you think, but they don't matter. What matters is you want a mentor."

"And you want a lover."

His nostrils flared. She didn't know if the reaction was due to her words or to the thrill of negotiation. "Yes, I want a lover. But I'll need an escort as well, someone to serve as my date at business-related functions."

Lela had no problems with that. "I'm sure those duties would prove educational."

He smiled as if he thought he had her on the ropes. "I'll give you an allowance."

"No." She pressed her hands, palm down, on either side of her plate. She wasn't sure why she felt so strongly about this, but she did. "No money. No gifts."

"But you'll have to dress the part."

Lela's laugh was as loose as her morals. "Honey, if there's one thing I've always found room for in my budget, it's nice clothes."

"Suppose I want to give you a gift?"

"I'd rather have a lesson."

"Then I'll try to restrain myself." His expression was sly, a boy planning mischief.

Lord, Lela thought. Did he have to be so cute?

Pushing the worry aside, she stood and dropped her napkin beside her plate. She'd made her bargain. Now she had to pay. Not that she minded. Her body pulsed with excitement, not just her pussy and breasts, but every inch of her skin. Even her scalp was thrumming. She was going to have him. She was going to strip off his tidy clothes and watch Mr. Big go wild. He must have sensed her intent because his gaze darkened as she stepped to his side. She put out her hand, an offer to help him rise. "Shall we seal the bargain?"

He curled his fingers over hers. "I'm not sure I can wait another minute."

Despite his words, when he stood he merely pulled her into his arms and held her, kissing her hair as if she were a long-lost sister. The ridge of flesh that pressed her belly, however, was not that of a brother.

Smiling to herself, Lela let her cheek settle to his shoulder. His embrace relaxed, and his breath rushed out in a sigh. His hands were as warm as summer sunshine. They rose and fell in sweeps beside her spine. Her vertebrae seemed to melt under the slow caress. Nice, she thought, too relaxed to resist. She surrounded him with her arms.

How comfortable this was. He was good to hold on to. His back was broad and solid. She stroked it through the nubby cotton of his shirt, measuring, admiring, then slipped her palms over his ass. Giving in to temptation, she squeezed the resilient muscle.

He groaned and put his mouth next to her ear. "You drive me mad."

She giggled. The declaration seemed out of character for the self-contained CEO. She liked that she could rattle him. Her fingers slid lower on his cheeks, following the curve until she could probe between his thighs. He jumped when she scratched the swell of his balls.

"Bed," he growled, and swung her into his arms as if she were a child. "An old man like me can't be doing it on the floor."

He carried her up the cast-iron stairs to her loft. She felt wonderfully passive, a rarity for her. She touched his stern lips with her finger, then the fine lines beside his eyes. Did he truly think he was old? She drew the back of her knuckles down his scratchy cheek. He seemed perfect to her.

He was smiling at her little touches when he laid her on the low bed. He backed away, leaving her sprawled on the covers to watch him peel his shirt over his head. He had a really nice chest: slabbed pecs and ripped abs and a pelt of hair she itched to stroke. Tonight he showed no shyness about displaying himself. Off came his shoes. Down went his trousers and socks. His cock bounced out from his clothes, hard and ready. Lela's nails curled into the bed-covers. He was a mouth-watering specimen, a genuine embarrassment of riches.

He tugged the hem of her dress, well stretched by the loll of her thighs. His eyes shone with silent laughter. "Guess you need some help."

Lela wagged her brows and rolled to her knees. The mattress creaked as he clambered onto it. She lifted her arms.

"Undress me, Daddy," she said teasingly, knowing she'd shock him.

Simon shook his finger. "Bad," he said, but he pulled the tank dress over her head. She wore nothing beneath it, only skin and sweat. His eyes drank her in, hands hesitating as if he couldn't choose what to touch. "I should have known."

Lela swept her hands up his chest. "What can I say? I'm a panty-less kind of girl."

"You're a wonderful kind of girl." His hands finally settled on her buttocks, pulling her weight up his thighs until his erection throbbed against her navel.

She watched the crown pulse for a moment, then met his extraordinary eyes. "You haven't kissed me yet."

His gaze dropped to her mouth. "I'm suffering from performance anxiety."

"I find it hard to believe you're a bad kisser. You strike me as a man who sets his mind to doing everything well."

"I try," he said, with a mischief she hadn't expected. "But there's only one first time. Making a good impression is seeming very important right now."

She laughed even as a lovely pang tightened her heart. He was worrying about their first kiss. He wanted it to be nice. Who'd have guessed Mr. Big could be romantic? She slipped her hands behind his neck. "Suppose I kiss you?"

"No." He shook his head, still teasing. "This is something I need to do myself."

He did it softly, lips whispering, then plucking. He pulled her closer and tilted his head. He paused, his mouth a millimeter from her own. Lela quivered with anticipation. Their breath washed together, warm and shallow. His hands tightened on her bottom.

"Lift up," he said. "I want you to take me when I kiss you. I want my tongue and my cock to enter you together."

If his words hadn't gotten to her, their huskiness would have. Flushed and liquid, Lela rose until his baby-soft crown split the lips of her sex. The broad curve stretched her entrance. She couldn't resist pushing against it, just enough to enjoy the pressure.

"Mm." His fingers dug in. "Yes, now."

He breached her mouth as he breached her pussy, one intrusion sleek and soft, the other sleek and hard. His width astonished, his heat. Simon grunted and worked deeper, rocking back and forth to make room for himself, drawing the oil of her arousal to ease his way. The huge head slid farther. Halfway home. Their tissues pulsed, rod against glove, both shaken by excitement. Lela's toes curled. She could not break the sensations apart, the kiss, the penetration, the eager wrap of his arms. They swirled in her head, in her veins. She clutched his shoulders like a drowning woman. Simon's kiss hardened, then broke free.

"All the way," he gasped, and widened her thighs to the edge of pain.

Moaning, she sank down the pounding shaft. He shuddered when she reached the base. The tendons in his neck stood out, and a strong blue vein ticked at his temple. Beneath the shadow of his beard, his skin was bronzed by blood as if some torment had him in its grip.

"What's wrong?" she asked, but her woman's instinct knew. The hold he had on his urges was about to break, violently, irrevocably. Far from fearing this event, Lela craved it. Moisture oozed from her sex, trickling warm to the place where their bodies met.

Simon felt it. Simon shut his eyes and trembled. His cock twitched wildly inside her.

"Fuck," he said. "Fuck."

"It's all right." Her hands smoothed his corded shoulders. "I want you to want me this badly."

His eyes opened, black with lust. "I want to fuck you. I want to fuck you as fast as I can. As hard as I can. I don't want to wait. I don't want to stop. I don't think I can."

She didn't have the breath to answer. She could only smile and lick his rigid neck. She set her teeth into the blood-darkened lobe of his ear.

The sting broke the tether that held him. With a strange, strangled growl, he pushed her onto her back. His cock withdrew, slammed forward, and again, and faster. He pounded into her as if fucking were a battle he had to win or die. All Lela had to do was hold on for the ride. His whole body buffeted hers. Every thrust jangled pleasure through her clit, through her cunt, through the diamond-hard tips of her breasts. She clung to him. His wildness thrilled her, his roughness, the way he strained to drive every penetration as deep as it could go.

"Lela," he gasped, kissing her mouth, her neck, squeezing her breast in rhythm to his thrusts. "Tight. So—" he jammed in hard "—fucking tight."

His admiration inspired her. She pulled with her inner muscles the next time he withdrew. The squeeze caught the hot spot under his glans.

His next thrust jarred her halfway up the bed. He panted and held deep, as if trying to grind his cock into her womb.

"Christ," he said, sounding panicked. His hand fumbled between their bodies, searching out her clit.

"No." She displaced his fingers with her own. "Let me. I want you to hold me as close as you can."

Groaning, he wrapped her in his arms and rolled them to their sides. His heart thundered against her ribs. The motion of his hips accelerated. Lela hooked her leg behind his, bracing to meet each desperate drive. Her calf slipped on his sweat. The muscles of his thighs were living steel, propelling him inward, upward. His excitement overwhelmed her. His chest labored for air. His cries were those of an animal. Her orgasm began to unfurl under the assault, red and thick and glittering with spikes of delight. The intensity of her rise was frightening, as if she were poised to plunge off a cliff. Higher she soared. Higher. Her clit swelled to bursting beneath her hand.

"Oh, God," he said. "I can feel your fingers. I can feel you rubbing yourself."

His cock stretched inside her, the pressure impossible, intoxicating. She couldn't focus on herself. She had to watch him go over. Hell, she had to push him. Pulse rocketing at the thought, she reached around and gently squeezed his balls.

"Shit," he gasped.

"Yes," she urged.

His scrotum tightened. Heat flashed over her palm. He cried out, and his cock slammed deep. She felt him fall, felt him pulse and shudder and twitch. His arms were bonds she did not wish to break. His growl of enjoyment was a prize beyond price. She stroked his thick, seal-black hair and kissed his dripping temple. His hips flexed one last time, savoring the last, fading spasm. He sighed.

"Damn," he said, pulling limply free. "I never do that."

His head was between her legs before she could protest

his withdrawal. The orgasm that had been hovering before he came flowered beneath his tongue. A matter of seconds and it broke. He grunted in approval, then slid two fingers into her sex. He pressed the juicy cushion behind her pubis, stroked, and just as quickly laved her to a second climax. This one was startlingly hard. It wrenched a gush of fluid from her sex.

His palm was sopping when he rose to lie beside her. He rubbed the moisture over his belly. The gesture seemed entirely unself-conscious, but Lela couldn't watch it without gaping. Surely she hadn't sprayed him so copiously, and surely he wasn't so happy to paint himself with her juice.

But it seemed he was.

"Better," he said, and coaxed her head onto his chest.

Lela lay there, stunned to silence, feeling his heart slow beneath her cheek, feeling his big, taut body relax. Their scents mingled in a strange, sensual perfume. Lela had had good sex before, plenty of times, but she'd never had sex like that. Simon was a sexual tornado who'd swept her helplessly in his wake. Now she felt disheveled inside and out. She stroked the curly hair that covered his ribs. She had more reasons than most not to trust her fellow man. But, with this man, she wanted to snuggle closer. She wanted to hide in his arms all night.

This, she thought, was not part of the plan.

Simon seemed immune to anxiety.

"Sorry," he said, stifling a yawn. "Can't keep my eyes open."

It was the first thing he'd done that did not fill her with alarm.

.   .   .

HIS HEART POUNDED him awake before he could begin to guess why. His groin was unnaturally warm. He opened his eyes. Lela knelt above him, naked, a straight razor in her hand.

"Oh, my God," he said, and she burst out laughing.

"I'm shaving you," she said.

"You certainly are not."

As if to contradict his statement, she rolled his balls in the cup of her palm. They were covered in hot shaving soap. That's why they were warm. In spite of his shock at this rude awakening, his cock hardened swiftly at her touch.

"Hm," she said, running the flat of the blade across her lips. "I think somebody likes my idea."

He grabbed the wrist that held the razor. "I think you're crazy."

Her eyes laughed at him. "You know, you have the greatest birthmark on your butt. It's shaped like a little horseshoe. I saw it when you rolled over."

"I'll roll you over," he threatened.

"Oh ho ho," she mocked. "Mr. Big can dish it out, but he can't take it."

" 'Mr. Big'?"

She licked her lips and somehow her hand slipped from his hold.

"Just here." She dragged the razor's blunt edge through his foamy pubic thatch. "Just let me shave you here." From belly to brow her body glowed. He could see the rose-kissed color in the light that spilled out from the bathroom door. She was so beautiful, his breath stalled in his lungs.

"Just here," she whispered, making the sharp edge rasp

on his tangled hair. His cock jolted, bumping the back of her hand. "I can tell you want it."

He could tell he wanted it, too.

"Have you done this before?" he asked, his voice as ragged as hers.

"No." She caught her lower lip between her teeth. "But I've always wanted to."

What could he say to this confession? What could he do? He stared at her, knowing he shouldn't, knowing he would.

"Hell." He closed his eyes. "What's a little blood between friends?"

The first scrape made the soles of his feet tingle. The second made him groan. He'd never dreamed he could feel this way, never thought such a dangerous touch could be so erotic. She stretched his skin taut with her hand, his perversely rigid cock pressed footward by her palm.

"Don't move," she said, her voice shaking, vibrant. "I don't want to nick you."

She crouched so close he could feel her shallow exhalations. Each stroke of the razor came slower than the last. His skin grew cold as she bared him, his body fevered. He was at her mercy. He was under her spell. But it was her he sensed unraveling.

"There," she said, a ghostly shred of sound. She closed the razor and set it down. She kissed his groin with trembling lips. "Smooth as silk."

He was on her before she could wipe him clean, in her before she could gasp, up her before she could moan. He wanted to say something, but words did not exist for what she'd done to him. She was no less shaken, a doe in the headlights, a temptress no more.

"Watch," he said, when she would have closed her eyes. "Watch me fuck you."

She craned her neck off the pillow and he pulled out halfway. His cock glistened, thick and veiny and broad, a bridge of flesh between their bodies. Its skin seemed to flush with pride at the eyes that watched it. He withdrew farther, to the sensitive rim of the head. The flare alone held them together, and the greedy kiss of her gate.

"Wow," she said. "You are some piece of meat, big guy."

Her voice shook when she said it, so he knew she meant it as a compliment. Still watching, she licked her lips. The involuntary gesture sent an aching jolt to his libido. He couldn't hang here like this. He had to kiss her, had to take her, and then neither could watch anymore. He sank into her mouth, into her body. She tasted of apples. She smelled of sex. His pace quickened, grew brutal. He couldn't do anything but pound her, her body hugging him in warmth, slicking him with cream. He was starving, he was full, and when she began to tremble he came in one long pulse of glory. Devastation. Salvation. A rill of pleasure that threatened to turn his genitals inside out.

His groan of ecstasy was not a human sound.

Oh, my God, he thought as the glow flooded through him.

This was not part of the plan.

Nine

A CAR SQUEALED around a corner in the night, jolting Lela awake. Light from the passing headlights swung across their bodies, saying: Look, look what you're doing. Lela looked. Her cheek was pillowed on Simon's chest. Her arm draped his belly. The skin where she'd shaved him was as smooth as a woman's. Awareness pinched her gently, deep inside. She was wet, as if she'd been dreaming of him. His nearest leg had lolled toward her, and she'd covered it with her own. The inside of their thighs lay pressed together. Her quadricep brushed the dangling curve of his cock. It was cool, but he was warm: a stoked male furnace.

He was also awake. She knew that the moment his arm tightened protectively around her back.

She ought to kick him out. Sleepovers weren't her thing. Sleepovers let a man think he owned a woman. No one owned Lela. Not even Bea.

She sat up. He was staring at her, quiet, watchful, a stranger who'd been inside her body, a stranger who'd let her take a razor to his groin. His hand closed the space between them and stroked the side of her breast. "You all right?"

The touch sent a soft shiver through her skin. Say it, she thought. Tell him it's time to go.

"We never had dessert," she said.

"Are you hungry?"

She shrugged.

"Well, then." He heaved himself up and offered his hand. "Let's have dessert."

A streetlight filtered through the grimy industrial window, outlining his shoulders and drawing a narrow blue halo around his head. Against her will, Lela's gaze traveled downward. His cock was a shadow between his legs, heavy with promise, fraught with danger. She couldn't look away. Her sex contracted, soft walls kissing each other in hopeless consolation. She wanted him too much. She wanted to drag him back to bed and keep him there till morning.

"Let's go," she said, and rose without taking his hand.

SIMON KNEW SHE was inches from asking him to leave. He knew because, in her place, he'd have done the same. Simon's mistresses never spent the night. Simon's mistresses never even came to his home.

I just have to clear this hurdle, he thought. If she lets me stay the night, I'll be all right.

She turned on the stove light, saving both their eyes from the glare of the overhead lamp. The glow painted her naked curves, her peachy breasts, her belly, and her slim, browned legs. His cock stirred, skin tightening in a reaction he could not hide. Neither of them had dressed before leaving the bedroom. Now Simon felt both free and vulnerable, both pleased and piqued. Did Lela traipse around this way with all her lovers?

It was a question he knew he shouldn't dwell on. He busied himself clearing their forgotten dinner dishes from the table. The memory of how he'd carried her straight to bed added an inch to the hang of his cock.

"I have ice cream," she said over the whirr of the kitchen fan. "Pralines and cream or chocolate chocolate chip."

"A little of both?"

She smiled and pulled out the dishes. When they sat at her crooked table, he saw she'd chosen the same. It seemed a good omen. They ate in silence, the only conversation metal clinking on china. Halfway through, Simon set down set his spoon.

"Lela."

She looked up at him, and, for an instant, her expression was as open as a child's. "Yes, Simon?"

"I'm not sure how to bring this up, but when you talked about your family, I thought you might— Well, I want you to know I'm not the Graveses' biological son. They adopted me. For a while, I was an orphan."

Her face was completely blank. Her lids came down, their lashes shadowing her cheeks. "Andrew knew."

"Yes, he was trying to throw us together. I thought he might have done it because we share a common background."

She shook her head. "I wasn't adopted."

But she didn't deny she'd been orphaned. Simon felt as if his heart had stopped beating. He thought of that awful year and a half, when his world had ended and it seemed as if nothing would ever be right again. He could sense the same hurt in her: lost, helpless, furious. Maybe he'd been sensing it all along. He looked at his hands, resting around his bowl. They were too big, too rough for the delicate task of comfort. He did not have his adopted father's kindness, only his will to help. He waited for Lela to meet his gaze. "How old were you when you lost your parents?"

"Eight," she said, and immediately jumped to her feet.

She took both their dishes to the sink, though neither of them had finished. Her motions were tight, as if her sinew had turned to wire. Simon held his tongue. Wait, he thought. Wait. If she was going to say more, it wouldn't be because he pushed. Finally, she shut off the tap and dried her hands on a checkered towel. When she spoke, she did not face him. Her voice was steady and low.

"My father was shot by the owner of the convenience store he was trying to rob. My mother went downhill fast after he died. She didn't have the skills to keep herself together, much less a kid. Her habit was her kid, if you know what I mean. She'd leave me by myself for days at a time while she turned tricks or tried to score. Sometimes I'd be on my own for weeks. Finally, one of the neighbors called Social Services. They put me in foster care. I never saw my mother again. They couldn't track her down. I imagine she's dead by now. Probably long dead."

Simon was clutching the edge of the table. "I'm sorry."

She opened the tap and closed it again, the motion a kind of shrug. "I was lucky, believe it or not. Most kids in foster care would give anything to reunite with their family, no matter how badly they're abused, no matter how little their relatives want them back. I never wasted time on that fantasy. I'd been counting on myself for years. I wasn't going to stop just because I got stuck in substitute care. I wasn't going to end up like her because I was too stupid to keep my distance."

She snorted. "You wouldn't believe how many kids hated me for not wanting to go back. For knowing she'd be bad for me. I was questioning their one, big dream. But I learned to keep the truth to myself. I learned to make friends. And I turned out all right. End of story."

He knew it wasn't the end of the story at all. He pushed from his chair, swept her hair aside, and kissed the back of her neck. "You're more than all right. You're strong."

And because he'd said so she clung to him as if she were not strong at all.

He was happy to hold her. She was warm and small and soft. She made him aware of his own maleness, of his own size. But the embrace quickly changed. Her body began to move, to ride and climb his thigh.

"Take me," she said hoarsely. "Take me right here."

He knew it was avoidance, but his body didn't care. What did he know of words, of talking things out? This need at least he could satisfy. He lifted her onto the counter and stepped between her legs. Their mouths tangled in a kiss. He fondled her hard-tipped breasts, then pulled her to his chest. He didn't mean to rush, but her hunger was catching. Her hands streaked over him: neck, shoulders, back. When she squeezed his buttocks, his skull nearly lifted off his head. By the time her ankles locked behind his waist, he was raging hard.

"Now," she said, guiding him to her gate. The pressure of her fingers made him grit his teeth. Her touch was impossibly good. He slid inside her, helpless to contain his sigh. Her body offered no resistance. She was wet and warm; tight, but easy. His cock flexed with delight when her curls pressed his. He was home. He was safe. He circled her with his arms and drew her closer yet.

"I can't get enough of you," he said.

He feared the rash words were true.

SHE WASN'T QUITE easy about seeing him again, but the next week proved Simon a good teacher, and a generous one. Whenever Lela had time off work, he rearranged his schedule for a lesson. They visited the city's high-end stores: Saks, Bergdorf's, Lord & Taylor. "Open your eyes," he'd say. "Who's shopping where? What do they touch? What do they buy? Which employees close the most sales? What are they doing that's different from the others?" When she answered his questions, he'd praise her for what she'd caught and coax her to discover what she'd missed. "When you know what you're saying is true," he said, "and not just theory, it's easier to convince other people to go along."

Together they walked the streets of the shopping district. He opened his mind to her, spilling out the lessons he'd learned from his years at Graves. Sometimes he'd be hoarse by the time they finished. His manner was unexpectedly shy, as if no one had asked him to share his knowledge before. He always gave credit to those who'd taught him. "My dad always says . . ." was his favorite opening line.

Clearly, Howard Graves was more than a father to Simon; he was a hero. One day, as they strolled past Rockefeller Center, Simon told her how they'd met.

"I was five," he said, "and I thought that orphanage was the scariest damn place I'd ever seen. Those kids! It seemed like they had to take out on each other every rotten thing that had ever been done to them. My parents had loved me, spoiled me. I fought back, but it was never enough. There was always someone bigger. Until Howard Graves came. He blew into that home like Superman. He was huge. Six-five. Red hair. Laugh like an earthquake. None of the other prospective parents had wanted me. I was not a cute kid. Or a nice one. But Howard took one look at me gawping and said, "That's the one. That's the boy we want."

The story was a fairy tale Lela had never let herself dream. She squeezed Simon's arm. "I bet you really were cute."

"Not in the least." He laughed; his happy ending had robbed the memories of their power to hurt. "The staff used to call me Scowly Boy. Said I had beady eyes."

"You have beautiful eyes!" she exclaimed, angered by the slight. "I love your eyes."

He smiled and kissed her cheek. Her heart swelled until it seemed to fill her throat. This is what it's like, she thought. This is what it's like to have a real boyfriend.

The prickling behind her eyes sent a warning she couldn't ignore.

If Lela wasn't careful, she'd fall in love with Simon Graves.

．　．　．

SIMON WAS IN New Orleans, troubleshooting at one of his stores. He'd invited her along, but she simply couldn't miss her hours at Meilleurs Amis. Despite what she'd thought was a shaky start, she and Nita were beginning to bond. One of Simon's female VPs had warned Lela not to socialize too much with her coworkers. She said it would make the transition from friend to boss too difficult. Lela thought she'd managed an acceptable balance. She could tell Nita liked her, but she also seemed to look up to her. She'd started copying her manner with customers. When Fran teased her about it, Nita told her to mind her own commissions; hers were up fifty percent. "That girl is going places," Lela overheard her say. "I want to go places, too."

Therese, poor cow, couldn't get over what a good influence Lela was. Pleased with her find, she took even more time off than before. If she hadn't been such an idiot, Lela would have felt sorry for her. The sight of her pregnant belly did elicit a guilty twinge, but she figured women like Therese, with their shrink boyfriends and their carefully cultivated inability to cope, always landed on their whiny feet. When Therese was fired, she'd simply peddle her incompetence elsewhere.

Lela, on the other hand, was going to be a good boss. Lela was going to turn this shop around. Already sales were up. She knew because, after the first week, Therese had turned all the accounts over to her.

Because of this, Lela had many happy dreams to occupy her thoughts. Just the same, she planned carefully for Simon's absence. They'd spent every night since the first at her apartment. If nothing else, her body had grown accustomed to his company. With distraction in mind, she stocked up on ice cream and magazines, and rented three action movies from the video place down the street. She had the makings for a pedicure, a manicure, and a cucumber-kiwi facial. She was not going to spend her weekend missing Simon.

Or so she vowed. Early Sunday morning, she was forced to admit defeat. She sprawled in her royal blue butterfly chair, pretending to read the latest *Elle*. The issue contained an article on the new crop of jewelry designers. The piece was relevant to her future aspirations, and fascinating, but she'd read the first paragraph a dozen times.

Her body ached for Simon in ways her trusty vibrator couldn't cure. She didn't even want to talk to him. She just wanted him here, in his favorite spot on her couch, where she could lay her head in his lap, maybe bite his thigh or nuzzle his crotch until his wonderful, monstrous cock strained to break through his zipper, strained for her wet, tonguey kisses, for her body, until they fell to the nearest rug, tore their clothes open, and did it, hot and fast, hard and sweaty, like manic wrestlers with an itch to get pinned.

Lela covered her face.

This was not a good sign.

She reached for the phone before she could stop herself. She and Bea hadn't exactly parted on a high note, but maybe a dose of girl talk was what they needed to mend their crooked fences.

Bea answered on the seventh ring. She was breathless.

"Did I catch you at a bad time?"

"No, no. I ran down from the studio. I've started a new painting." She laughed, sounding younger and happier than Lela had ever heard her. "Actually, I've started it three times, and each time it's gotten bigger. Now it's big enough to fill my studio. I'm obsessed. You wouldn't believe the amount of paint I've wasted. It's a good thing *maman* left me an heiress, or I'd be broke."

Lela swallowed her automatic defense of Bea's mother. Bea was never in the mood for that. "I'm glad it's going well."

"It's going fantastic!" Bea's voice dropped as if sharing a secret. "Lela, I really think this picture is going to be special. I mean, the good Lord knows what the critics will think, but this is the best thing I've done. The best."

Lela started to murmur something supportive when Bea broke in again.

"Oh! I almost forgot. The strangest thing happened. Some man called from America and asked for slides of all my pictures. He said he'd seen a painting of mine at Meilleurs Amis. Is that what you did with the one I gave you?"

"Yes. I hope you don't mind. The boutique was about as interesting as a monk's cell. Anyway, the manager said I could hang it."

"Right, right, you're working at the store." Lela pictured Bea nodding. "How's that going?"

"It's going well." Suddenly she felt reluctant to share her triumphs. Was she blowing them out of proportion? Would they all come to nothing? She twisted around in the slinglike chair and squeezed the phone between her shoulder and ear. She grabbed one ankle in her hand. Her vixen-red pedicure was quite the thing. Tell her about Simon, she thought, ignoring the quickened thump of her heart. That's what you called for. "Something else happened at the store. I've met a man."

"Let me guess," Bea chortled. "He's tall, dark, handsome, and rich."

She was sure Bea didn't mean to insult her, but the back of Lela's eyes burned. She pinched her lower lip to quash the threat of tears. This was Simon's doing. He'd turned her into a bundle of raging, weepy hormones. Bea had every right to assume this man was the same as all the rest. Her joke was just that: a joke.

"Actually," she said, feigning lightness, "he's all that and more. He's also Andrew's boss. Remember? The man he was trying to fix me up with? Andrew engineered a meeting, and we really did hit it off. He's been helping me learn the ropes of retail."

"And what ropes have you been helping him learn?"

This time Bea's archness made her laugh. "We haven't advanced to bondage yet, though we did do it in the bathroom at Bergdorf's."

"Oh, Lord, I don't want to know. Well, I do. But ladies shouldn't kiss and tell."

"I like him," Lela said. "He's a decent, sexy man."

"Of course he is. You've always had good taste. Andrew was a sweetheart. A flirt, but a sweetheart."

"Yes." Lela pinched her mouth again. Why couldn't she say it? She was falling in love with Simon. For the first time in her life, she was falling in love.

She'd loved people before, of course, or supposed she had. But those loves had faded through time and circumstance and the occasional betrayal. Her attachment to Bea was her most enduring experience with the emotion. She had not, however, ever been *in* love with anyone. From what she could tell, being in love was a kind of terror, frequently a delicious terror, but a terror just the same.

Simon, damn him, showed no signs of suffering from a similar ailment. Oh, he showed signs of lust and affection, even respect. He'd opened the cracks of his gruff exterior to reveal the kindness he hid within. But he betrayed no signs of terror. Or joy, for that matter. He was quietly happy to be with her, enthusiastically happy to share her bed—neither of which added up to the giddy, tumultuous maelstrom of emotion above which she was trying to keep her head.

The scariest part was she wanted to drown.

It was all too melodramatic to share. Bea wouldn't believe her. She might pretend she did, but she wouldn't. In her current emotional state, Lela wasn't sure she could stand that.

"How's Philip?" she said instead, and settled in to hear Bea's latest attempt to convince herself she wasn't totally mad for the man.

SIMON MISSED HER all weekend. New Orleans could have been New Jersey for all the charm it held. His mind worked away at business, but his heart yearned for Lela. He missed the way she smelled. He missed the way she snuggled against him in her sleep. He missed the way she'd try to comb the morning spikes out of his hair with her fingers. She was adorable in the morning, sleepy and slightly grumpy, but always willing to be coaxed into a quick bump and grind. In the morning, her muscles were soft and warm like rising bread. When he sank into her, he'd feel completely embraced, completely content.

He was beginning to think he'd enjoy waking up that way every morning.

The flight back to La Guardia took an eternity. Business completed, his mind turned and twisted with fantasies of Lela. It might have been his imagination, but his crotch still seemed to itch from the night she'd shaved him. She was a wild woman, and she made him want to be wild as well. He wanted to take her in the fountain at Central Park. He wanted to lock her in a cage and force her to suck him through the bars. He wanted to paint her breasts with sperm, to take her in the ass on the back of a Harley. The images were strange, unprecedented, and inordinately powerful. They made him harden and sweat and clench his fists with unquenchable lust.

It was all her doing. He'd barely scratched the surface of her sexual adventurism. He wanted to dig down to the bottom. He wanted it so bad it hurt.

It was two in the morning when he buzzed her loft. He didn't know whether she'd let him in or curse him out, but he knew he couldn't go home without trying to see her first.

God willing, she'd have missed him a little, too.

Her voice was muzzy when she finally answered. "Simon?"

"Yes," he said, leaning in to the speaker. "If it's too late, I'll go, but I really wanted to see you."

A crackle issued from the box. He could almost feel Lela thinking. His cock thickened inside his trousers. Please, he thought. Let me in.

"All right," she said. "I'll meet you at the elevator."

His cock shot up so fast it should have had vertigo. Something pinched the tip, but he was too busy shoving through the buzzing door to care. She was meeting him at the elevator. Lela was letting him in. His penis throbbed in time to the words. Lord, lord, lord, he was going to fuck her until she cried.

Lela, however, had a different game in mind.

She met him in the hall in a long red gown, silk, cut on the bias, with straps like angel hair pasta. Simon grinned and shoved at the gate, but it was jammed.

"I can't get this open," he said.

She stepped closer and licked her lips. "I know."

That's when he noticed the cuffs. They dangled from her fingers: black velvet with trailing satin ties. His pulse pressed his ears as if his veins were swelling. His palms went damp, his thighs heavy. When he spoke, his voice seemed to come from far away. "What are those for, Lela?"

She swung them back and forth. "A little game. If you want to play, you have to grab the bars with both hands."

He thought of the fantasy he'd had on the plane. She'd been in the cage then. Apparently, as far as his snarling prick was concerned, this was just as good. He turned his head and tried to see past the reach of the dim, cracked hall light. Two other apartments shared this floor. Conceivably, one of the neighbors could walk out. It seemed unlikely, but his cock didn't mind that prospect, either. His briefs were sticking to the head, plastered there by a trickle of pre-come and sweat.

"What'll it be," Lela purred. "Mouse or man?"

Simon gripped the bars of the cage.

"Man," he said, and Lela licked her upper lip.

The velvet cuffs passed around metal and wrist. She secured them with the satin ties. Then she pressed her face into one diamond-shaped opening and claimed his mouth. Her kiss was aggressive, masculine. The point of her tongue swept past his teeth, overwhelming his, dueling with his. In seconds he was gasping for air, deliciously dizzy, achingly hard. She pulled back long before he wanted her to, but he didn't have the power to stop her.

Her eyes raked him up and down, lingering on the swollen thrust of his erection. "You look good like that, big guy. Real good. But I don't think I've seen enough."

"I can't show you any more," he said. "My hands are tied."

That ploy was worse than useless. She reached through the bars and undid his belt. Grasping the buckle, she pulled the leather free so fast it hissed. She tossed the belt behind her, through the open door of her apartment. The clunk of it hitting the floor made him wince.

"Ooh," she said. "I think Mr. Big is a little nervous. That's all right, though. I'm sure I can distract you from your fears."

This time when she reached, her hands surrounded his crotch, kneading and stroking his painfully engorged flesh. He moaned at the pleasure she inspired. Such strong hands, such firm squeezes. She knew what he liked. She knew exactly. He widened his stride and rolled his hips against her palms. God, she was good.

"Want me to kiss it?" she said.

He closed his eyes. "I want you to suck it. I want you to open my zipper and take it in your mouth."

If he'd shocked her, she didn't show it. Her tongue reached through the cage to lick his cheek. Her fingers caught the tab of his zipper. She began to tug. Blood screamed in his veins, through his cock. She drew the zipper down. A long sigh escaped him as his overloaded shaft fell into her hand. He opened his eyes and watched her hold him. Her nails matched the red of her gown. Her palms were almost as silky.

"That's good," he said. "I missed you touching me."

Her hands moved gently up and down. She was looking straight at him, her expression soft. She bit her lower lip. "I missed this, too. Mr. Vibe's got nothing on you."

He was laughing as she knelt, but the first kiss cut his amusement short. The liquid stroke of her tongue, the satin clasp of her lips, sent him straight to heaven. The grate dug through his clothes as he struggled closer. Even without the cage between them, she couldn't take much more than the head. Like the rest of her, her mouth was small. Rather than try to swallow him, she worked his shaft with her fist, slowly, almost a tease. Only the crown received her tender oral care. It didn't matter. The things she did with her tongue and teeth made his nerves shriek with excitement. She had a knack for fluttering just the right spot beneath his glans, then rubbing it with her lip.

"Oh, yeah," he said, neck sagging. "Oh, yeah."

But he was drawing too close to climax. Much as he enjoyed what she was doing, this wasn't the welcome he'd craved.

"Lela." His hands rattled the grate. "Let me out. I want to make love to you. I want us to come together."

"How much do you want it?"

"Don't tease. Not now. I missed you."

Her eyes were stars shining up at him. "Will you let me tie you to the bed?"

"If you have to."

"I don't have to; I want to."

"Then you can. Just let me out, Lela. Let me hug you hello."

As soon as he was free, he held her as if they hadn't hugged in years, held her so tightly she squeaked. Then he carried her inside and kicked the door shut behind him. He plastered his mouth over hers, moaning, sucking, taking charge the way she hadn't let him before. Their kiss was everything he'd dreamed. At last he was with her, alone. Her hands slid up his back and clung.

"Mm," she said, a happy sigh. "You're distracting me."

"Upstairs then. You can do your worst there."

They climbed the stairs hand in hand, with Lela leading the way. She finished undressing him, scolding when he tried to help.

"You're my present," she said. "You have to let me unwrap you."

He shivered as she circled him, running her hands up and down his naked body. He'd never been as conscious of it as he was now: its strength, its size, the life that beat beneath its skin. He wished he were more beautiful for her, more graceful, but nothing in her manner betrayed the least disappointment. When she cupped his face and lightly kissed his chin, he felt as if she kissed his ugliness away.

"Simon," she said, just his name, and led him to the bed. With the trailing ties, she attached one of his wrists to the simple, mission-style frame. The other she left free. He wiggled it in question, offering it to her.

She shook her head. "I know you. You don't want to give up all your control. You wouldn't enjoy it."

"Maybe I would." The words were husky. He thought they might be true.

She straddled him and hiked her red gown to the top of her thighs. "Maybe we'll test that theory later. Maybe tonight I want my prisoner to touch me."

When she lowered her weight to his belly, her wetness warmed his skin. He slid his free hand to that crux, slid his fingers between her slickened folds. "You want me to touch you here?"

"Yes," she sighed, and arched her back.

He didn't have to ask if she wanted it slow. Her languorous movements told him, the sultry droop of her eyes. Her gown shimmered in the light from a chipped Tiffany lamp. Her dark hair gleamed. Her breasts swayed. He dragged his hand up the silk and touched them, brushing the hardened tips with his knuckles, painting their cleavage with her cream.

"You're so beautiful," he said. "I've never known a woman who could make me want her the way you do."

Her smile was warm and pleased. She swayed forward and kissed his mouth as softly as a child. When she backed away, he thought she would speak, but she merely caught her breath. She pressed her tongue to her upper lip. She reached between her legs. His cock jumped when she grasped it, alive in every cell. Oh, her touch. It was oil on a runaway fire. She tilted him, positioned him, and slowly pressed him to his hilt. She lay still then, breathing deeply against his neck. This had always been his favorite moment, the moment he filled a woman so deeply he could go no farther. But tonight the suspense was unbearable. He needed to come. He needed to feel her come. Without thinking, he yanked his bound hand against the headboard. Lela shivered.

"Can I move?" he rasped.

"Only your free hand. The rest of you belongs to me."

He gripped her hair and lifted her head. He wanted to

do as she asked, but he couldn't bear this immobility. "You move then. Please."

Her compliance was almost worse than her resistance. Her thrusts were a ripple of silk in a gentle breeze. Slowly she rocked. Inexorably he rose. When he began to groan, she kissed him hard. He poured his frustration into her mouth, willing his body to remain still, to obey her desire. He moved his hand between her legs, but she would not hasten.

"Slower," she said, guiding his fingers over her swollen bud. "Don't rush me."

"I'm dying."

"Not yet, you're not. Not till I say."

She didn't say. She wouldn't say. Sweat rolled down his skin and hers. Her pussy seemed to shimmer over his cock, undulating ripples of involuntary movement. It was torture. It was heaven. It was shredding the last threads of his control.

"Come," he begged, but she shook her head. She didn't speak. She only groaned. The sound tightened the skin of his sex until it stung. He touched her breast, pinched her nipples until they tightened like little stones. Still she resisted. She pulled her gown over her head and rode him bare, hands on his chest, hips rolling smoothly, gently. Her head fell back on her shoulders.

"Soon," she whispered. "Soon. It's so good. I love this. I love you inside me. You're so big I feel like I could burst."

He squeezed the headboard until the wood creaked under his hand. His molars ground together. He tried to relax, tried to breathe himself calm, but his orgasm was winding up too fast, the tension too sweet to bear, too strong to resist.

"No more," he said through gritted teeth. "I can't." He gripped the back of her neck and pulled her close. He had to make her understand. "I can't wait."

She closed her eyes and put her hand to the place they met. Her fingers moved. Knowing what she was doing was the last straw. His pleasure exploded, copper in his mouth, lemon syrup in his sex. Dimly he felt her shudder, felt her come, but his climax blinded with its strength. The spasms were sharp and deep. They pulsed upward from his gut, like slow ball lightning, rolling up, rolling out, one burst, then another. Each gush of seed stroked his cock from the inside. His spine was melting. His body went limp.

"Simon," she said. "Simon, Simon."

He came back to himself like a deep-sea diver. Her weight was sweet against his chest. She rubbed her face from side to side, smooth cheeks rasping on his hair. They were still joined, but he was slipping. He didn't want to lose the connection. Fortunately, he had just enough strength to drag his hand to the small of her back and snug her closer. She wriggled, then sighed. Her sex dripped down his balls.

I love you, he thought, and shivered at a sudden chill.

WHEN HE RETURNED from his shower, she was sitting up in bed with her laptop, a cranky machine she had, so far, not allowed him to replace. Simon scrubbed the towel over his wet hair. The room smelled of sex. This was not how he'd hoped to find her.

"I'm wide awake," she said. "But you go to sleep."

"Not tired," he grumped. He wasn't hard, but with a little encouragement he could be.

"If you're not tired, maybe you'd like to help me with this."

He knew she was playing games, refusing him to keep his interest keen. Nonetheless, he sat beside her and peered over her shoulder at the spreadsheet on the screen. He straightened. "Lela, that's this year's budget for Meilleurs Amis."

"I know. I'm trying to figure out how the New York store fits in with the rest."

"But that's sensitive information. You shouldn't have it."

"Tell that to Therese. She's the one who gave me all her passwords."

He scratched his scalp through the wet spikes of his hair. It was proof of the befuddled state Lela had him in that this was the first time he'd realized what a conflict of interest being her mentor had created. She was trying to help the company he meant to take over. And now she was putting confidential financial information in his hands. If he told her what he intended, she'd almost certainly refuse to see him again. If he didn't, he'd be engaged in a breach of his own personal ethics. Lela was not a player. All was not fair when it came to her.

Of course—he stilled and stared at the wall of photographs below—nothing said he had to use what he'd learned. He could keep it to himself. The money boys never had to know. They were good enough to clinch the buyout without compromising Lela's confidence.

Perfect, he thought, and ignored the little voice that

said silence was a compromise, too. He couldn't risk losing her. Not now. Not when the bond between them was so fragile.

The truth would simply have to wait.

Ten

IMON WENT HOME for a change of clothes. As had happened more and more often lately, a cloud of depression settled over him as soon as he opened the door. The maid had come and gone. The suite was dust-free, clutter-free, and smelled like cleaning solution. It could have been a hotel room for all it conveyed about its inhabitant.

He hated this place. He'd never thought about it before, but he did. He stopped in the center of the living room, keys dangling from his hand, and looked at the heavy, masculine furniture. The decorator had chosen it, said it reflected his personality. Apparently, his personality was very brown. The carpet was brown. The sofa was brown. The cabinets and tables sported a strange, mottled tortoiseshell effect. The walls were gold, but it was a chill gold, like gilt. Perhaps the decorator had thought the paint would remind him of money.

With a sigh, he tossed his keys onto an end table and rubbed his hair back and forth. If Lela could see this place, she'd run screaming in horror. He was beginning, just beginning, to think about asking her to live with him. But she'd never live with him here. Hell, she'd looked at him funny when he'd left a toothbrush in her bathroom. She probably wouldn't agree to live with him anywhere.

Snivel, snivel, he thought, and strode determinedly to his closet. Business rivals didn't call him Glacier Graves for nothing. He knew how to be patient. He knew how to grind down the opposition. If only he didn't feel as if he lost some vital part of himself every time he left her side.

He grimaced at a brown silk tie. Life had been so much easier with Diane.

The phone rang just as he grabbed his briefcase. Lela, he thought, heart surging as if he'd downed a pot of espresso.

But the caller wasn't Lela. The caller was his mother.

"Good. I caught you," she said in her warm, kind voice. "Your secretary is so unnerving to speak to. She acts as if she's afraid of me."

Simon sat on the arm of the couch. "It's me she's afraid of, Mom. She probably thinks the apple doesn't fall far from the tree."

"And it doesn't, you darling boy!"

Simon smiled. Tess was the only person in the world who'd ever called him darling, or who thought he was anything like her. "What's up, Mom? Is Dad all right?"

"Of course, darling. Fit as a fiddle. You can hardly hear

him slur anymore. I'm calling because our fortieth wedding anniversary is coming up. We've decided to throw a big party. Show everyone your dad is up to snuff."

"Just tell me when and I'll clear my calendar."

"We-ell." His mother drew the word out the way she did when she was embarrassed to ask a favor. "I was hoping you'd do more than that. I was hoping you'd bring that nice Diane girl we met at the Children's Fund ball. Oh, Simon, I know it's interfering, but your dad worries you aren't getting out and having fun, and he thought she was such a princess. Talked about her for weeks. How sweet she was, and how pretty."

Simon pushed the skin of his forehead against the bone beneath. "I'm afraid Diane and I aren't seeing each other anymore. She's engaged."

"Well, it was just a thought. You know your dad will be happy to see you with or without a date."

Her disappointment, gentle as it was, brought a dull ache to his brow. Tess and Howard Graves had given him so much, more than he could ever repay. He hated worrying either one of them.

"I'll see if I can bring another date," he said. "I've been seeing someone new."

"Have you?" Tess couldn't keep the motherly interest from her voice. "Is she nice? No. Never mind. I'm sure she's nice. All your girlfriends are nice."

Simon rolled his eyes at that. All his mistresses had been nice. His girlfriend, if that's what Lela was, was another story. "I can't promise she'll make it, Mom. She may have other plans."

A short silence greeted this announcement. Obviously,

Tess couldn't imagine anyone turning her darling down. "Oh. Of course. Modern women don't build their lives around a man, do they?"

"No, they don't, but I'll do my best to bring this modern woman to your party. And now I really have to go, before my employees accuse me of slacking." He listened to her burble of leave-taking, a smile warming his face. "I love you," he said when she was done.

Her breath caught. "I love you, too, darling."

He set the phone in its cradle. Her gasp told him something he should have known. He didn't say those words enough. Not nearly.

LELA DIDN'T UNDERSTAND why Simon was so nervous about attending a charity function. He seemed inordinately relieved when she agreed to accompany him. Then, two days before the event, he insisted on going through her closet to choose what she would wear.

"These aren't quite right," he'd said, after pawing through every dress. "I'll pick something up for you at Graves."

"I said no gifts."

"Fine. When you get that managerial position, you can pay me back."

"If I have to pay you back, I should be able to choose."

"Please, Lela. I know I don't have Andrew's flair, but I do have a sense of what's appropriate. Trust me. You won't hate what I buy."

When he asked in such an earnest, humble way, she didn't have the heart to refuse him. And she didn't hate what he bought. It was a cocktail-length sheath in raw lavender silk that suited her coloring to a tee. The style was very simple, very classic: sleeveless and fitted, with a clean, square neck. Lela would have worn it without underwear, but Simon forestalled that choice by providing a strapless body briefer, which was so beautifully constructed and so sexy she couldn't even pretend to mind wearing it. The clever thing actually gave her cleavage.

Simon had swallowed hard when she modeled it for him.

Now, however, he just looked grim. His knuckles were white on the wheel of his big bronze Mercedes. God forbid if she had wanted to talk to him. She would have been out of luck.

The event was being held on Long Island, at an estate on the north shore. An hour of driving took them to a large, half-timbered house with rolling, landscaped grounds and a cobbled roundabout before the door. Though it was a private home, a uniformed valet whisked the Mercedes away.

"Well," said Simon and tugged his jacket straight. He was dressed casually for him, in a brown linen suit and black sport shirt. He was gangster handsome but hardly relaxed. If he'd been any stiffer, his tie might as well have been a noose. With one hand at the small of her back, he guided her through a trellised garden. Behind the house, across a lawn as green and groomed as a golf course, spilled a crowd of chattering well-dressed people, most of them older than herself. Beyond them, the Long Island Sound lapped against a short dock. A sailboat bobbed in its berth, the single mast as graceful as a beech. Champagne glasses sparkled in the sun, and pearls, and cuff links, and straight white teeth. Lela felt as if she'd stepped into a scene from *The Great Gatsby*.

Not that it mattered. Lela had hobnobbed with the rich and snobby before. She knew how to behave. If she felt a shiver of nerves, well, that was Simon's anxiety rubbing off.

She was about to venture into the fray when Simon caught her arm and pulled her under a rose-covered arch. His expression was intensely sheepish.

"I have to tell you something," he said.

Lela folded her arms beneath her breasts. "Yes?"

He took a deep breath. "This isn't a charity function. It's a party for my parents' anniversary. My dad's been worried about me. He thinks I don't date."

Lela burst out laughing. She couldn't help it. This was the last thing she'd expected him to say. "I can't believe you couldn't get another date."

His lips thinned stubbornly. "I didn't want another date. I wanted you. I figured you wouldn't come if you knew it was nothing to do with business."

"All you had to do was ask."

"But our agreement—"

"Simon." She squeezed his shoulder. "I would have said yes. I like you."

He blinked in surprise. God, he was adorable. The thought that he wanted her to meet his parents, even if it was under duress, sparked a heartwarming glow inside her breast. She couldn't remember the last time one of her lovers had wanted to show her off to anyone but his drinking buddies.

"I like you," she said again. "It's not just the agreement."

A hint of color stained his cheeks. He cleared his throat. "Good," he said. "I like you, too."

SIMON'S MOTHER WAS a dear, and his father was a flirt. They made a handsome couple. Howard's ginger hair had gone to gray, and Tess's was an unlikely silver-white. They were both fit and tall and generous with their smiles. Tess was the quieter of the two. Lela knew right off that she ruled Howard's roost. She suspected most of his rakish banter was designed to entertain his wife. The first thing he did on meeting Lela was declare Simon didn't deserve her.

"Run away with me," he urged. "I know how to treat a beautiful woman."

"Don't you mind him," said his wife. "He's incorrigible."

He insisted on grilling her steak with his own two hands. "Nothing but the best for Simon's date." His voice was halting, but loud. Two minutes after they'd met, he'd explained he was recovering from a stroke. "Can't charm the girls the way I used to."

Lela assured him he was doing fine. Indeed, he was everything Simon said: big and big-hearted and as open as his son was reserved. The shyest guest seemed to love his teasing, seemed to love him. Simon's mother, Tess, glowed like a rose every time he looked at her. Of course, she glowed for Simon, too.

Simon was different around his parents, more relaxed. When he smiled at them, the love he felt shone clear as sunshine. Lela's eyes pricked so fiercely she had to look away. She didn't want this tightness in her chest, didn't want to be haunted by this old, impossible longing. But what she wanted didn't matter. The dream refused to be shoved aside. She wanted a love like this, a family like this. She wanted someone to devote his heart to her.

When the sun sank behind the house, they lit the Chinese lanterns. Strings of them decorated the lawn: rose and white and green. Fireflies wheeled before the stars. An oldies band set up on a small platform. Listening to them play was like stepping back in time. Simon danced her around the lawn to "Volare" and "Till There Was You" and other loopy songs she couldn't have put a name to.

"Courting songs," Howard teased, elbowing his son as he and Tess swept smoothly by.

Neither she nor Simon were good at this kind of dancing. All they could do was shuffle. Simon didn't seem to mind. In fact, he didn't seem to want to stop. He nuzzled her hair as they moved in their little circle, his trousers going shush-shush-shush against her dress. By the end of the first dance, he had an erection and had to hold her close. Lela liked that. His hand was warm at the small of her back, his lips soft against her cheek.

"This is nice," he said, though he must have been uncomfortable.

If she hadn't known better, she'd have said he was being romantic.

Apparently, Simon's mother thought so, too. She cornered Lela on her way back from a trip to the bathroom. Lela wasn't sure how it happened, but a minute later, she and Tess were having a tête-à-tête on a secluded garden bench. Tess patted Lela's hand.

"I'm so glad you could come, dear," she said. "Simon's never brought a girlfriend home before."

Lela squirmed at that. "I'm not sure you can call me his

girlfriend. We're friends, I guess, but it's really not more than that."

Simon's mother smiled as if she knew a secret. "Be that as it may, I'm very pleased to meet you. Simon doesn't have many friends, not close ones." She leaned toward Lela and lowered her voice. "I think he's afraid that loving anyone but us would be disloyal."

Lela's throat was thick. She had a hard time meeting Tess's eyes, which were somehow merry and serious at once. "He certainly does love you."

"Yes," Tess agreed, "but he has more love to give than he knows." Then she shrugged, the hint of sobriety leaving her expression. "Tell me about you, Lela. Do your folks live in New York?"

It was a question she'd faced a hundred times, but this time, this night, it hit her hard. She looked at her hands, wound together in the lap of her lilac dress. "They're not around anymore. They died when I was young."

"You poor thing," Tess clucked. Her arm hugged Lela's shoulders. "So you were an orphan, too?"

But there was no "too" about it. Lela was not the creature Simon was. Lela hadn't been saved in time, and she couldn't pretend she had been, least of all to this kind woman.

People always called her a success story, one of the foster kids who'd "made it." Lela knew better. She was a wolf waiting to bite the hand that fed her, because part of her could never trust. Every relationship she had was stained by that flaw. She was stained. The crack ran through her like a fault in the earth.

"I'm sorry," she said, unable to sit a moment longer. "I need to make a call."

. . .

SIMON FOUND HER in the library, trying to find a cab service that took credit. Silvery tear tracks striped her cheeks, but her voice was perfectly businesslike. When she saw him at the door, she averted her face. Relief and worry mingled in his breast. He took the phone from her and hung it up.

"You don't need to do that," he said as gently as he could. "If you want to go home, I'll drive you."

Her shoulders began to shake. She seemed incapable of facing him. "Your parents— The party—"

He pulled her against him and rubbed her back. Her arms folded up between them, stiff and self-protective.

"They'll understand," he said. She curled closer. Oh, his heart ached for her. If he could have made love to her then, he would have. "My mother didn't mean to upset you, you know."

Her head turned back and forth across his shirt. "I don't know why I'm being like this."

"Sure you do." He kissed the top of her head. "One of my college roommates confessed once that he'd never been so jealous as the Christmas he spent at my house. Howard and Tess are great. Believe me, I know how lucky I am."

"You deserve them." She pushed back and swiped at her nose. "God, I hate feeling this way. It's so stupid. I know better. I am what I am, and it's not so bad."

His brows furrowed together. "Of course, it's not bad. You're wonderful, Lela."

She made a face. He wished he were clever with words like his father, like Andrew. He wished he were clever with women. But he wasn't. He had to do the best he could with what he had. Leaning down to look her in the eye, he braced her shoulders with his hands.

"You're wonderful, Lela. To me, you're wonderful."

He must have said something right because she sniffed hard and smiled. "I'd be more wonderful if I had a Kleenex."

He found one for her on the library desk. "Want to go home now or stay a little longer?"

She finished wiping her nose. Its tip was pink, as were her eyes, but she looked surprisingly pretty for a woman who'd just been crying. Or maybe, to him, she'd always look pretty.

"Let's stay," she said, her shoulders relaxing. "Your father promised me another dance."

IT ENDED UP being one of the nicest nights she'd ever had, maybe *the* nicest. She loved being treated like Simon's girlfriend, loved leaning into his side and listening to him talk in his low, careful voice. He barely let go of her all night. He held her to him as if he were her personal mooring.

Just this once, she thought, I'll let myself pretend.

They left at midnight, to the protests of Simon's father.

"The night's young," he said.

Simon smiled and shook his head. "Lela has to work tomorrow. She needs her beauty sleep. So do you, Pops. I want you to take care of yourself."

"I take care," said his father, and he let his son enfold him in a hug.

They drove in silence again, but this silence was as comfortable as a favorite robe. Simon sat her close to him and kept his hand on her thigh, rubbing her now and then as if to assure her she wasn't forgotten. She watched his profile in the highway lights: rough and strong and strangely beautiful. His parents, his real parents, would have been so proud if they'd seen how he'd grown up. She was terribly glad she hadn't missed out on knowing him.

My God, she thought, I love him to pieces.

The knowledge wasn't as scary as it might have been. The only true scare was how big the feeling was, how it rose like a tidal wave, demanding to be let out. How could she feel so much for one person? How would she ever keep it inside? Her sex was tight with it, hot with it. She wanted him more than she ever had. She wanted to show him how she felt.

She turned on the seat and put her hand on his leg. "Ever had a blow job at the wheel?"

He snorted. "Don't even think it, Miss Thing. My father would never forgive me if I totaled the car with you in it. You made quite an impression on him."

"I did, didn't I?" Her hand slid higher, up his muscled thigh, into the valley of his groin. He shifted on the seat. Smiling to herself, she cupped the swell of his balls. Something soft moved under her hand and began to grow hard. She strafed it gently with her nails. It lengthened.

"Lela."

"I'm just warming you up. We'll have to get a quick start when we get home. Since I need my beauty sleep."

"Lela."

"Hush. I'm working." She tucked one leg under her bottom and licked the lobe of his ear. Her nails trailed down his rising shaft. She pushed them under his crotch, then squeezed him in her palm. A drop of sweat trickled down his neck, but she wasn't satisfied yet. "You were harder than this when we were dancing. I could feel it. Did you wonder if people would see? Is that why you held me so close?"

"I wanted to hold you close. I like holding you."

Lela smiled and bit the ear she'd been licking. Simon jumped. She used the distraction to whip open his trousers. "You can be so sweet, Simon. I wonder if people know that about you."

"I doubt it," he said, and groaned as her fingers wrapped his sweaty, straining skin. He was silk in her hands, silk and steel. "Lela, if you keep that up, you're going to get more than you bargained for."

"Promise?" She lowered her head. She breathed on him, then inhaled his musky scent. It heightened as she did. Pleased, her tongue curled out, found his tiny slit and licked.

The car swerved, almost throwing her against the dash. Lela's heart thumped with fear, but he was only pulling onto the shoulder.

"That's enough," he said, sounding genuinely angry.

But he couldn't have been too angry because he threw her back on the seat, shoved up her dress and popped the snaps that fastened her body briefer. She had an instant to register the leather beneath her bare buttocks and then he was over her. His cock burned between her legs, against her mons. Fluid trickled from her sex. He slipped in it, and groaned, and lurched too eagerly forward. The gear shift jabbed her thigh. The window bonked his head. He cursed as she'd never heard him curse before. Then, when she was about to reach to guide him, he found his way in. She moaned with relief. His entry was as dramatic and as welcome as ever. Thick, impatient, he sawed back and forth until he could seat himself fully, to the root, the way he liked best. As always, he had to stop then, throbbing inside her with his eyes closed and his mouth slack, as if he never wanted to forget how good she felt around him. Feeling rather good herself, Lela scratched her hands down his back and made a growly cat noise.

"Want to try a new trick?" she offered.

He panted at her. She circled his mouth with the longest finger of her hand. "Get this wet, big guy." His lack of comprehension excited her all the more. "Suck it. I'm going to put it somewhere nice."

When he did as she asked, she put her hand down his pants and searched the long crease between his buttocks. She knew the moment his fog cleared because his cock twitched violently inside her.

"You're going to do this now? By the side of the high-way?"

She grinned and tickled his sphincter. "You know what they say. Don't put off until tomorrow . . ."

He squirmed. "Whatever happened to 'haste makes waste'?"

"Just tell me when it gets good, big guy."

His resistance seemed to disappear all at once. Her finger slid into the webbing. He groaned, then stiffened.

"My leg is cramping," he whispered, but his cock was marble hard, and his pelvis was grinding hers.

"Do you want to pull out and massage it?"

The shake of his head was small but definite. "No. Just kiss me until it goes away."

She did as he asked and more, gently circling the satiny

walls of his anus, getting him used to the feel, probing for
the little gland that made this bed trick fun.

"Ah," he said, his spine rolling, then: "Oh, my God."

She laughed. "Leg better?"

"Oh, yes."

"Want another finger?"

"Oh, yes. Oh, yes. My God, that's incredible." He
huffed with pleasure as her second finger slid into place
and stroked the tiny swelling. "I've never felt anything like
that."

"Good," she said. "I always wanted to be the first."

A blare of light approached, an eighteen-wheeler coming up behind them.

"Damn it," he said, beginning to move in long, heavy
thrusts. "If that trucker honks, I'm strangling you."

The trucker did honk. Lela tossed her head and laughed.
"Come on, big guy. Give it to me. Give it to me good."

Simon pumped so vigorously the seat chirruped as if it
was sprung.

"You'll have to take it yourself," he warned. "I'm not
waiting for you and getting arrested by the side of the
road."

She hitched her legs higher on his waist. "Faster, big
guy. I think I see a state trooper."

His laugh was shaken by his thrusts. "God, I love you."

The world seemed to stop turning. He loved her? Her
eyes filled with tears. She touched his face, trying to probe
his shadowed gaze. It couldn't be true. It was too soon, too
ridiculous that a man like him could love a woman like
her. As if he knew what she was thinking, he smiled and
bit her thumb. Below the waist his movements slowed.

"Oh, no you don't," she said, her voice as shaky as her limbs. "You've got to hurry. I want to get you home and do this right."

He wouldn't hurry, but it didn't matter; her buried fingers hurried him against his will. She stroked the hidden gland until he moaned and shook, until his balls pulled up and hardened.

"Shit," he said.

"Do it," she whispered, hot in his ear. "Blast me with your come, Simon. Shoot it up my cunt. I want to feel it, Simon. I want to feel your cock explode."

Her dirty talk made him laugh, but it got to him. He cursed again and tensed and swelled as if he really was going to explode. His cock was so stiff she felt bruised, deliciously bruised. Yes, she thought, her climax lost in anticipating his. She bit his shoulder and worked her fingers faster. He couldn't resist the added friction. He broke on a groan, then laughed as he spasmed hard.

"You're crazy," he said, his grin distorting the kisses he pressed to her face.

"Crazy like a fox."

He sighed, and settled, and held her like a treasure he thought he'd never find. The moment ended long before she was ready.

"Oh, man," he said. "I've got to get you home."

He didn't seem embarrassed, but the tenderness was gone. She wondered if he was sorry for what he'd said.

Rome

Eleven

*B*ÉATRIX WONDERED IF she should have called
Philip. They stood together in her rooftop studio, bathed
by the smell of turpentine and the pearly Paris light. It
would rain soon. It would ease the summery heat and water her wild red roses and end the silence that had fallen
over them both.

The painting was finished. Ten by twelve feet, it was
larger than anything she'd attempted. For the last month,
it had been her life. She'd skipped sleep and food and
company because she couldn't bear to put down the
brushes. Five more minutes, she'd say, only to come to
herself at dawn. The figures, a teenage girl and her two
younger brothers, were as vivid as she could make them.
The canal was as wet, the sky as blue, the grasses as green

and lush. The paint was laid on thickly, as if even in that she'd been compelled to generosity. She'd poured her sweat and blood into each stroke, and, to her, each stroke seemed to radiate her passion back. She knew these people. This little family had seen love and loss, war and now peace. In a way, this was her dream of what a family could be.

Whether anyone else could see what she did, she didn't know. She hoped, but the memory of the critics' lukewarm reception to her first show still burned.

It's good, she thought when she laid the last daub of white in the youngest boy's eye. It's the best thing I've done. If the critics don't like it, I'll never make them like anything. The realization brought an odd peace. If she gave up on pleasing them, she'd be free to paint what she wished. Fear washed through her, but it was a good fear, an exciting fear. All her future canvases were blank.

She'd dialed Philip's cell phone before she could stop herself. Even though she caught him at work, he'd agreed to come at once. They hadn't spoken in three weeks, not since their fateful cab ride to Versailles. She'd buried her ache for him in painting, but now she wondered what his quick acceptance meant. Had he missed her? And, if so, which part of her had he missed? His stepdaughter? His erstwhile lover? His friend?

She did consider him her friend. Their separation had taught her that. She'd taken his kindness for granted, abused it even, but when he withheld it she'd missed it as much as she missed his touch.

Now he stared at her painting, his expression inscrutable, his high brow pleated in a single fold.

"Well?" she said, unable to bear the wait.

He turned to her, smiling, his fine gray eyes agleam. "It's beautiful." His voice was thick. He cleared his throat and looked back at the painting. "My grandfather lived in London during the Blitz. He used to tell me stories about the blackouts and air raids. When I see pictures like that, I remember him."

"You don't think it's too mawkish?"

Slowly, he shook his head. "No. It's you, Bea. It has your edge. There's wit in this. There's pain and hope and a wonderful humanity. You painted this from your heart. As you should."

Tears pressed behind her eyes. She hadn't imagined he saw her so clearly, or admired her so much. She looked down at the paint-smeared floor. He touched her cheek, a feather-light brush of knuckles. Then his hand fell away. When he spoke, his voice was low. "Thank you for calling. I was afraid you wouldn't want to see me again after . . . after the last time."

"I was afraid you wouldn't want to see me." The admission took all her courage. He reached for her hand and squeezed it. When she looked up, he was studying the painting again, almost as if he didn't dare look at her. He did not, however, let go.

"What's happening between us is trouble, Bea."

"I know."

"If people knew we were fooling around—"

"They'd think you were feeling insecure and trying to cement your position by sleeping with the Clouet heir."

His gaze was startled. He choked out a laugh. "That particular construction hadn't occurred to me, but since it's no worse than anything I came up with, I won't take offense."

"I don't believe those things, Philip. I know you've worked for everything you have."

He took her other hand and faced her, as if they were children at a dance. "I'm glad." For a moment, his eyes searched hers. His expression was serious. "I haven't been able to forget what we did in that taxi. It's the most amazing thing that ever happened to me."

"Me, too," she said, though she wondered if he meant it the way she did. What they'd done hadn't amazed her as much the fact that they'd done anything. After all these years, to have Philip wanting her! His beautiful eyes did not clear up the mystery. The affection she saw had always been there. She couldn't tell how deeply his feelings ran.

Not as deeply as mine, she thought. He could never match her there.

He nodded toward her painting with the side of his golden head. "I'm going to buy this. I want to hang it at headquarters."

He named a sum that made her eyes widen.

"Philip!"

"That's the going rate for corporate art. Unless you want to charge me a penalty for having the nerve to call it corporate art."

"Of course, I don't. But—"

He wasn't listening. He rubbed the lean, straight line of his jaw. "I think I'll notify the press."

"The press!"

His sudden grin told her he was enjoying this. "Surely you wouldn't begrudge Meilleurs Amis the attention? It's not every day the daughter of a famous fashion institution turns out to be a gifted artist."

Bea blushed with pleasure. "I couldn't trade on my connections."

He hugged her. "You could, Bea, and you will."

PHILIP SIGNED THE check with a flourish and slid it across his desk. He smiled to himself as Bea shook her head in wonderment. He'd paid few artisans before; purchasing wasn't his responsibility. Now he saw what he'd been missing. Playing benefactor definitely had its charm.

"This is a lot of money," she said.

"It's no more than you're worth."

She grimaced. "According to you."

"Yes, according to me." He grinned at her, the bubble of enjoyment expanding. "I'll have you know I was tempted to write that check from my personal account and hang your painting on my wall. But then I'd be the only one who got to enjoy it. This way, the whole company can feel a pride of ownership."

Bea's grimace tilted into a smile. She shot a glance through her lashes. "Taking money from Meilleurs Amis seems vaguely incestuous."

"It is vaguely incestuous." He came around the desk and sat on its edge. "Bea. This is only your first big check. There will be more. Ten years from now, you'll say I robbed you."

"We can but hope."

The sparkle in her eyes made him want to kiss her. What a wisecracker. God, he'd missed her. And, God, he wanted her. He ached from dreaming of her. He'd relived that hour in the taxi a thousand times, awake, asleep, as if she'd been in his blood for years, building, gathering, un-til—like some arcane aphrodisiac reaching critical mass—the effect was too strong to ignore. Maybe she had been in his blood for years. Maybe he'd wanted her all along and had misread the feeling as affection, as sympathy. He'd always enjoyed her company. Even when she was at her grumpiest, Bea was someone whose presence pleased him. When she was sunny, as she was now, her happiness meant more to him than his own.

Maybe he didn't just love her. Maybe—he touched the length of cotton that covered his heart—maybe he'd fallen in love with her. Lord. He wasn't ready for that. The wounds Eve had inflicted had not yet healed. To be hurt like that again, by Bea, might be more than he could stand.

"Hey." She gave his shoulder a light punch. "Why don't I take you to dinner tonight and we'll spend my ill-gotten gains."

"I'd love to, but I have to catch a flight to Rome. I'm visiting one of our suppliers."

"Nothing wrong, I hope."

He pulled a decorative pen from the stand behind him and tapped it rapidly on his thigh.

"No," he said. "But I haven't done the courtesies in a while. I don't want *signor* Amalfi to think we've forgotten him."

"Ah." She nodded wisely. "The cobbler."

"Yes." He forced the beating pen to still by taking it in both hands. Old Mr. Amalfi supplied one-of-a-kind shoes to Meilleurs Amis. Sometimes he reproduced examples of historic footwear, as in their recent Marie Antoinette dis-play, and sometimes he concocted fantastical creations of his own. His shoes were marginally comfortable, ruinously expensive, and perennial bestsellers at all the boutiques.

But visiting him was not a matter of courtesy. Young Mr. Amalfi, the grandson, the accountant, was a bottom-line man. In light of Philip's recent expenditures—the Beijing store and the refurbishment of Milan—he'd expressed some concerns about their line of credit. Credit was lifeblood to a business like theirs. Philip frequently couldn't pay for goods until he'd sold them. Since the markup was five, six times what he'd paid, the risk was acceptable. If required, they could live without Amalfi shoes, even pay on receipt with the cash flow from other sales. But if he agreed to that, chances were the news would spread among their suppliers. If more insisted on cash up front, Philip would be royally screwed. Far better, he thought, to nip this problem in the bud.

And nip it he would, especially if he could speak to the senior Amalfi. Once upon a time, Alberto had been Sophie's lover. A happy one, by all accounts. Ever since, he and the Clouets had enjoyed a profitable relationship. Philip would remind him of that. He'd explain how sensible his recent expansions were, the thought that had gone into them, and the projections for future earnings. The business was sound; it was merely growing. Meilleurs Amis was still the best showcase for his shoes. Most of all, though, he'd let Alberto Amalfi know how deeply he respected his talent. The old man was an artist. Philip wouldn't even have to pretend.

So there was no reason to worry Bea with this little setback.

"It's just a quick trip," he assured her. "I'm sure I'll be back by Monday."

"You should stay longer," she said. "It is Rome. When was the last time you just had fun?"

"With you," he said, unable to stop the words. Her blush made him glad he hadn't. Cupping her glowing cheeks, he let impulse take him. To hell with being careful. He'd been without her too long. "Come with me. We'll eat pasta. Stroll the piazzas. Soak up the Italian sun. Who knows? Maybe you'll find the inspiration for your next masterpiece."

She rolled her eyes but she was smiling. "I have had a craving for *gelato* . . . ."

"I know a fabulous place on the Via Veneto. Their apricot-peach will make you swoon."

"Such emotion," Bea teased. "You'll make me think you've forgotten your roots."

He squeezed her shoulders and kissed her once on the cheek. "Say you'll come. Otherwise I'll have to eat it all without you."

"I'll come," she said.

Her answer made him happier than he had any right to be.

SHE FELT AS if she were running off with a married man. The guilty thrill refused to fade, and she would not, could not dwell on what they might be risking. Rome was another world. Rome was the moon. Once they'd bowed and scraped to Mr. Amalfi, they'd be on their own, away from prying Paris eyes.

Anything might happen. Philip looked at her differently now, hungrily. Maybe it was only hunger for a repeat of the thrill he'd discovered in the cab. But maybe it was something more.

In Rome, she'd know.

The refrain danced through her head as she hastily packed a weekend bag. Her sketchbook went in first, followed by a bouquet of pretty dresses, her sexiest underwear, her pills, and an optimistic supply of condoms.

I'll have him, she thought, firming her jaw. At the very least, I'll have him in my arms. Her pussy shimmered at the prospect. Outside her window, the bell at Sacré-Coeur tolled the hour. Her blood rushed faster. Philip was waiting with a taxi downstairs. She tossed in her one pair of slingback Amalfi shoes, zipped the leather case, and was off.

To the eternal city! In Rome, she'd know.

THEY TRADED STORIES they'd never told before: tales from their childhoods, from places they'd been and people they'd known. The glories of nighttime Rome were merely backdrop to this other exploration. They marveled at how much they didn't know about each other, about how much they had in common.

They returned late to their hotel on the vìa Veneto. Bea had stayed at the Excelsior before. It was not as trendy as it had been during the days of *La Dolce Vita*, but the fashion world remained loyal. They held an annual show there, and it was still the height of luxury. Philip had rented one room, never even discussed getting another for her. His assumption pleased her, or perhaps he was just determined not to be denied. Either way she didn't mind, though she couldn't resist teasing him.

"One bed?" she said, raising her brow at the satin-covered expanse.

"Two pillows."

"I need two for myself."

"We'll steal one from the couch."

"I could sleep on the couch."

His mouth curled with lazy amusement. "Don't even think it, Miss Bea."

She liked that he knew she was teasing. The rhythm of their banter put her at ease.

"Take your shower," he said, hand rising to her cheek. "I'll be waiting. I'm going to take my time with you tonight."

The promise kept her company, eroticizing the silky flow of soap and water. He'd be undressing now, peeling his clothes from his gorgeous body, baring the muscle of his belly, his delicious hand-sized buttocks, his graceful legs and arms. Maybe he'd imagine her in here. Maybe he'd start to rise and touch himself, wanting to be big for her, wanting to be ready. She closed her eyes and stroked herself for him. Her nipples were hard, her thighs taut. At that moment she loved her body for the pleasure it would bring them both.

When she emerged, hair wet, body wrapped in a towel, she found him naked by the bed. It was the first time she'd seen him without clothes, and the sight stopped her in her tracks.

"Come here," he said, a gentle order.

As she walked, his penis filled, lengthening first over the hang of his balls, then wavering upward, higher and thicker, until he stood firm for her, the tip throbbing like a little heart. The crown was rosy and full. It looked hard, like rubber. Entranced, she watched it pulse as he un-wrapped her towel. She barely noticed her own nudity. A vein was ticking in his groin, and his tiny cock slit had be-gun to shine.

He chuckled. "You like looking at me, don't you?"

She opened her mouth to make a smart remark, then said, "I've dreamed of how you'd look for a long time."

He sighed, a sound she couldn't interpret, though she didn't think it was regret. His thumbs trailed down the valley of her cleavage. "I love your breasts." He trailed back up to cup them. "They make me weak in the knees."

His mouth sank to hers, and their bodies seemed to melt together, bellies pressing, arms wrapping, feet sidling close for the perfect, skin-melding fit.

"What else?" she whispered against his lips. "What else makes you weak?"

With a low moan, he lifted her and laid her on the bed. "Everything." He stretched over her and stroked her with one hand, down her side, along her leg to coax her knee to bend and fall wide. Access gained, he drew light, twist-ing patterns on her inner thigh. "Everything about you makes me weak. Your breasts, your thighs, the way your belly feels like silk under my hand. The way your hair curls. The scent of your neck. The sound of your laugh. The curve at the small of your back."

She laughed, but he was kissing each place he praised, tenderly, skillfully, until she could not laugh but only squirm with uncontainable pleasure. His hand found her wet, and there, too, he petted. He slid one finger in and out, then painted her clinging folds.

"You make me weak when you come," he said, husky and low.

"And when I touch you?" She wrapped her hand around his shaft.

His penis leapt against her palm. He closed his eyes. Pleasure flickered across his face as she pulled gently toward the tip.

"Then, especially." He sighed, then eased her hand away and wriggled down to suck her breasts. He settled in and latched on, his arms going round her with a strange intensity. The sounds that broke in his throat were pained. She stroked his hair, loose now, down his neck, over his shoulders. He held her tight and rocked her. Such emotions welled inside her, she feared she'd weep. She felt as if they were comforting each other for hurts they'd never voiced, for hurts others had inflicted, for hurts they'd only feared. This was the kind of healing that could break one's heart.

"Come inside," she said, kissing the baby-fine waves at his temple. "I can't wait any longer."

He lifted over her. "I want to be naked like before. Is it all right? I'll be careful."

She touched the curve of his lower lip. "It's all right."

He shuddered at her answer, then again when she reached down to part herself for him. He entered slowly, sweetly, trembling as she closed around his questing shaft. His weight rested on his elbows. His fingers combed her hair. His bare skin was an extraordinary intimacy, too new to take for granted. The sensation of his satiny cock head pushing through her folds, opening her, touching her hidden flesh, brought a moan to her throat.

"Bea," he sighed, stretching for the final inch. "This makes me weak. This makes me weakest of all."

Then he was home—home and hers. She hugged him

with her knees and ran her hands down the length of his back. Her fingertips circled the solid muscles of his buttocks. He shivered.

"You feel strong," she said. "You feel like heaven."

He smiled with all his old fondness and began to stroke, his hips beating softly, his eyes steady and clear on hers. He did not look away. He did not hide or let her hide. With anyone else, the directness of that gaze would have been intolerable. With Philip, she felt only elation. For once, the beauty of his face did not overwhelm her, only his kindness, only the quiet strength of his soul.

She had never loved him more, nor felt so beautiful, as she did with him inside her. When she saw the pleasure she brought him, in the tensing of his mouth, in the flush of his skin, in the deepening thrust and draw of his hips, she couldn't help but love herself.

"I wish we could stay like this," he said. "I wish this never had to end."

But it did. Neither of them could hold off climax forever, Béatrix least of all. Her body wasn't made to wait, not the first time, not when the tug and plunder of her sex worked so steadily on her nerves. He knew her finish was near. He pushed deep, deeper, with a little more pressure, a little more speed. She clenched her hands behind his back, coasting on the lush, aching edge. He smiled into her eyes, half a grimace because he was close himself. His knees dug into the sheets. He braced her shoulders. For the first time since they'd started making love, his eyes squeezed shut. Then, without warning, he thrust so quick and hard her climax seemed to explode.

She cried out and a second later he did, too, a raw,

pained grunt. He ground against her so desperately it hurt. Only when his warmth spurted over her belly did she realize he'd pulled out.

He collapsed, panting, then rolled off her to the side. Turning toward him, she pulled two curled fingers down the softening underside of his cock. He twitched when her thumb brushed the dripping slit. She gentled her touch, smearing the last of his seed across his crown.

"Philip," she said. "You're being medieval."

"I'm being careful."

She laughed, resignation in it. "You can't possibly have more faith in withdrawal than you do in my birth control pills."

"Just in case," he insisted.

But she wasn't convinced her safety was foremost in his mind. She trusted him when he said he'd never had unprotected sex. There wasn't another man on the planet she would have believed, but she believed him. She was pretty sure he believed her. Hell, they both got tested every time Meilleurs Amis ran a blood drive. So the problem had to lie elsewhere. If a man pulled out when every instinct must be screaming for him to thrust, his crisis of faith ran deep. Had she shown him the sharp of her tongue too often? Did he doubt she truly cared for him? She stroked the golden curls of his chest, reluctant to push the issue but wanting at least to bring it up.

"It feels like you're holding back," she said.

His mouth opened and shut. He pulled her closer and kissed her hair.

"It's a risk," he said, which wasn't an answer at all.

. . .

WAKING UP BESIDE him the next morning did much to lift her cloud. They made love, quickly this time, with teasing and laughter, then dressed for their day. The visit to *signor* Amalfi's villa passed like a dream. They charmed the old man in tandem, like a well-oiled machine. Then, while Philip and the two Albertos discussed "serious" business on their own, Béatrix kicked off her shoes and snoozed on a lounger by the terraced, terra-cotta pool.

Hibiscus scented the air, and olive oil from their lovely cold lunch. The Mediterranean sun was a drug to make her forget her troubles, a warmth that stole through her veins and coiled around her sex. For the first time in ages, she allowed herself to revel in fantasies of Philip. She thought about how she wanted to touch him, about what she'd do if he were baking by her side. His skin was smooth and caressable, his muscles firm, his cock a temptation to the hand. She wanted to drive him so wild he wouldn't have the will to pull back. She wanted to make him hers completely. By the time he came to collect her, her motor was purring like a cat.

His business must have gone well. He smiled down at her, at ease with himself and her. "Have a nice nap?"

"Oh, yes," she said, letting him watch her stretch.

As soon as they left the villa, he took her hand. The kiss he pressed to her knuckles was sweet. Mine, it seemed to say. Mine.

PHILIP HAD RENTED a Vespa. They putted through the empty streets while the natives indulged in their daily siesta. All but a few tourists were sleeping off a leisurely lunch. At three, the city and its traffic would reawaken, but for now the sights were theirs.

They rode north past Giancolense Park with its shady palms and scented gardens. They swept around the Piazza San Pietro at the Vatican, gawked at the Castel Sant'Angelo's ochre fortress, and crossed the Tiber. The moped rattled on the cobbles of a beautiful piazza. Despite the day's heat, Philip pulled her arms more snugly around his waist.

"Hold on," he said, and she laid her cheek against his back.

They stopped at a plain-faced church to admire two stunning Caravaggio's. The three-hundred-year-old paintings were in wonderful condition. This artist had not been afraid of the dark. Great masses of it made his figures stand out like beacons, their colors rich, their modeling more convincing than a photograph. The power of his work moved her beyond words. I'm not even close to this, she thought. I have lifetimes to go.

The distance did not depress her. A dream was a worthy thing.

Philip stood behind her while she gazed at the old master, his chin resting on her hair, his arms crossed over hers. His presence doubled her pleasure. She knew he appreciated genius. He had been an artist once himself. He had studied enough to understand. Neither of them spoke. The church was cool and quiet, and the weight of the past was all around them, slightly crumbling, often stained, but no less awe-inspiring.

Caravaggio had walked these streets, like Michelangelo and Mussolini. Like Julius Caesar and the inimitable Sophie Clouet. Like Béatrix.

Finally, Philip kissed her hair. "Shall we drive to the vìa Condotti and check on Meilleurs Amis?"

"Yes," she said, though she didn't give a damn about the boutique.

Happily, the visit was brief. The locals ran things their way, and, since the shop was thriving, Philip wasn't inclined to interfere. He bought a straw hat for Béatrix, a silly schoolgirlish concoction with a trailing yellow ribbon. It made her look like a large plump Madeleine.

"Your cheeks are getting burned," he said as he settled it on her hair.

The manager winked at her the way women do when they think a man is smitten.

Béatrix smiled back and ducked her head. It wasn't true, but she didn't mind the woman thinking it was.

"Where to now?" Philip asked.

"Just drive," she said. "Drive to where it's shady."

He knew the city well, and he knew the rumbling machine on which they rode. Even when the cars poured back through the streets, she felt perfectly safe. He took her south again, past the Colosseum and onto the Appian Way. At first the traffic was unrelenting, but as it thinned out she grew more aware of the vibration of the moped and of Philip's body pressing hers. Tie-less, he wore his old pub-crawling clothes: faded jeans and a loose white shirt rolled to the elbows. His chest was hard beneath her forearms, his thighs warm between her legs. He seemed the man he'd been before he married her mother, the man she'd fallen for on sight. Today she wanted him even more. Today she knew what lay beneath those casual clothes.

As if he sensed when her awareness changed, his chest

began to rise and fall. She dropped one hand to the bend where his leg met his torso. A shiver rolled down his spine. Pleased, she licked a bead of sweat from the back of his neck.

He said something she couldn't hear over the engine. His hand covered hers, thumb stroking down one finger before returning to guide the bike.

Béatrix smiled against his back. Knowing Philip, her public display of affection had been enough to get him hard. She shifted her forefinger to brush the side of his balls. It seemed the Vespa's rumble shook his flesh just as thoroughly as it shook hers. How nice, she thought, and rubbed the thinning denim. His knuckles whitened on the handlebars. His thighs tensed.

As soon as the shade thickened, Philip pulled off to the side of the road. They'd reached an old tomb. Portraits of the family who were buried there, their marble faces worn, still clung to the crumbling brick. This was a tomb from the days of the Republic, when city burials had been banned. Sadly, pollution had turned half the carvings to limestone.

But Philip wasn't concerned with the state of antiquities. He swung off the moped with a groan and rubbed his overburdened crotch. "Bloody thing goes through you like a vibrator."

Béatrix laughed and brushed her fingers over his. She'd never seen him rub himself in public. He looked around for possible witnesses, then—finding none—gave her a quick hard kiss.

"Come on," he said, and helped her onto a worn, weedy path. He kept her hand as he led her deeper into the trees, deeper into the shade of the low, scattered buildings. Leaves whispered secrets in the breeze, and the smell of sunbaked earth filled her nose. Béatrix held on to her hat as they trod the uneven ground. Philip's shirt was plastered to his back in a single line, the dampness diving under his waistband in a way that made her flush. She hoped he had more than sight-seeing planned for this stop.

"Have you been here before?" she asked.

He favored her with an odd half smile.

"No," he said, his eyes slumberous. "But I've heard people talk about the place."

He wasn't the only one.

As they approached the shadow of another wall, she spotted a couple groping each other so furiously, full intercourse seemed seconds away. Philip barred her from going forward with his arm, but she'd already stopped. He whispered over his shoulder, not looking away from the writhing pair. "This cemetery is a famous lover's lane. Apparently, people come here at all hours."

Apparently. Still attached to his partner's mouth, the male half of the pair kneed the woman's legs apart and wrenched down his zipper. His cock sprang out, long and red and curved upward like a hook. Eager to take this marvel on, the woman gathered up her dress, grabbed his shaft, and pulled him between her thighs.

"*Bene!,*" growled the man, breaking the kiss. His hips moved as if he were rubbing his shaft up and down her slit. Then he shifted.

The pair groaned in unison as he shoved home and began to pump. His speed was impressive, his rhythm as steady as a turbine. But it seemed the angle wasn't right. A minute later, he cursed and changed position. The woman urged him to push.

"*È troppo grande,*" she added.

Béatrix snickered to herself as she translated. It's too big. If this woman thought he was too big, she'd hate to see what she'd make of Philip.

The man grunted and thrust harder, sweat rolling down his florid face. He must have made headway because the woman moaned.

"*Sì,*" she praised, leg climbing his hip. They kissed with open mouths. Béatrix could see their twining tongues.

She tugged the sleeve Philip had rolled up his arm.

"Come on," she said. "Let's leave these lovebirds alone."

With a sheepish grin, he followed her around the corner of the tomb. Someone was there before them, a young Italian man. Philip almost tripped over his foot. Their fellow sightseer was alone, his back pressed to the wall in a patch of sun. He was brown and lean, with curly black hair and eyes that flashed mischief like a pagan Pan. Béatrix doubted he'd seen twenty yet. The picture of sexual challenge, he had one foot on the ground, and the other propped on the ancient brick. His thumbs hooked the pockets of his skin-tight white jeans, while his fingers fanned the ridge of a full-blown, man-size erection. He was not, by any stretch of the imagination, trying to hide it.

"Nice show, eh?" he said in charmingly accented English. He must have heard them speaking around the corner. Without a hint of embarrassment, his gaze raked Béatrix from head to toe, then Philip. His inspection stopped at the bulge of Philip's crotch. He cocked his head. "But maybe you two could put on an even better show."

Philip's British reflexes kicked into gear. His spine stiffened like a poker, and his arm curved protectively around Béatrix's back.

"I don't think—" he began.

"Yes, you do." Taking advantage of Philip's astonishment, the man reached lazily out. He trailed his hand down Philip's chest until his fingers stopped just above his straining cock. "And when you think about it, it makes you hard."

His boldness reduced Philip to spluttering, but that didn't discourage him, either.

"I'll take you both on," he said, pushing off the wall so he could cup Philip fully. "In fact, it will take both of you to handle what I've got."

Béatrix didn't doubt him. He was obviously at his hormonal peak. His eyes burned like obsidian in his dark olive face, drinking in Philip's reaction. Shorter than Philip by a head, he displayed no fear as he fondled the taller man. He used a lot of force, but it didn't seem to hurt. At any rate, Philip didn't draw away. Further emboldened, the man pushed his face as close to Philip's as it could get.

"Are you man enough?" he whispered, fingers working his cock and balls. "Are you man enough to see what I can do?"

Philip looked at Béatrix, helplessly aroused. Two spots of color stained his cheeks. She could see he wanted permission and that wanting it had confused him. Without her to give the push, he'd be too embarrassed to play this out. To her surprise, she found she wanted to push. His pleasure was her pleasure. If this had anything near the effect their cab ride had, she was all for it. However long or short their time together, he'd never forget his adventures with her.

And, after all, the young man got her pulse racing, too. Seeing she held the key, the Italian turned to her.

"He's never been with a man before," she said, knowing this as surely as if he'd told her. "But if he wants you, I'm willing to share."

The man grinned back at Philip. "It's up to you then, *signore*. Do you want me?" He did something with his hand, simultaneously squeezing and rubbing Philip's crotch. Philip's eyes almost crossed.

"He likes to be watched," she added. "That's his favorite game."

"What a coincidence." The Italian leaned up to run his tongue along Philip's jaw. "That is also one of my favorite games. To watch and to be watched. I like that almost as much as I like sharing."

"Oh, God." Philip raked back his hair. "What are you getting me into now?"

Twelve

HILIP WASN'T AT all sure he should be doing this. On the other hand, he wasn't certain he could stop. Chills of excitement swept his body. Each time Bea smiled at him, his cock seemed to grow another inch. If he didn't open his trousers soon, he'd strangle.

Lord knew what the Italian was suffering. His white jeans were plastered with X-rated loyalty to his bulge.

"*Scusi*," he said now, flashing teeth and squeezing a brown hand in to adjust his shaft. When he withdrew it, the head was up, peeping obscenely over his waistband. Philip looked away and wished he had the nerve to do the same.

The Italian told them to call him Cesare. Agile as a goat, he scrambled ahead of them over tussocks of grass and fallen stones. He was leading them to a special place, he said, a place to which his cousin—a trusted guard—had the key. Past the last tomb and over a hill they reached it. Shaded by trees, the subterranean door was dug into the slope. Cesare fit a large bronze key into the lock.

"Here," he said, "we will be private."

Lighting an old bull's-eye lantern, he beckoned them inside. The stone-lined space was long and low, like the hull of a boat turned upside down. Two stone benches lined either side. Between them, at the far end, a cube of white marble glowed in the shadows. It looked like an ancient altar. Images had been carved around the pedestal, but Philip couldn't make out what they were.

Bea laid her hat on one of the benches. "This isn't a tomb."

The young man confirmed her guess. "No, this was a Temple of Mithras." Setting down the lantern, he led Bea to the plinth and knelt down. "See?" His finger traced a carving. "Here is the god killing the sacrificial bull. As you can see, this bull has a big *belino*, a big penis. He will make Mithras very strong."

"Mm," said Bea, in that dry, humorous way she had. "The question is, how strong has Mithras made you?"

Cesare rose and rubbed his hands to either side of his erection. "Open my jeans and see."

Philip's breath caught in his throat. The sight of Cesare's excitement, and Bea's, thickened the musty air.

"I couldn't undress you without help," Bea said. As if her coyness were a cue, she and the boy turned together to smile at him.

This, he knew, was his moment of decision. He would join in now or Bea and the boy would play alone. Or maybe the adventure would simply end. As Bea had said, he'd never had a man before. He'd been asked, of course. In his business, half the men one met were gay. The thought didn't repel him. Now and then he'd been curious. He'd simply never been tempted to change his life that way. Women were complicated enough, and rewarding enough. He didn't need to turn to men. But now this boy, and Bea, were offering him a chance to taste that foreign fare: without strings, without expectations beyond the pleasure of an afternoon. Philip's groin throbbed strongly at the thought. His body knew what it wanted him to choose.

Almost without his will, his feet shuffled forward on the dusty stone. He couldn't speak, could barely swallow. With shaky hands, he reached for the young man's zipper and tugged it gingerly down. The pressure as it gave way made his own balls tighten.

"Ah." Cesare sighed and pulled himself free. With both hands he stroked his long, blood-darkened shaft, obviously enjoying his own touch. The skin of his penis was creased with cloth marks. Each wrinkle seemed to require a slow massage.

Philip's fingers twitched to help.

"He is pretty, isn't he?" said Cesare, nodding toward his *belino*. "I think you should kiss him."

Philip shook his head even as his knees folded beneath him. The boy held the thing out to him, the eye seeming to stare and wink. Nervously, Philip licked his lips. As soon as he stopped, Cesare rubbed the pulsing head around his mouth.

"Yes," he coaxed. "Open for me."

Philip opened. The cock slid between his lips like a

sapling wrapped in oil. It was so smooth, so warm. Philip felt as if he'd been waiting all his life to taste this salty heat. Its textures were as familiar as masturbation, as alien as a snake at supper. He found the creases Cesare's zip had left and rubbed them with his tongue. Like magic, Cesare swelled in his mouth. Philip couldn't control himself. He sucked hard and shivered to Cesare's moan.

Behind him, Bea stroked the back of his neck, encouraging him, reminding him that she was there and he was safe. The tips of her fingers were hot. At this evidence of her arousal, pain spiked Philip's cock. He was so hard he had to bend forward from the hips.

"Poor *bandeur*," Bea soothed, using the French slang for erection. "He hurts, doesn't he?"

Her words inflamed Cesare. He pressed inward, testing the verge of Philip's throat. Philip didn't think; he merely sucked, firmly, caressingly, drawing the boy's pleasure through his tongue.

Cesare moaned. "Your mouth was made for this, *signore*."

For untold minutes, Philip fellated him, hypnotized by the silken push and pull, by the sound of harsh breathing, by the smell of sexual sweat. The cock made a noise going in and out, a noise of saliva and suction, a noise that shot sparks from his ear to his groin. Philip knew he would never forget it.

Finally, with a flattering wince of reluctance, Cesare pulled free. His cock throbbed a protest, visibly yearning toward Philip's mouth. Cesare ignored its complaint. "We should not keep the *signorina* waiting. I want to see you take her. I want to see what pleasure an *inglese* can bring."

His words were a teasing challenge. No self-respecting

Italian believed an Englishman could best him in bed. But Philip had no insecurities on that score. He was a man of much experience, and this Italian, however lusty, was still a stripling. He smiled at Cesare. "Shall I undress her? Would you like to see her body?"

"Oh, yes," said the young man. "Very much."

Bea was blushing furiously. Philip suspected the idea of being naked made her self-conscious. He kissed her and held her burning cheeks between his hands. He spoke in French to make it private.

"Trust me," he said, "when this Italian sees how gorgeous you are, he'll thank all the saints in Rome."

She laughed, and her embarrassment cooled beneath his palms. Philip undressed her gently, first the dress, then the pretty underthings beneath. Her body was generous, lush and round and sensual. He wondered that he'd ever thought it less than perfect. Even her freckles inspired his ardor, as if a horde of adoring fairies had kissed her at her birth. She was so beautiful, his Irish-Parisienne. The Italian seemed to agree. All through her disrobing he wanked himself, a long corkscrew motion like a baker stretching dough.

"Keeping the motor running?" Philip said.

Cesare flashed a smile. "No, no. This one could keep all the motors in Rome running by herself. This—" he nodded at his working hand "—is to help me bear the pain of waiting."

"You're not getting inside her," Philip warned. "She's mine."

"Believe me," Cesare soothed, "I understand completely."

Bea crossed her arms.

"You're mine," he repeated to her this time. Her eyebrows rose, but he would not call back the words. She lowered her head and smiled, and he realized she wasn't angry. She was pleased. She wanted to be his.

"Bea," he said, the sound all throaty hunger. She held off his approach by pressing one finger to the center of his chest. She retreated a step, sat on the bench where he'd dropped her flowery dress, then swung up on her knees. She planted them wide, curled one hand between her breasts and the other over her mons. Her lower hand tightened until her labia split around two fingers. A steam-like pressure filled Philip's head.

"Is this what you want?" she said.

He couldn't wait a moment longer. His hands flew to the placket of his jeans, popping the button, yanking down the zipper. His cock swelled with relief, blood racing to the newly unconstricted flesh. The pleasure was exquisite, almost as exquisite as the single thrust that drove him to her core. Her breath rushed out in a gasp. Her thighs were cool and soft, her pussy molten. For a second he feared he'd come, but, thankfully, the sensation of imminence faded. Her hands clutched his shoulders from behind.

"This," he said, holding her buttocks to grind against her. "This is what I want."

Bea couldn't pull back from coming the way he had. She was too close. He knew the signs by now: the flush that crept over her breasts, the shimmers of movement inside her sex. Her nails pricked his skin as she fought to delay.

"Take him," she groaned. "Take him now."

Suddenly Cesare was behind him. He felt the brush of

a condom-covered cock, then hands parting his buttocks, then something greasy and slick dripping over his hole.

"You do want it, don't you?" she said, the question ragged. "You do want him to take you?"

Philip bowed his head. Cesare's probing stilled. Against his chest, her breasts shook with the beating of her heart, so fast, so precious. He cupped one globe and pinched its rigid nipple. She wanted this. It excited her. Maybe because she knew it excited him. The last of his doubts slipped away.

"Yes," he said. "Yes."

He'd been taken from behind before, but never by a living cock. Then he'd liked the added stimulation. Now he found it devastating. This intrusion was warm. Cesare moved. Cesare pulsed. Cesare groaned as he forged, inch by inch, through his resistance. Soon Philip's limbs were shaking as if he had a palsy. His body could scarcely process so much pleasure. Cesare steadied his hips with both hands.

"Is all right?" he gasped. "I'm not hurting you?"

Philip groaned, completely beyond speech. He held Bea tight and panted against her neck.

"Keep going," she said. "He's hard as a poker."

Cesare kept going, filling Philip even as Philip filled Bea. The boy's glans nudged something that had Philip crying out, the pleasure so intense it hurt.

"Like that?" Cesare chuckled, his groin finally snuggling close. "Like me to rub you right there?"

Philip could only moan but Cesare understood. He began to stroke, in and out, not long thrusts but deft. Each motion prodded Philip's prostate. Light flashed behind his eyes, and a sound like a dog's whine squeezed from his throat.

"Yes," said Cesare. "Feel me fuck you."

His thrusts pushed Philip into Bea. Bea thrust back in the same rhythm, as if she were fucking Cesare and Philip's body had gotten in the way. Philip did not have to move. He only had to stand and brace, and unutterable pleasure beat at him from every side. Bea didn't take long to reach her peak. She went over with a gasp, squeezing him in soft, juicy ripples, drawing the pressure of his orgasm to the brink.

"Bea," he croaked, head sagging back to an unfamiliar shoulder.

Fingers dug into his hipbones. Lips pressed his neck. Hardness met his back, softness his front. Cesare thrust faster, jarred harder. He's going to come, Philip thought, his heart racing wildly. He's going to come, and he's going to see me come. He's going to feel it on his prick. He's going to hear the sounds I make. He's going to know. It was a fantasy he hadn't known he had. His anus contracted around the cock that pounded it. Cesare couldn't resist the tighter clasp. He grunted and shuddered and shot his load with a low Italian curse.

Philip yearned to follow. The tip of his cock tingled, almost, almost spewing. Now, he thought. Now. He grabbed onto Bea, jamming her hips against him. He had to get closer. He needed to fuck her deepest core. He bore down with his inner muscles, pushing even before his seed would come. In his mind, he could picture the tip of his penis, straining, ready, the little slit a burning brand.

Come, he thought, grinding into her. Come. Come. Come.

"Yes," she gasped, clutching him. "In me. In me."

The words were an order only his penis understood. Its pressure rose, insanely high, unbearable, a sweet, impossible pain. Come, he thought. Jesus, come.

Then her pussy clenched and kissed his struggling glans and together they burst through the final barrier. His orgasm roared through his cock with frightening force, through his body, as if his very cells shared the spasm of joy.

Minutes passed before he could move. Bea stroked his head where it rested on her shoulder. The Italian had pulled free. Philip heard him tidying himself.

Before he left, he slapped Philip's back.

"*Grazie*," he said as if Philip had stood him a beer. "I will lock up after you go."

When he was gone, Philip eased from Bea's hold. A silvery trail of sperm slid down her inner thigh. His heart stopped. He'd forgotten to withdraw. More than forgotten. He'd reveled in filling her with his seed.

"Bea," he said.

She covered his lips. "Don't be sorry. I wanted you to do it."

He wasn't sorry. Emotions boiled inside him, but none involved regret. The feelings were so strong he didn't know how to put them into words. He went to his knees and hugged her thighs and pressed his cheek to her naked belly. Ironically, despite the presence of a stranger at their play, he'd never felt closer to a woman. Without Bea, he never would have dared this experience. With Bea, he'd felt astonishingly safe. He knew then that what he felt for her was more than lust, more even than love. He knew he couldn't ignore it. He must act. He must secure her as his own. But precisely how he ought to do that was beyond his capacity to see.

THE RIDE BACK to the hotel was very quiet. To say that Philip was distracted did not do his muteness justice. With bitter clarity, Béatrix remembered her own embarrassment following the threesome Lela had engineered. Did Philip feel like she had now that the excitement had drained away? Had she once again pushed him further than he cared to go? One thing was certain. She was going to have to forgive Lela. Whatever lapse of judgment she might have shown, Bea's treatment of Philip was a hundred times worse.

They ate in the hotel dining room. Béatrix would have preferred a local *trattoria*, like they'd eaten in the night before. There, amid the color and the noise, the silence that hung between them wouldn't have been so obvious. But Philip hadn't consulted her. In fact, Philip didn't seem to have his mind on her at all. When the waiter brought their *antipasti*, he raised the last topic she wanted to discuss.

"I forgot to tell you," he said, fork and knife poised over a roast pepper. "I received Lela's report on the New York shop."

"Did you?" Bea shoved half a *bruschetta* in her mouth. She chewed. The oil-drenched toast and tomatoes clung to her throat. Only the garlic allowed her to swallow.

Unlike her, Philip wasn't given to nervous eating. He set his utensils down. "She did a good job. Surprisingly thorough. She has some interesting ideas about buying from local artisans to give the New York shop a New York identity."

"You're going to hire her on as manager then?"

"I don't know. It's a big responsibility. Do you think she can handle it?"

The hair on the back of her neck prickled. She should have expected this question, but she hadn't. "You're asking me?"

Philip seemed surprised by her reaction. "Yes. You know her better than I do. I'd like to know if you think we can rely on her."

This was it. Bea could shoot Lela down, and Lela would never know. Philip was far too sensitive to reveal who'd helped him make his choice. But Bea would know. She'd know she'd hurt her friend out of the fear of being outshone. On the other hand, expecting more of Lela than she could give wouldn't do her any good. If Lela failed, everyone would end up hurt. She had to be objective. She had to decide what was best for Lela and for Meilleurs Amis. She took a sip of wine, then a swallow of water.

"I think you shouldn't give her the responsibility all at once," she said, thinking as she spoke, ignoring the rapid thudding of her heart. "Dominique Pomier has a brother in New York. Why don't you transfer her there and let them work side by side for a while? I doubt the current manager will train Lela properly once she discovers she's being replaced."

When she looked up, she was surprised to find Philip beaming at her. "What a wonderful idea. I'll talk to Dominique tomorrow. You know, Bea, you've got a good head for business. If you weren't so damn talented with a paintbrush, I'd wish you were more interested in Meilleurs Amis."

"I am interested," she said. "You can ask me to help out any time you like."

"Well," he said, "I may run things by you now and then, but I would never get in the way of your dream. I'm only sorry I didn't see before how much your art meant to you, and how good you were at it. I'm proud of you, Bea. Really proud."

He patted her hand in his old paternal way. Béatrix couldn't bear it, that he would turn fatherly on her after all they'd done together! She looked down at her plate. Somehow, without her knowing it, another *bruschetta* had disappeared. She set her jaw. She wasn't going to do this, wasn't going to hate herself for eating a piece of toast, or for putting her foot wrong with Philip. So she wasn't perfect. Who was? She'd only meant to give him a new pleasure. If he couldn't handle it, that was his problem, just like her jealousy for Lela was hers. If he cared about her, really cared, he'd get over it. He wouldn't let the chance to share something real slip through his fingers.

She was beginning to fume in earnest when he reached across the table to cup her cheek. "What is it Bea? What's wrong?"

The answer burst from her. "You regret this afternoon, don't you? You think I tricked you into it."

Philip's mouth dropped. He blinked. Then, in a flash he scooted his chair next to hers. He took her hands between his own. "No, Bea. I don't think that at all."

"Then why didn't you say something?" Out of the corner of her eye, she saw someone at the next table glance at her. She lowered her voice. "Why were you so horrified to have come inside me?"

"I wasn't, Bea." He kissed her hand and pressed it to his breast. "I don't regret anything we've done together. It means more to me than I can put in words. Maybe at first I was afraid to trust you, but I was even more afraid to trust myself. You know my judgment hasn't always been the best." He drew a heavy breath and then released it. "Maybe I shouldn't say this, but I don't know how else to make you understand. I loved your mother. Perhaps I didn't understand her as well as I should have, but I loved her."

Bea wanted to sink through the floor. "I know that."

"I don't think you do. It isn't fair to make comparisons, but what I feel for you is different. I trust you, Bea. If today isn't proof of that, I don't know what is. I trust you. You make me happy. And even when you make me miserable, it's a clean kind of miserable. I don't feel dirty for loving you. I feel lucky. I feel proud."

He felt proud? Proud to *love her*? Bea's heart was thundering in her ears. She'd been swept from depression to joy to disbelief in the space of seconds. The room seemed to spin even though she was sitting down.

"You love me?" she said, almost choking on the words. She looked into his beautiful gray eyes, willing them to tell the truth. As always, they shone with kindness, with affection. But tonight they also shone with tears.

"I love you," he said, his voice as rough as hers. "I love you the way a man loves the woman he wants to spend his life with."

"Oh," she said, a pitiful gulp of sound. She touched his

cheek with trembling fingers. "I love you, too. I've always loved you."

Awareness flickered across his face, first a question, then wonder. He hadn't known. He hadn't known. Pain filled his eyes, and a terrible understanding. Then he smiled.

"Bea," he said and kissed her, French-kissed her, in the middle of the restaurant, in front of the world. His arms came around her, and he pulled her close. She was making that little "oh" noise again, though it was muffled by the delicious twining of his tongue. When he finally released her, she was shaking so hard he laughed. "Bea, Bea, Bea. I think we're going to have to order room service." He touched her quivering lip. "Right now I've got a hunger only you can quench."

Béatrix was more than ready to go along. It was not, however, to be. A voice cut through her happiness like a snow-chilled blade.

"*Bonsoir*, Philip," it said in insinuating upper-class French.

The voice belonged to Marie d'Ardennes, Evangeline's best friend and the wife of Meilleurs Amis's banker. She was a small, birdlike woman, a young Nancy Reagan in a chic Chanel suit. She was also a bitch of the first water, a recommender of fat farms, a cunt in the nastiest sense of the word. Her tentacles reached to every corner of Paris society: fashion, finance, politics. At the sound of her voice, all the color drained from Philip's face. No one had to tell him how bad this was.

True to form, Marie did not wait for him to recover. "How long has it been, Philip? Not since Eve's funeral, *non*? Six long months."

"Seven," said Philip, his mouth tight.

"So many as that! Well, no wonder you have found it in your hearts to comfort each other." She turned to Béatrix, her smile pursed. Her eyes, both knowing and scornful, seemed to take in every ounce of flesh that lay beneath Bea's simple flowered dress. "And you, Bea, you're looking . . . healthy. As always."

"Thank you." Béatrix kept her voice as bland as she could. "I hope you haven't been ill. You look as if you've lost weight."

Philip coughed into his napkin. Marie's stingy mouth opened to respond, but she could not. Most likely, she was too accustomed to her thinness being a source of envy. Instead, she returned her attention to Philip. He had recovered from his fit, and she pressed his shoulder familiarly. "You must come see Gustave and me sometime. He was saying just the other night how long it's been since we had dinner."

Her hand caressed the shoulder of his jacket, the little motions both threatening and sexual. Her nails were a thick, bright red, as if to distract from the signs that her hands had aged. Marie was not a woman who embraced her years contentedly. Of all Eve's friends, she'd been the least able to choke down her jealousy over Philip. Naturally, Eve had done everything she could to feed the reaction. Watching her friends turn green was a large part of the pleasure she'd gained from marrying a younger man. The way Marie touched Philip now made Béatrix shudder, as if with Eve out of the way, the old vulture thought he was hers for the taking. The fact that she'd seen him kissing Béatrix moments earlier did not seem to matter. Perhaps she believed the highest bidder could bring him home.

But Philip wasn't a prize. He never had been. Béatrix was hardly immune to his beauty, but his beauty hadn't made her fall in love, nor had his marriage to her mother. Those things had made her distrust him; the person he was inside had made her fall in love.

She reached across the table and squeezed his hand. "I'm sure Philip would be happy to take you and Gustave out. Your husband must be interested to hear the latest developments at Meilleurs Amis."

With obvious reluctance, Marie released Philip's shoulder.

"Oh, yes," she said, her lips stretching in a grim parody of a smile. "The latest developments should interest him very much."

DESPITE THE EXCELSIOR'S powerful air-conditioning, Philip was dripping sweat by the time they reached their suite. The champagne-colored carpet did not soothe him, nor the graceful gilded swirls of the wall molding. He headed straight for the stocked bar and poured himself a stiff Glenlivet. As soon as he'd tossed it back, he poured another. He delayed drinking it just long enough to wrench off his jacket and tie. He only wished the memory of that bitch's clawlike grip were as easy to remove.

Marie d'Ardennes had tried more than once to seduce him. He'd always managed to fend her off, but it seemed the time to pay for those rejections had come. When Eve had been alive, Marie hadn't dared strike at him, but now . . . He took another swallow of scotch and forced himself to breathe. It would be all right. Gustave wasn't an idiot.

He wouldn't pull their loans just because Philip refused to screw his wife.

Unless Marie gave her husband another reason to doubt him. Unless she managed to twist his relationship to Bea into some sort of business ploy. Unless—he shivered at a sudden chill—unless she discovered the real reason for his trip to Rome.

"Hey," said Bea, her arms coming around him from behind. She pulled up in surprise when her cheek brushed his clammy shirt. Tutting in concern, she turned him in her arms and began to undo his buttons. "I'm sorry she walked in on us, Philip. That was terrible. But we'll find some way to undo the damage."

"I don't want to undo the damage. Not if it means lying about how I feel for you."

"I wasn't going to suggest you lie, but maybe—"

"No." He covered her hands. "I'm not going to hide our relationship. The world will simply have to get used to the idea."

"Well," she said, then nothing. Brow puckered, she drew away and plopped down on the cream and gold sofa.

Sensing her distraction, Philip finished removing his shirt himself. He immediately felt better, especially when Bea snuck a look at his muscles and blushed. He sat beside her and pulled her against him. "Please don't worry about this. We shouldn't let anything spoil tonight."

"I just wish there were some way we could defuse her."

Philip snorted. "I'm afraid the only way to defuse Marie d'Ardennes would be a promise to fuck her on a regular basis."

"Oh," said Bea, then began to laugh, softly, her breasts

shaking against his side. "A little like sleeping with the Wicked Witch of the West."

"Quite. And, believe me, I'm not up for it."

She nuzzled his chest, still chuckling. "What are you up for, Philip?"

Her words were enough to harden him. He moved her hand from his side and pressed it over his crotch. "I'm up for showing you how much I love you."

At once she grew quiet. He doubted he'd ever tire of seeing that shining wonder fill her eyes.

"I'm up for that, too," she said and he groaned at a sudden surge of want.

"Tell me," he said. "Tell me again."

She told him many times before the night was through. She told him shyly, and teasingly. She told him huskily and in a broken, breathless whisper. She told him as she wrapped him with arms and legs and pussy. The words spilled back from him in just as many guises. They were as sweet to say as they were to hear.

For one blissful night he ignored the precipice on which he, and everything he'd worked for, was poised.

SIMON SAT IN his office reading a long report from Legal. For the last quarter hour, he'd been fighting an urge to smash something. The New Orleans store was being sued for discriminatory hiring practices. Simon knew the charge was bullshit. Neither he nor his father had tolerated bigotry. Graves Department Stores were among the first businesses in the South to promote minorities and women into upper management, and to do their utmost to keep them there. Simon believed in equal opportunity, and he made sure the people who worked for him believed in it, too.

The lawyers were advising him to settle.

That alone made him see red. What the fuck good was a lawyer who wasn't up for a fight? Did they think he cared what it cost to clear the Graves name? Did they think heads wouldn't roll if they couldn't get this nuisance suit dismissed?

He grabbed a paperweight, clenched it with an intent to throw. But then his father's photo seemed to chide him from the corner of the desk. Simon, it said gently. It's up to you to create an atmosphere where your employees can act courageously. If you lose your temper and scare the bejesus out of them, how is that going to help? It was an old lesson, one of the first Howard taught him. Simon had brought the anger with him from the orphanage. Maybe he'd been born with it, because even the home Tess and Howard made hadn't allowed him to outgrow it. They had, however, taught him self-control.

Simon unclenched his hands and his teeth and drew a deep, calming breath. Carefully, deliberately, he pulled a notepad from his drawer and began jotting down discussion points. He'd explain his position to Legal. He'd ask how they intended to support it. Then he'd decide if heads needed to roll.

He was well into point number four when Andrew stuck his head around the door.

"What!" Simon snapped without thinking.

Andrew grinned. "Mrs. Winters told me Legal had dropped that off. I thought you might welcome some good news."

Simon sighed. "I'd love some good news. Come in."

Andrew practically bounced across the carpet. As always, he sat on the corner of Simon's desk. He leaned close enough to rap Simon's notepad. "We've got them."

"Got them?" asked Simon, but he knew. His stomach was sinking already.

"Meilleurs Amis!" Andrew crowed. "My contact tells me the bank just called their loan. Apparently, one of their vendors got nervous about their cash-flow situation. They cut off his credit. The news spread and, *voilà*, there isn't a lender in the region who'll touch him."

"What about outside the region?"

"He hasn't got the connections. Oh, man." Andrew rubbed his hands together. "He is screwed but good!"

The point of Simon's pencil snapped. He looked down at his pad and found he'd drawn a large *L* with a heavy line through it. Shit. How the fuck was he going to explain this to Lela?

"What's the matter?" said Andrew. "I thought you'd be happy."

"I'm happy," Simon said, not happily at all. He looked into Andrew's crestfallen face. "You didn't engineer this, did you?"

The younger man stiffened. "No, I did not. Philip Carmichael shot himself in the foot, just like I knew he would. The man is not a political animal, and that's what you've got to be to survive in Paris."

"Okay." Simon patted his knee. "I had to ask."

"I wouldn't," Andrew said. "You told us no dirty tricks. You said you wanted a clean win."

And if I hadn't? Simon wondered, but there was no point worrying about that now. Somewhere in Paris a business was about to go under. If Simon didn't drag it from the depths, someone else would. Or no one else would. Either way, Simon would be morally responsible for his decision.

He looked down at his hands and remembered the last time they'd touched Lela's lean, racy curves. He'd never felt for a woman what he felt for her. She'd become part of his life, someone he wanted to share things with, someone he loved. His hands curled into fists. There was no way to avoid it. Lela's reaction would be bad. But he wouldn't give her up without a fight. He wouldn't give her up at all.

Unconsciously, he thumped the desk. He pointed at Andrew. "Get the file to me. I want to handle the negotiations myself."

Andrew nodded, then hesitated. "I'm not going to tell Lela, you know. That you had this takeover in mind before you met her."

"I never thought you would," he said.

Andrew smiled unsurely, nodded again, and left.

Simon released a long sigh and sagged back in his chair. It wouldn't matter whether Andrew told Lela or not. The girl was smart enough to add two and two.

Thirteen

PHILIP STOOD BEFORE the floor-to-ceiling window and gazed down twenty floors: Office workers scurried between the towers of La Défense, through shadow to light and back. They looked as small and powerless as he felt.

His wife's old friend had talked to the Amalfis.

All morning he'd scrambled for alternate financing, to no avail. Though the business climate had changed of late, for the most part Paris still ran as an old boy's network. Philip, alas, had never been an old boy, and never would be now. The news Marie d'Ardennes was spreading had shredded the last of his credibility. No doubt Eve could have mended the damage, but Philip didn't have her clout, as he'd known before he tried. The attempt had left him so weary he swayed on his feet. He steadied himself by pressing the tips of his fingers to the glass, but the pain remained, a cold, hard stone beneath his heart. Two of his nails were bleeding, bitten through during the Sisyphean calls.

This catastrophe outdid both the first showing of his designs and his humiliation by the press after Evangeline's death. Then only he had suffered. Now a whole company would. Livelihoods would be lost: futures and pasts. Most would survive, but some would not. Because he'd been reckless. Because he'd never been able to inspire the confidence his wife had. He simply wasn't tough enough. Even now, if he could have turned back the clock and erased their weekend in Rome, he wouldn't have done it. Love meant more to him than business, people more than pride.

He dreaded the thought of telling Bea. He knew she'd feel guilty. She'd wonder if she was worth what he was losing. And she'd worry for him, which was the last thing he wanted. At the moment, he didn't give a bloody damn about himself. His employees were his priority. He had to salvage what he could for them. Maybe he could sell off some assets. Or license Meilleurs Amis's name. Anything to meet a few more payrolls. Anything to buy a little time.

He strode to his desk, intent on returning the accountant's frantic call. Instead, Bea's number sprang to mind. As unpleasant as his news was, he had such a yearning to hear her voice his eyes pricked with the strength of it. This is what love is, he thought: wanting to share the bad and the good. A smile tugged his mouth. It was a useful lesson, but one he gladly would have forgone.

He jumped when his secretary buzzed him.

"A call from America," she said. "A Mr. Simon Graves."

Simon Graves. Where had he heard that name before? Not a banker, he didn't think. Or one of their suppliers. Shrugging, he picked up the line. Whoever it was, his morning couldn't get any worse.

LELA WAS SCRUBBING the kitchen floor when Simon let himself in. Her pulse had picked up at the rattle of the elevator. She knew the sounds he made, the decisive force of his steps. She knew his aftershave, lime and spice and underneath the bone-melting scent that was him: her lover. The word called forth warmth and wetness, deep inside, both comfort and thrill.

She didn't move from her hands and knees. "I knew I shouldn't have given you a key."

He didn't seem to mind her less-than-glamorous state. She heard a thunk, and he was on his knees behind her, folding his body around her, pretending to bite the back of her neck. The stirring at the crotch of his trousers told her he wasn't entirely teasing.

"You have the most adorable bottom," he said, and groaned as she rubbed it against his rapidly stretching cock. His arms tightened around her waist, the feel of his suit jacket incongruous but exciting.

When she spoke her voice was husky. "I wasn't expecting you tonight."

He nuzzled through her hair to lick the spot beneath her ear. "I'm on my way to the airport. I wanted to talk to you first."

"Talk?"

His hips pressed and subsided in the rhythm of love-making. "Can't right now. Too distracted."

Lela bit her lip against a laugh of pleasure. "Is this going to make you late for your flight?"

"Don't know." His hands slipped under her boxer-style shorts, first petting her curls, then pushing the brief garment over her hips. She shifted to take them off, but Simon stopped her.

"Don't move," he said, his breathing abruptly heavy. "I'm going to cut them away."

He pulled her big meat shears from the drawer and snipped not just her shorts but her tank top as well. His hands shook, and she knew she'd inadvertently stumbled into one of his fantasies. She shivered as the shears moved over her, cool and hard. His silence was exciting, his intensity. She was woozy with arousal, imagining what he was seeing, imagining what he was feeling. When he'd finished cutting, his hands swept her body. His palms were hot and slightly damp. Between touches, she heard him discarding his clothes.

"Don't move," he said again when she would have turned her head. "You're too beautiful to look at me."

"I like looking at you. I like seeing how big you get. I like watching you grow."

"No," he growled and curled his body around her again: his broad hairy chest, his strong arms, his shifting, clenching thighs. "You can't see me. You can only feel."

"You feel beautiful," she said. "You feel strong and warm."

He shuddered and pressed his erection to the crease between her buttocks. He was fully hard, dripping with excitement as he rubbed her lushest curves. Lela thought she might dissolve. She could feel the veins that twined his shaft, the weighty hang of his balls, the quick in and out of his lungs. The tips of his fingers burrowed through her pubic hair. He found her sticky, and swollen. When he stroked her clinging folds, she had to arch her back.

"You're wet," he whispered, one hot inch from her ear. he slid two fingers inside her, then pressed his thumb to her soft, slippery hood. She squirmed and drove him farther.

"I'm wet because I want you."

"It's hard to believe you could want a man like me."

"Believe it, big guy. You make me hot."

His breathing grew harsher. "Open your legs."

She opened them. His stroking continued, into her pussy, over her clit. He pressed closer, squeezing his cock against her cheeks. She could count every beat of his pulse. But he still wasn't satisfied.

"Wider," he demanded. "Arch back for me."

She lifted her hips until her breasts nearly brushed the cleanser-swirled floor.

"That smell," he said. "Jesus."

She didn't know if he meant her opened pussy or the Comet. Not that it mattered. The crown of him was prodding her longing mouth, pushing past that first resistance and into her sheath. In he slid, deeper and deeper, so alive, so thick and long he seemed to press her heart. She hugged the corded arm he'd wrapped beneath her breasts. He kissed her shoulder.

"I love you," he said, holding deep, holding tight. "Never forget that. No matter what."

"No matter what," she agreed, the words moaning out of her.

Something broke in him at the sound. He began to thrust like a man pounding railroad spikes.

"Fuck," he said, jamming deep. "Yes. Open for me. Let me fuck you. Let me. Ah, God, that's good."

The force of it startled her, the cries he made, the strength of his grip. She had to brace her elbows on the floor and even then each blow jarred her forward. Finally, she was up against the oven door. She'd never even had a chance to take off her yellow rubber gloves. Apparently, this wasn't a problem for Simon.

"Squeeze my balls," he gasped. "Squeeze my balls with your glove."

She squeezed him, and his breath immediately choked out.

"Yes," he moaned. "Yes. You are so fucking sexy."

She laughed, but it was exciting to hear him talk that way, to feel him lose control. She could see him in the window of the oven door. His face was barely recognizable: dark, taut, twisted with passion. He didn't know she could see him. He hid nothing. Her arousal soared at the distortion of his features. He was gritting his teeth. Wanting more, wanting everything, she compressed his scrotum and pressed one rubber finger to the ridge behind his balls.

"Lela!" he cried, slapping forward, fingers frantic on her clit.

But he couldn't get her fast enough. He was on the edge. He was swelling inside her, his whole body clenching with his need to come. He panted hard, ground into her. She tightened her pussy and dragged him over the brink.

His fall was noisy, a long growl of orgasm that tingled through her ear.

"Lela." He sighed, and finished her with his hand, still inside her, still half hard. When she came, his cock twitched deliciously in reaction.

After that, she couldn't hold herself up. She rolled onto her back beneath him, the linoleum gritty, his heat shadow warm. She touched the sweat-matted hair over his breastbone. "Not that I'm complaining. But what brought that on?"

"Uh," he said, and evaded her eye.

"You're blushing! Now I really want to know." She scooted out from under him and tweaked his chin. "Did the family maid seduce you on the kitchen floor?"

His cheeks were crimson. Lela thought for sure he wouldn't answer, but he sat back and squared his shoulders. "We didn't have a maid when I was growing up. My, uh, foster mother used to scrub the floors that way. The first time I saw her do it, I knew I'd found a real home."

His gaze met hers, defenseless, open. She discovered she couldn't tease him, funny as it was to have a fetish for floor scrubbing. Instead, her throat tightened for the boy he'd been, for the love he was capable of feeling.

"You're home with me," she said.

His dark eyes glittered, the navy seeming black. He swallowed hard and opened his arms. They hugged each other for a long time, naked, on their knees.

"I want to be your home, too," he said, and her tears spilled onto his chest.

A moment later, he cursed. "Damn, look at the time."

He pushed her back and held her shoulders. "I have to go, but we'll talk when I get back."

He seemed so serious her heart tripped over itself. She hardly dared think what he meant. Refusing to hope for too much, refusing even to admit what she hoped for, she helped him dress, gathering his scattered clothes and straightening his crooked tie. Despite her resolve, she reveled in the feeling of ownership she got from these simple tasks.

They stopped one last time by the door. He smoothed her hair with his big, gentle hands. "Remember what I told you."

She nodded, though she wasn't sure which thing he meant. Suddenly she didn't want him to go. Her hands had settled lightly on his lapels, but she longed to grab them and hold him prisoner. She felt as if he were going off to war.

"I love you," he said, searching her face as if he meant to imprint her image in his brain. "Remember, I love you."

"I love you, too," she said shyly.

The brilliance of his smile washed away her fears.

Bea was sobbing so hard Lela could barely understand her. She'd heard her friend cry before but never like this.

"Slow down," she said, unconsciously gripping the phone. "Tell me what's wrong."

"Ph-Philip," she managed, and broke down again.

"Is Philip all right?" Lela asked, wondering if he'd found a new girlfriend. If he had, she'd strangle the handsome creep.

"He's fine. Sort of. But the company—" Bea hiccuped once and pulled herself together. "Someone saw Philip and me together in Rome. One of Mother's cronies. We've been, well, we've been seeing each other. She spread all sorts of rumors—which were totally untrue. Philip's done a fantastic job for Meilleurs Amis. But now someone's trying to buy the company out from under us!" Her frustration escaped in an angry growl. "I'd like to shove those slides down his throat!"

"What slides?" said Lela, still trying to process the fact that Philip and Bea were an item.

"The slides of my paintings. It's the same man who called from America wanting to buy my work. Andrew's boss! Andrew must have been planning this all along, even before he slept with me."

Lela sat on the arm of her secondhand sofa, suddenly too weak to stand. She stared at the tape on her VCR, a movie she and Simon had rented last weekend. She had to return it. It was late. She pressed her palm to her forehead.

"You mean Simon Graves is trying to buy Meilleurs Amis?"

"Yes, Simon Graves. That *connard*. They're all bastards. The banker especially. We were having a cash-flow pinch is all. We could have pulled out of it. We could have been making money for them. Even more than before. Sales at the Beijing store are just starting to pick up. Damn it, Lela. It's not fair. Philip has worked so hard, and now he's going to lose everything, just because he fell in love with me!"

Lela slid off the arm and into the couch. Despite the summery heat, she was shivering. She remembered all the "help" Simon had given her. That night, when she'd brought her laptop to bed, she'd shown him the yearly budget for Meilleurs Amis. He'd explained it item by item, his patience boundless. And no wonder: all along he'd been planning this! Pain throbbed behind her forehead. With an effort, she focused on the continuing rush of Bea's words.

"I keep asking myself what we talked about the night Andrew came to dinner. What we might have said to let him know we were vulnerable."

Nausea swelled in Lela's throat. "I hope you don't think I—"

"*Ça, non!*" Bea exclaimed. "Of course not. How could you have known what Andrew would do? He used you. He used all of us."

Lela closed her eyes. Andrew wasn't the only user. He wasn't even the worst. She, of all people, should have known better. She couldn't believe how gullible she'd been. She put her best friend's business at risk. And for what? Some gangster-faced suit who wanted to own the world. She was glad now she'd never told Bea her new boyfriend's name. Bea might not be so quick to exonerate her if she knew, and where would Lela be then?

Nowhere, she thought, shaking her head in despair. Alone without a soul to care if she lived or died. But she shouldn't be thinking of herself. Not now. Not when Bea needed her.

"I'm coming," she said.

"What?" Bea sounded startled.

"I'm taking the next flight to Paris."

"Oh, Lela." Her friend's voice had gone teary again. "It would be good to see you."

Once Bea's gratitude would have meant the world.

Today her misery was too dark to be lightened. She clenched her jaw as she hung up the phone.

I'll survive this, she swore.

And I'll never trust that man again.

PHILIP HADN'T WANTED the men from Graves Incorporated in his office. Instead, he'd had them shown to the grand conference room, the one he rarely used. Eve had loved it. Its elaborately carved walls recalled an old-fashioned ballroom, white and gilt and a cool Delft blue that had matched his dead wife's eyes. Instinctively, he sought her inner coldness for himself.

If you ever cared for me, he thought, help me now. Help me save as much of your company as I can.

For a second, he thought he felt a brush of something, sorrow perhaps, or a ghostly apology. The hair on his arms prickled, and then the sensation was gone. The block of ice that steadied his heart was entirely his own.

Simon Graves followed his retinue into the ornate room. With his entrance, he eclipsed everyone and everything. He was a dark, solid presence with a hard face and blazing eyes. He spoke little, letting the lawyers do the talking, but his gaze took in everything Philip did.

Philip wasn't sure whether the American meant to rattle him or take his measure. His intentions scarcely mattered. Philip knew how to use his beauty, and his British blandness, as a shield. He had the distinct pleasure of watching the older man fight not to lose his temper at his demands.

"You're in no position to ask for these concessions," Andrew said, the only familiar face among the crowd. "If you don't find a buyer soon, Meilleurs Amis is going to fold."

Philip remembered that this man had slept with Bea. His face grew even cooler. He waited until Andrew began to flush at his expressionless stare.

"Your boss," he said, emphasizing the word, "has a reputation for valuing competence. My employees are more than competent; they're specialists. They understand the high-end luxury trade in ways that Graves employees, for all their skills, cannot. If you wish to integrate Meilleurs Amis into your organization, you're going to need their expertise."

"But to insist that we keep unprofitable stores open—"

"For a year. In any case, only the New York store is losing money. You can't close that because you need a presence in Manhattan to be taken seriously."

"If you're such an expert," Andrew sneered, "why are you about to go bankrupt?"

Like the ruler of a feudal court, Simon lifted one hand to silence him. Andrew subsided in his chair, his gaze now fastened—pleadingly, Philip thought—on the face of Simon Graves. His boss did not return the look. He spread his broad hands across the list of demands Philip's lawyers had drawn up. "Why have you placed so large a price on the use of Meilleurs Amis's name?"

"Because that's the asset you want most."

A muscle twitched at the corner of Simon's mouth. Then, as if giving himself permission, he smiled. The expression took years from his face. Philip could see the mischievous boy he must have been.

"Give them what they want," said the CEO, without looking away from Philip. His employees set up a chorus of protests, Andrew's loudest of all. Simon put his hand on the southerner's shoulder. "See that they settle it. I want an essential agreement by the end of the day."

Andrew's face twisted with reluctance, then cleared. He dropped his head, the picture of a chastised courtier.

"Yes, sir," he said.

Simon snorted and slapped his shoulder. He turned to Philip. "All right then. Why don't you and I have a drink while these boys wrangle?"

Philip felt as if a rug had been yanked out from under him at precisely the moment a chair had been shoved behind his knees. He struggled not to appear off-balance. "We can go to my office."

"Good," said Simon Graves, and broke into a brilliant smile.

PHILIP CARMICHAEL WASN'T what Simon expected. True, as Andrew said, he wasn't a shark. He was, however, capable of putting up a fight when pushed to the wall. And he inspired an unexpected protectiveness. Maybe his sad gray eyes were the reason, or his air of embattled British pluck. Whatever the cause, every employee they passed, from lobby guard to secretary to executive VP, glared at Simon as if he were the devil incarnate, come to cast down their golden prince. The man inspired loyalty. He just didn't know what to do with it.

Simon accepted a whiskey from Philip's private stash and relaxed into a sleek but comfortable chair. True to his heritage, or perhaps just wary, Philip sat stiffly behind his desk.

"I'd like to keep you on," Simon said. Philip's jaw

dropped so comically Simon had to fight a smile. "You'd be a pain in the ass to replace, and I really don't see why I should. You've made a few mistakes, but, all in all, you've done a good job. Plus, you don't strike me as the back-stabbing type." He took another sip and let his smile win free. "I've read your file, Mr. Carmichael. You're a man who works best with someone else's clout backing him up. I may not be the barracuda your wife was, but since I'm about a hundred times as big, an alliance between us ought to work out fine. I'll pay you a half again what I pay Andrew. You'll continue to oversee the original Meilleurs Amis, plus consult on their integration into Graves Department Stores."

Philip had shut his mouth and was now blinking rapidly. As if he realized this, he calmed. "I'm probably going to marry my stepdaughter."

The words were a quiet challenge. Suddenly cautious, Simon set his drink on the edge of Philip's desk. "I hear she's a nice girl."

"Very nice, but our marriage is bound to cause a media furor. I can't imagine that's what you were hoping for when you made your offer."

Everything he said was true. Simon had been hoping for positive press, a nice pop to drive the Graves name to the next level of public awareness. He looked at the man who was proposing to threaten that good press, at the nails he'd bitten to the quick, at the stubborn set of his jaw and the steadiness of his clear gray eyes. Those eyes were older than his pretty face, which did nothing to detract from his movie star looks.

Lela knew this man, he remembered, the thought coming out of nowhere. Lela had gazed into that sad angel's face and still fell in love with Simon. He asked himself what sort of scandal he'd risk for her sake. Any sort, he thought. Even if she never forgave him for this takeover.

"Who you marry is your business," he said. "If you work for me, I back you a hundred percent."

Philip's slow smile would have made a teeny-bopper swoon. "If I work for you, I want twice what Andrew makes."

Simon laughed. Who said the British didn't have balls?

THEY KILLED ONE bottle of rich, dark burgundy, then opened another. Béatrix grew drunker as the story spilled out. Slurred and jumbled, her anger caught on the shards of injustice.

"I hate that this happened," she said, not for the first time. Wine sloshed in her glass as she set it on the marble-topped coffee table, the table she'd bargained down by a third at the St.-Ouen flea market. Half a year ago that was. She'd been so proud of her independence, so determined to leave her feelings for Philip behind. She rested her elbows on her knees and stared at the quivering surface of the wine.

Life never turned out the way you planned.

"I hate that it's because of me," she said, swiping at her nose. "I hate that he's losing everything he worked for because he cares for me."

Lela rubbed her back, between the shoulder blades, the way she used to when Béatrix had failed a test or been dumped by a boyfriend. How simple those hurts had been compared to the hurt she was feeling now.

"It's not your fault," Lela said. "It's that woman's, that Marie d'Ardennes's. And maybe it's Philip's for not being the ball buster your mother was. Maybe this is for the best."

Béatrix stared at her in amazement. "How can it be for the best? Philip is ruined!"

"He's not ruined, Bea. He lost a business. Whether he realizes it or not, I think he chose to give it up. I think he chose to keep you instead."

Thoughts slid behind Lela's eyes that Béatrix didn't understand. Gradually, her words sank in. Philip had chosen her. She began to cry again, choked, involuntary sobs. She hid her face in Lela's shoulder and held on tight. "What if I'm not worth it? What if he ends up being sorry?"

"Oh, Bea." Lela kissed her hair, then her cheek, and finally the quivering softness of her mouth. The kiss tasted of wine and tears. For a moment, Bea accepted it, wanting that sweet stroke of tongues, that friend's tenderness. *Sometimes it's the only way you can show how much you love someone,* Lela had said. And maybe sometimes it was the only way you could prove how lovable someone was.

But Béatrix couldn't accept this proof. Not anymore. Philip trusted her, and kissing Lela was not the same as sharing the young Italian. This was not a stranger who would disappear at the end of the day. As gently as she could, she pushed back from Lela's hold.

Lela turned her head away and pressed one fist to her mouth as if holding something in. Worried, Béatrix touched her shoulder. When Lela turned back, her eyes were rimmed in red.

"Simon Graves is the man I've been seeing," she said.

"The one I thought was special. I didn't know he was planning to do this. I think he used me to get information on Meilleurs Amis. I was feeling betrayed. I wanted . . . I wanted to touch someone who really loved me. But I shouldn't have kissed you like that. I never will again, Bea. Never. Your friendship means too much to me." She clenched her hand in front of her mouth again, fighting tears. "If I lose you, I think I'll die."

Béatrix knew then, really knew, how important she was to Lela, her more beautiful, more glamorous, more charming friend. A part of her was savagely, childishly pleased, but another—the grown-up part, the part Philip called from her—knew her friend needed help.

She cupped Lela's face the way Philip would have cupped hers. "You won't lose me. I'll always be your friend. And if I did like girls, you're the only one I'd sleep with. Assuming I wouldn't be cheating on Philip."

"Well, that's something," said Lela, with her old ironic smile.

"Not that I'd want you on the rebound," Bea added.

Lela rolled her eyes at her lame attempt at humor, then sobered. She toyed with the rim of her glass. "He really fooled me, Bea. I really thought he cared."

"Maybe he did care. Maybe he just couldn't find a way to explain."

Lela shook her head. "He lied to me, like all the others. I could never trust him now."

Béatrix had never heard Lela sound so defeated. This Graves character had something to answer for, quite a few somethings!

.   .   .

THAT EVENING PHILIP called her to his office and told her about Simon's offer. He seemed stunned with relief, his body made awkward by the turmoil of his emotions. He turned two stretched rubber bands between his fingers. "It might not be a bad thing. He seems a decent sort."

"For a corporate raider, you mean."

"Yes," he said, but didn't smile. He leaned forward across his desk, his weight resting on his forearms. "I know it will mean a big adjustment for everyone, but I think he's our best chance to preserve the company. At least I'll be there to look out for our people."

Béatrix knew he would. He was a better defender of others than he was of himself. Behind him, the office window yawned over the Paris night. Beside him, one small lamp shed a circle of light on a stack of transfer papers. As part owner, she'd be obliged to sign them, too.

"It's up to you," he said. "If you want to call it off and try for a better offer, we will."

She smiled at him, amused and touched by his deference. In the dim light, his hair shone like tarnished gold. He looked so young, younger than she did.

"You can't afford to leave it up to me," she said. "What if my decision hurt the company? You own the majority interest, Philip. You're the one who's been running Meilleurs Amis. Besides, we both know the chance for a better offer is slim."

He dropped the rubber bands and stared glumly at his nails. "I won't bully you into signing away your inheritance."

"Philip." She covered his hand. "I was born into this business. You've earned your place in it. You've earned my trust." His mouth pinched in protest, but she wouldn't let him run himself down. "You didn't ask Simon Graves to keep you on; he volunteered. If you can stand to work for him, I can stand to let you."

Philip sagged back in his chair and closed his eyes. The sigh he let out told her a lot about the weight he'd been carrying, not just recently, but for years. He turned his hand to clasp her own.

"I wouldn't mind being his employee," he said, eyes closed, head rocking from side to side.

"Then we'll do it," she said. "We'll sell."

First, however, Béatrix Clouet would beard the lion in his den.

SHE DRESSED CAREFULLY in her best Balenciaga suit and her finest Ferragamo shoes. Her curls were tamed into a thick chignon, and she'd painted her face with a subtle hand. Thus armored, she sauntered through the Sofitel's lobby as her mother would have, as fashion mogul and seductress, as businesswoman and siren. People stared as she passed, obviously wondering who she was and why she seemed important. The effect was so easily achieved she could have laughed. Power belonged to those who acted as if they had it.

Had her mother discovered that truth? Or had she believed power belonged to the woman with the longest claws?

But what Evangeline believed didn't matter. Bea had come into her own because, like Philip, she would defend to the death the people she loved. She exited the elevator and strode down a plush, silent hall. The door numbers were etched in brass. She knocked on 1217 and waited for her best friend's lover to appear.

He seemed unsurprised to see her, though she'd caught him in a brown silk dressing gown. He held the door wide.

"Come in," he said.

A laptop sat open on the dining room table, but other than that the suite seemed uninhabited. Pristine gray carpet stretched to beige-and-pink walls. No socks lay on the floor, no books, no souvenirs. She had a hard time imagining someone as flamboyant as Lela being attracted to this somber man. Or maybe not. His walk conveyed a sense of power, controlled power. His gaze, though fleeting, was intense.

She refused his offer of a drink.

He sat on a pale Art Deco couch, its back a fluid curve with bold black accents. He waited patiently while she prowled the supremely uninformative room.

"I suppose you're here to size me up," he said.

She was, but she didn't bother to admit it. She halted in front of a blurry portrait of the Eiffel Tower. Hack work. "Philip tells me your offer is generous."

Simon's weight shifted on the couch. "I wasn't in the mood to fight."

When she turned back to him, he'd crossed one ankle over his knee. The posture bared his hairy, muscular calf. More dark hair emerged from the V of silk at his neck. Without even trying, he radiated maleness. He seemed more than capable of physically overpowering a girl like Lela. Had he done so? Was this stone-faced brute the man who'd won, then broken her heart?

"I want to buy back 'The Big Sister,' " she said.

His brows rose. "The painting that's hanging at your headquarters?"

"Yes."

He smiled. "No."

"No?"

"No," he repeated just as calmly. "That painting is a Meilleurs Amis asset I'm particularly interested in acquiring." He twitched his robe back over his shin. "If it makes you feel any better, your fiancé did try to exclude it from our deal."

The floor quaked under her feet. "My fiancé?"

Simon's smile broadened. "He did mention he intended to marry you."

Béatrix sat, not realizing on what until Simon extracted a pile of contracts from beneath her hip.

"I'm sorry for spoiling the surprise," he said, his voice suddenly gentle. "And I'm sorry to be meeting you under these circumstances. I've been wanting to for some time, not only because I admire your work, but because someone who is dear to you is also dear to me."

He had hunkered down beside her chair, his face earnest and somehow shy. He could only mean Lela. This ultramasculine man would hardly refer to Andrew as someone "dear." But was he telling the truth?

"Your company needs me," he said, his hand resting warm on her arm. "I won't lie to you. If you sell to me, Meilleurs Amis will change. It won't be your grandmother's company any more, or your mother's, or even Philip Carmichael's. It will be bigger, more modern, less exclusive. But it won't be dead. Meilleurs Amis will live to see another hundred years."

The passion in his voice decided her.

"I won't sell you my interest," she said, enjoying for just one moment the way he stiffened. "I'll *trade* my interest for stock in Graves Incorporated."

His shoulders relaxed then, and his eyes gleamed. They truly were the windows to his soul. No other feature betrayed his feelings so keenly. She'd expected to please him, not to move him to the edge of tears. She found herself surprisingly glad she had.

"Thank you," he said, taking her hand between his own. "I appreciate your faith in me."

He seemed to be speaking of more than business. Did he love Lela? Was he hoping Béatrix would speak on his behalf? Was he even aware that Lela knew of his betrayal?

Wait, she cautioned herself before the questions could rush out. Wait and see how he conducts himself tomorrow.

Lela's heart was too precious to trust to an impulse.

Fourteen

SIMON DREAMED OF his father. They sat at the back of the old church in Setauket, the church of Simon's childhood. The air had a strange, aqueous shimmer—green and gold. It reminded him of sunlight bouncing off a lazy river. Though empty, the church was decorated for a wedding. A pale lavender runner stretched down the aisle, and the end of each pew trailed white satin ribbons and snowdrops: his father's favorite flower.

Howard Graves looked better than he had in years.

"You did the right thing," he said, his big hands pressed to his knees. "When you see a man stumble and you know you're the best one to help him up, well, you've just got to do it. Besides, your mother always did like shoes."

"Shoes?"

His father grinned. "Bet you never guessed I knew old Amalfi. Almost worked for Graves 'cept we couldn't afford him back then. Hah!" He slapped his thighs. "Couldn't compete with what old Sophie Clouet was giving away."

Simon didn't question the information. He was simply grateful for his father's company. He'd been working too hard lately. It was good just to sit, shoulder to shoulder, soaking up the peace.

"The altar's glowing," he said, pointing out the faint pearly radiance.

His father nodded. "Going to be a wedding."

"Yes," said Simon.

"Better catch the garter. If you drop it, your mother will never forgive you."

"Wouldn't want that," said Simon.

They sat for a while longer in companionable silence. Then his father braced his hands on his thighs and stood. "Come on, son. Let's take a walk up the aisle."

The nave was longer than it should have been, but Simon didn't mind. Dust motes spun through the sunlight as they passed. The air smelled of oranges and old wood. The lilac runner was soft beneath his feet. Bare feet, he saw. When they finally reached the end, the glow was so bright it enclosed them like a bubble.

"Nice," said his father, looking around in approval.

Simon touched the heap of snowdrops that spilled across the altar. Their petals were wet and cool. He saw now that the light was coming from them. "I thought these were hard to keep fresh."

"Not in this church," said his father.

Something tightened in Simon's chest, a slow presentiment.

"No," he said.

His father smiled at him, the seams in his face silvered by the glowing flowers. "Take care of your mother. And remember I'll always love you."

SIMON JOLTED UP in the hotel bed. His cheeks were wet. He wiped them on his palms and tried to calm his breathing. It was just past dawn. He touched the side of the bed where Lela would have slept if she'd come along, if he'd had the courage to ask her. The sheets were cool and smooth. He looked at the phone, then the bedside clock. He made a quick calculation. It was far too late to call New York.

He decided he'd call his father after today's meeting. And he'd call Lela, as well. A dream was just a dream, but if his subconscious was sending him a message, he'd be a fool to stop his ears.

A STILL-DISAPPROVING SECRETARY ushered Simon and his team to the stately conference room they'd met in the day before. They were offered coffee and croissants and left to admire the overwhelming decor. Simon tipped back in his chair and contemplated the gilded ceiling. Usually he enjoyed closing a deal, but today he wanted it over with. Today he wanted to go home.

Philip and his stepdaughter were the last to arrive.

Simon's stomach dropped when he saw who'd come in with them. Lela. Lela was here.

Lela knew.

Bastard, said her contemptuous stare.

Denials fought for exit from his throat. He hadn't done what she thought. He hadn't used her to betray her friends. Come to that, he hadn't hurt her friends. Meilleurs Amis would be better off because of him. Because of him, Meilleurs Amis would survive.

But the table was circled by accountants and lawyers, and the only pleas he could make were with his eyes. Lela's response was a lowering of her brows. She took the seat next to Philip and Bea, as far from him as she could get. She crossed her lissome arms. I'm with them, her posture said, and you can go to hell.

Sweat broke out under his arms. He blinked to clear his vision. He could barely follow the discussion, signing whatever papers Andrew slid in front of him. Lela. He had to talk to Lela. He had to make her understand. Not until he reached the last section of the contract did he realize both Bea and Philip were smiling at him. Bea's expression in particular seemed fond.

If they weren't angry at him, why was Lela?

Because you weren't honest with her, he told his foolish self. You put it off and you put it off, and now it's too damn late.

Dismal beyond belief, he watched Philip Carmichael sign the final line. The Englishman stood, graceful as a dancer. As he balanced his fingertips atop the sheaf of paper, a lock of gold hair fell over his noble brow. Simon had a feeling this beautiful young man never lied to the people he loved.

"Since we're in Paris," Philip said, "and since these negotiations were so much more pleasant than they might have been, I believe it's time to open the champagne."

The table laughed and applauded, but the merrymaking was cut short by a tap on the conference room door. The ill-tempered secretary ventured inside, looking for once more worried than disapproving.

"I'm sorry for interrupting," she said. "But there's an emergency call for *Monsieur* Graves. Line three."

Simon didn't wait for Philip to tell him he could take the call in his office. Hands gone icy, he grabbed the phone that sat beside the coffee carafe and punched the blinking line.

"Yes," he said, the word scraping his throat like sandpaper.

The voice that answered was his mother's. He closed his eyes. He knew even before she spoke that the news he'd feared had come.

BÉATRIX HAD NEVER seen anyone go as pale as Simon Graves. He looked positively spectral as he responded to the call, his voice sharp with what sounded like anger, though she suspected it was fear.

"How bad is it?" he said, knuckles clenched on the receiver, body turned slightly away from the room.

Everyone had fallen silent. Most looked down at their notes or hands. Only Lela and Bea and Andrew watched the ashen CEO. Bea doubted Simon noticed. His focus was entirely on his call. "Which hospital? Is he conscious?"

He paused, wincing, at the answer from the other end.

With the hand that didn't hold the phone, he rubbed the groove beneath his lower lip.

"Mom," he said, interrupting a burst of sound. "Call Aunt Grace and Uncle Pete. Have them wait with you in the hospital. I'll be there as soon as I can. I'll be on the next plane."

Like a sleepwalker, he set the phone back in its cradle and stared at them as if he couldn't think why they were there. His gaze, still blank, locked on Lela's. Gone was the plea Bea had seen there before. All that remained was his instinct to connect. Whether he knew it or not, this man was crazy for Béatrix's friend.

"I'm sorry," he said, voice dazed. "My father has had a stroke. I'm afraid I have to leave."

A murmur of sympathy ran around the room. Philip circled the table and gripped Simon's shoulder. "I'll have my secretary call the airlines for you. She'll get you on the next flight out."

At this Simon's chin shook, the tremor so like a boy's her heart went out to him.

"Yes," he said, stiffening his jaw. "That would be helpful."

As if Simon were an invalid, Philip and Andrew led him from the room, one bolstering either side. Béatrix watched them go, then turned to Lela. Her friend's eyes glittered with hovering tears. She'd clasped her hands like a girl at prayer.

"His father," she whispered. "He adores that man."

Bea laid her hand over Lela's. "You could go with him. He might need your support."

"He wouldn't want me to."

Bea didn't believe that. Bea thought Simon would want

her more than anyone. "He does love you. I could see it in his eyes the moment you walked in."

"I wish that were true," Lela said, and shook her head as if wishing were a crime.

LELA SPENT A fortune on the cab from JFK. Not that it mattered, considering she'd just paid full fare for the last-minute flight from Paris. She was lucky the machine hadn't spit out her credit card.

The taxi rolled to a halt in front of the low, landscaped stretch of a private clinic. Idiot, she thought for the hundredth time. Simon didn't want her here. Simon didn't love her. Even if he did, this was a family crisis. Family. Lela had no part in that.

Most of all, though, she cursed the hour she'd wasted pacing Bea's apartment, fighting the urge to throw herself in Simon's wake. She could have been here already. This could have been over with.

"This is it," said the cabbie.

Reluctantly, knees wobbling, Lela paid him and got out. She was groggy from the long, sleepless flight, from the double time change and the fear of what she'd face. A hysterical laugh pushed up beneath her breast. She'd just spent the last of her cash. If Simon didn't want her here, she'd have to walk to Brooklyn Heights.

Pushing away the thought, she slammed the door behind her.

"Good luck," said the cabbie, with a kindness that pricked her eyes.

Unable to speak, she nodded and headed up the smooth, flower-bordered walk. Inside, the clinic was as fancy as some hotels, with antique gold walls and floors so polished she could see her reflection in the marble squares. Only the smell marked it as a hospital: a combination of antiseptic and anxiety. The crisply dressed nurse behind the reception desk directed her toward the appropriate wing.

"You won't be able to see him," she warned. "Only immediate family can do that."

"I understand," Lela said, her voice rusty to her ears.

The waiting area was lined with flourishing green plants and bland modern art. Lela recognized Simon's mother from the back. She was speaking to a tall, white-haired couple. The aunt and uncle, Lela presumed. Simon was nowhere in sight. Lela's heart thumped in her chest. She didn't know if his absence made it easier or harder to approach the intimate group. She'd tidied herself as well as she could in the airplane bathroom, but suddenly she felt a grubby wreck. An interloper. An orphan no one would adopt.

Stop it, she ordered, as angry at herself as she'd ever been in her life. This wasn't about her. If the Graves's wanted her to stay, she'd stay. If they didn't, she'd hitch her way home. End of story.

That resolved, she clenched her hands and approached Simon's mother.

The older couple spotted her first. At a word from them, Tess Graves turned. Lela's breath caught in her throat. Tess's face was not the face of the woman who'd welcomed Lela to her home. Grief had ravaged it, and the knowledge of coming loss. She seemed startled to see her, perhaps unsure of who she was.

"Lela?" she said, hand to her naked mouth. "Oh! My dear. How kind of you to come."

"I'm sorry," she said, the words barely coming out. "I don't meant to intrude."

"Nonsense," Tess demurred. Before Lela knew it, she was wrapped in Tess's arms. Though her hold trembled, it was strong. "Simon will be so glad. He'll be so very, very glad."

She pushed Lela back and wiped her cheeks.

"Silly," she said. "I know Howard's in a better place. And I know one day we'll be together again."

Lela swallowed. "Mr. Graves is gone?"

Tess dabbed her nose, then made an impatient gesture with the tissue. "It's just the machines keeping him going. Simon is saying good-bye, and then we'll give the doctors permission to turn them off." She smiled at Lela, eyes bright as diamonds. "I'm so glad you're here. I won't worry about him now."

Lela looked at her shoes. "I'm not sure Simon will want to see me."

Tess surprised her with a breathy laugh. "I wouldn't worry about that, dear. We've all guessed how Simon feels. Now, come sit." She took Lela's arm and led her to a circle of dark green chairs. "Simon could be a while. He's never had an easy time letting go." She laughed again, a memory taking her. "Do you know, the night we brought him home, Simon refused to release my husband's hand. He was five then. Hair like a scrub brush, pitch black, and the biggest eyes I'd ever seen. I suppose he thought Howard would disappear if he didn't keep a good grip on him. I had the devil of a time serving dinner—and never mind getting that boy through his bath! Howard was so patient. He held Simon's hand till he fell asleep, then made sure he was sitting by his bed first thing in the morning. They adored each other, those two. Love at first sight."

"He loves you, too," Lela said. "You're the woman all the others have to live up to."

Tess dabbed her eyes and smiled. "Yes, but he's a papa's boy. Always has been, God bless him. This will be hard on him. I hope you have a good deal of patience yourself."

"For him I do," she said, and Tess patted her knee. The truth of the promise caught her by surprise. Even if Simon didn't love her, even if he only needed her, she would stick by him through this. Lela loved him, and maybe she could ease his pain. For now, that was all she had to know.

LELA HAD FORGOTTEN about Andrew until he rounded the corner carrying a boxed quartet of Starbucks coffee. His feet shuffled to a halt.

"Lela," he said, nearly staring his eyes out of his head.

Under different circumstances, the reaction would have been comical.

"I bought this down the street," he said, as if she were entitled to an explanation of his presence. "Here." He thrust one cup at her. "Double latte with cinnamon."

"That's yours," she said, aware that Tess and the others were gazing curiously at their exchange.

"Please," he said. "I don't need it. I only got it because—"

"Because you're a nice man," Tess finished, rescuing him. She took the coffee from his hand and placed it in Lela's. "Why don't you two young people take a walk in the garden? We can see you from the window. We'll call you if we need anything."

Tess's gentle suggestion may as well have been an order. Lela felt both dismissed and reprieved, and utterly incapable of defying the request. She followed Andrew out a side door onto the sunny grounds.

Green grass, bright as poison, stretched to a small parking lot. Flower beds snaked through the perfectly groomed expanse: azaleas, tulips, and one small weeping willow. Without discussion, she and Andrew headed for the patch of shade.

When they reached it, Andrew rested his back on the twisting trunk. He seemed awkward, not the same man who'd slept with her many times, who'd been a friend of sorts. He didn't even seem the man who'd sat at Simon's right hand. Something had stolen his glow.

Lela wondered if, in his grief, Simon had pushed his right hand away.

"I'm glad Tess did that," he said. "Ever since I saw your face at the meeting, I knew I needed to talk to you."

"Did you?" Lela squinted through the glowing leaves. She was not feeling kindly toward him. The anger she'd resolved to turn from Simon moved restlessly inside her, searching for a target. Andrew would do, she thought. Andrew would do very well.

"Yes," he said, and cleared his throat. "I want you to know it was my idea to buy Meilleurs Amis, not Simon's. I know he was helping you at the New York boutique, but he never shared anything that passed between you with the acquisitions team. We did our own research. Simon never broke your confidence."

"Maybe not, but he also never told me what he was planning." She hadn't meant to say the words, but she didn't take them back. They were true. Shoulders tight, she lobbed the untouched coffee into a trash receptacle. Metal clanged as it hit. Simon hadn't told her. And he should have. She wasn't a casual acquaintance. She was his lover. He knew what Bea meant to her. He should have told her what was going on.

Andrew scuffed his loafer through the grass. "If you'd been in Simon's shoes, would you have risked telling him?"

"Yes," she said.

Andrew's expression called her on the lie. She turned away, angry because she couldn't deny it and because she didn't want to be angry at all. She crossed her arms and watched a delivery van roll out of the parking lot. NEW YORK FLOWERS, it said, in cheery blue and white. Her temper snapped.

"What about you?" she said. "You sat at Philip's table. You broke bread with him. You slept with his stepdaughter. And then, like any decent human being, you said to yourself: I think I'll get my boss to take over their business. And all to impress a man you've got a crush on."

"I do not have a—"

"You do!" She rounded on him. "You do, damn you. I could hear it in your voice every time you said his name. You wanted me to sleep with him only because you couldn't do it yourself!"

More than the heat reddened Andrew's face.

"I admire Simon Graves," he said, every muscle stiff. "I love him like the father I never had."

That was all he had to say. The lightning burst of fury drained away. She understood the longing for absent family, for a spur to cling to in the sea. That he was lying to himself didn't matter. She could not force him to face his feelings, not if it meant destroying his closest human tie. When it came right down to it, she didn't have the heart.

"Why are you defending him to me?" she said instead. "I'd think you'd be happy to see my back."

"But he loves you."

For Andrew this was reason enough. Whatever Simon wanted, Andrew would do his best to provide. His devotion was that deep—and that dangerous. There lay the difference between them. Lela would not hurt a friend for Simon's sake. Lela loved him, but her love made her want to be a better person, not a worse one.

"Don't give Simon your soul," she said. "He wouldn't want that from you."

Andrew blinked at her. She didn't know if he understood, if he *could* understand. She sighed and patted his arm. "I'm going back inside. I want to wait for Simon."

He didn't follow. He stood in the shadow of the rustling leaves, lean and tall and lonely. She discovered it was a deeper punishment than she wished to inflict.

Unable to sit still, Lela walked the shining corridor. How did you say good-bye to someone you'd loved since you were five? Lela didn't even know anyone she'd known when she was five. Those people existed somewhere—social workers, foster families—but her ties to them had been severed long ago.

How did you tell a doctor you were ready for him to shut off the machines that were keeping your father alive?

She turned at the murky portrait of the clinic's founder and strode the other way. Halfway down the hall, a door opened. Simon stepped out and shut it carefully behind him, as if the person who lay inside could be disturbed.

He paused, head down, hand resting on the knob. Then he looked up. His eyes met hers as if he'd known where she stood. His lips formed her name.

She'd never seen such shadows in his face, nor felt such a deep, visceral tug at her being. She walked to him, because he couldn't seem to move, and took him in her arms. Though he was taller and larger than she was he bent to her as if they were the same. His embrace squeezed the breath from her.

"Lela," he whispered. "He's gone."

She had no words for this. She held him, rubbed his back, kissed the shell of his ear. His breath hitched. He turned his head and sealed his mouth over hers. She didn't resist, not when his tongue sought hers, not when his tears ran down her cheeks, not when the press of his sex changed from soft to hard against her belly.

Abruptly, he pushed away, looked away, though one of his hands reached blindly for hers.

"You're staying, aren't you?" he said, wiping his cheeks with the same impatience his mother had shown.

"Yes, I'm staying."

He faced her again, more composed. "Lela, there's so much I want to explain. About Meilleurs Amis. About us."

Lela smiled and shrugged one shoulder. None of that mattered. Even if Andrew hadn't spoken to her, she couldn't have held her anger now. "You said you loved me. You said I mustn't forget, no matter what. I haven't."

His eyes searched hers. "I want to take you home. I want to spend the night with you."

"I think you'll have to, big guy. I blew the last of my bankroll on the cab."

He smiled at that and clasped her face between his palms. "I doubt I'll be good company."

"You don't have to be, honey. You just have to be near."

For a second he closed his eyes. "Come on," he said, wrapping her waist within his arm. "Let's go tell my mother I'm done."

WHEN HE'D SAID he wanted to spend the night with her, Simon had been thinking of Lela's apartment, of the air and space and the comfortable nest of a bed in her loft. The urge to curl up with her there had been illogical, of course. He could not leave his mother. Emotional issues aside, they had a service to plan and literally hundreds of people to call. The press would have to be notified, and the members of the board. As kind as they were, Aunt Grace and Uncle Pete couldn't handle all that.

So they returned to the house on the North Shore. Once there, Simon meant to look after Lela, he really did, but his mind could focus on nothing but the logistics of what they had to arrange. Even that required the occasional prompt. His mind wandered from the simplest task, not to his father, but to a gray, foggy numbness. Through all of it, Andrew was a rock. Simon hadn't wanted his company on the plane; he'd been a reminder of the misstep he thought had cost him Lela's love. He'd snapped at him on the flight, then refused to speak, a childish response that Andrew seemed to forgive as easily as breathing.

He was kinder than Simon deserved, as was Lela.

She brought sandwiches to the library where he and

Andrew worked through their lists of things to do. He was dimly aware that she and his mother were cooking. He heard the pots rattling and smelled the smells. At one point, he gave her the keys to his car, but for what he didn't know. When she coaxed them to the dinner table, he went. Though he barely tasted what he put in his mouth, the food calmed the tremor in his hands. Then he made another round of calls.

He wearied of saying the words. My father has died. Howard Graves, founder of Graves Incorporated, has passed away. When they finished for the night, he ached as if he'd spent the day digging ditches. He went in to see his mother, kissed her, and plodded down the silent hall toward the guest room his parents always saved for his use.

Andrew, wearing a white T-shirt and bright red boxers, stopped him at the corner. Simon and Andrew had traveled together many times, but suddenly it seemed strange to see him undressed. If a suit was a kind of armor, Andrew's was gone.

"Do you need something?" Simon asked. "Did Aunt Grace find you a room?"

"Yes," he said. "I just— Is your mama all right?"

"As all right as she can be."

Andrew nodded and chewed his lower lip. Obviously, Tess's well-being wasn't the only thing on his mind.

Simon put a hand on his shoulder. "What is it? What's bothering you?"

In the moment before he looked down, Andrew's eyes were tortured. "Do you want my resignation?"

"Your resignation! What the hell for?"

"For my part in the takeover."

Simon tried to shake the cobwebs from his brain. "You told me you and Acquisitions played it straight. No dirty tricks. That wasn't a lie, was it?"

"No."

"Then I don't want your resignation."

"But Lela—"

"Lela is not such a child that she needs a scapegoat for my actions. Nor am I." Andrew still looked forlorn. Simon gripped the side of the younger man's neck, feeling eerily like his father. "I made my own choices, Andrew, and I'll clean up my own mistakes. Besides, how could I get on without you? You're my right hand. And my friend. I need you to stick around."

Andrew nodded and swallowed. He straightened his shoulders. "I'm here for you, Simon. Always."

"Good." Simon slapped his arm. When Andrew walked away, he stood and watched him, an unaccustomed awareness nagging at his mind. He needs someone, he thought. Someone of his own. He tapped his lips. He knew a number of women who had crushes on the handsome southerner: secretaries, vice presidents, the night guard in New Orleans. If Simon had noticed that many, there were probably dozens more. Surely one of these people could be more than a plaything to Andrew, if Andrew could be coaxed into letting them.

He frowned and rubbed his nose. Maybe it was ridiculous to imagine he could play matchmaker, but today had brought home just how much he owed the man. If nothing else, Andrew had thrown Simon and Lela together. Yes, their relationship was shaky, but it might have been far worse. With all his charm, Andrew could have made Lela fall in love with him.

． ． ．

THE GUEST ROOM was furnished in navy and green plaid, in honor of some Scots ancestor Simon had never known. Far lovelier than the bagpipe that hung from the wall was the sight of Lela sitting up in the double bed. One of his old shirts, with an ink stain on the collar, covered her slender form. As soon as she saw him, her face pinched with worry.

"Oh," she said, scrambling to her knees. "Come here, honey. Come here."

This was a welcome he hadn't dared hope for. He let her undress him, let her baby him. His blood warmed. He hadn't thought himself capable, but he began to want her. His head fell back, too heavy to hold upright, as she caressed his torso with her hands. Shirt gone, she dragged his trousers down his legs and pulled off his shoes. She was on her knees before him. A pulse beat over his skin, from scalp to toes. His cock was more than half hard. He wanted to hold her, but he couldn't seem to move.

"It's all right," she murmured, nuzzling the hang of his balls. "Let Lela make it feel all right."

She slipped the tip of his cock into her mouth, plucking him there, just there, before sliding extravagantly down. Simon groaned at the soft, sucking pull. Was anything kinder than the warm, wet stroke of a woman's tongue? Heat poured through his thighs. She rubbed the back of his legs as she rose and fell, spreading the tingle of pleasure where she touched.

In minutes, his cock felt full enough to burst.

"Stand up," he said, roused from his stupor. "I need to kiss you."

Too impatient to wait, he lifted her by her wrists. She twined them behind his neck. A flush of arousal warmed her face. He pulled her to him. He opened her mouth with his own. The taste of her was sweet. She writhed against him and climbed his leg. She was naked beneath the old shirt, wet against his thigh, soft beneath his hands. He squeezed the tight curve of her bottom and earned a heated gush as his reward.

"Take me, Simon," she said. "Make love to me."

The words were a lick of fire. He laid her back on the bed and unbuttoned the cotton shirt. Within its frame, her body was perfect living silk. She called him to explore, to savor each blush and sigh. Obeying the urge, he traced the sweet spots under her ribs. He licked the delicate skin at the bend of her arm. He teased her clit with his finger and drew on her breasts with his tongue. Her body arched with want. The knowledge that he could please her inspired a soul-deep satisfaction.

My hand stirs her shiver, he thought. My kiss is the reason for her moan.

"Ready?" he said, the question deepened by desire. He knew the answer even before he slid his finger into her sheath.

"Yes," she sighed, spine rolling. "Yes."

Their eyes met as he hung above her. Gold streaked the blue of her irises, framed the gleaming circles of jet. He could see his own reflection in her pupils, tiny but clear. For the first time in his life, he marveled at the deeper meaning of this act. This was more than an exchange of pleasure, more even than an exchange of love. This was the joining of two separate beings into one. He wanted her to help. He wanted her to make it happen.

"Put me inside you," he said. "Take me in your hand and draw me in."

She grasped his shaft, the touch causing him to jump. She laughed, breathlessly, and set his swollen glans against her flesh. Past the first quivering ring of resistance she pulled him. Her muscles clung to the skin beneath his ridge. Then she removed her hand.

"Your turn," she said, all honey and half-closed eyes.

Simon set his knees. Her hair had spilled across the tartan pillowcase, dark against the blue and green. He speared its silk with his fingers, sucked in a breath and pushed. In he slid, in, until their hips and their groins met, and a sheet of paper could not have fit between them. Her warmth throbbed around him, inside him. She locked one leg behind his buttock and stretched the other straight. The fit was so sweet, he couldn't bear to pull back.

"I'm staying here," he growled, hand clamping around her bottom. "I'm staying right here until you come."

She did not argue. Her eyes slid shut, and her neck arched with pleasure. They ground together, bodies struggling for the closest friction they could get.

Rock by rock, his climax rose from deep inside him. Her contractions pulled it upward, the circling of her pubis, the press of her womb against his glans. The peak was a slow gathering of sensation, a dark ache of need. He could not hurry it. He could only gasp and strain and know she did the same.

"Closer," she urged, wrapping him with her other leg.

Her pussy tugged him like a fist. He ground his teeth and pressed his forehead to her own. He was hurting close, desperately close. He tightened his inner muscles the way she had, needing this release as he'd never needed any in his life.

They were panting in unison, trembling. She slid one hand between them, over his chest. Her nails raked his hair. His skin tingled. His pubis ached like heaven and hell. She drew a winding coil around his nipples.

"Now?" she whispered.

He could only grunt in answer. He wanted to shove his whole body inside her. He wanted them both to go up in flames. He strove a fraction deeper, rubbing, reaching.

"Oh, God," she groaned, and pinched his puckered nipple.

He needed no more provocation. A moan wrenched from him, a throb of pleasure-pain, a gush of hot relief. A second later, she shuddered out her pleasure, silent but intense.

As good as it was, the release did not relax him. His body wanted the impossible. His body wanted more. As if she sensed this, she pushed his weight upward and rolled them to their sides. Crooking her leg over his, she began a gentle thrusting, not enough to unlink them, but enough to encourage his flagging sex. With its resurgence, his tension eased.

Her smile was a teasing curve against his neck. "Shall we stay like this all night?"

"All year," he said, and hugged her close. What a miracle she was: to forgive him; to love him, despite his foibles and his flaws. He didn't know how he would have faced his father's death without her. The emotion that welled inside him was too huge to contain.

"Until I met you," he said, "I didn't know how lonely I was."

She pulled back and gazed at him. "Oh, Simon, until I met you, I didn't know how much love my heart could hold."

They both sniffed at the same time. Simon laughed. "Jesus, what a pair of saps."

Lela's fist punched his chest. "It's not sappy, it's nice. And you can't tell me you don't like to hear me say it."

"I do like it," he admitted. "And I love you."

Suddenly she was quiet. She hid her face against his chest and drew a shaky breath. "Be my family," she said, low and shy. "Be my home."

His heart tightened at her bravery. He knew what those words meant to her. He knew what they meant to him. The gratification he felt was fierce. She asked him to be his home: no one else, him.

"I will, Lela," he said. "For as long as you'll have me, I will."

Lela hoped he knew just how long that was.

IN THE ABANDONED conference room, Philip lifted a champagne bottle from a half-melted bucket of ice. Bea watched him from her seat on the edge of the table. She wore a patient half smile he'd never seen on her before. He found it disconcerting, even troubling. Now of all times he wanted to be able to read her. He let the magnum sink back into the slush.

"Well," he said, his voice too loud. "More for us."

Bea rubbed his shirtsleeve. "I doubt you want to celebrate any more than I do."

"No." He played with the foil that sheathed the cork. "It's odd. I'll still be here, still be doing most of the job I did before, but everything's changed. Ultimately, the weight won't be on me."

"And you'll miss that?"

"Maybe a little."

She scooted around until she caught his knees between her own, then gathered his hands together and kissed their knuckles. "You'll have new challenges. The expansion into Graves Department Stores should be exciting. I wouldn't mind helping with that myself."

He smiled down at her. "I'm not used to you comforting me."

She blushed, but the line of her jaw was firm. "You have to stop thinking of me as someone you need to take care of."

"I know. I'm just afraid you'll think less of me for this. I can't help feeling I've failed you."

"Failed me!" She seemed genuinely taken aback by this assessment. "Philip. You made a hard decision, and you made the best of it you could. You got more from Simon Graves than I thought possible. I suspect he'll be pleasantly surprised when he discovers what a prize he won in you."

"But—"

"But nothing." She braced his shoulders and forced him to look at her. "Some people make better captains than generals. There's no shame in that."

"But wouldn't you rather have a general?"

Her laugh was rich and full.

"*Mais non*," she teased. "I'd rather have you."

For a moment, he bridled. He'd wanted her to see him as he wasn't. Instead, she loved him as he was. With a rueful grin, he pulled the clip from her hair and watched her curls tumble wildly over her shoulders. This was how he'd always wanted to see her: happy and confident and full of life. He brushed the trio of freckles beside her mouth.

"Bea," he said, heart thundering in his chest. "Will you marry me?"

She crossed her hands over her breast, a spontaneous gesture of joy. "Philip!"

He laughed. "Is that a yes?"

She flung her arms around him. "*Oui, mon capitaine!*"

Fortunately, he was too busy kissing her to mind her little joke.

London

Fifteen

IF THE WEDDING had taken place in Paris, it would have been an event. In the pretty Gothic church in Blackheath, it escaped the notice of all but the nosiest residents, most of whom had been invited. Philip's parents had lived in this picturesque village since their retirement, though their cockney accents were still as thick as London fog.

They'd welcomed Lela into their home, all sweetness and bustle, as if Lela were Bea's sister instead of her friend. She had only to think of wanting a thing to be offered it. Sensing her anxiety, they made sure Simon had a seat up front where she could see him.

But even his encouraging grin couldn't calm her butterflies.

Lela Turner had never been a bridesmaid. She'd never stood at the front of a church while hundreds of strangers smiled at her and nodded. But she was a manager now, officially, since last week, a woman of responsibility. She wasn't going to lose her nerve over a few friendly stares.

Willing her stomach to stop fluttering, she smoothed the pale yellow column of her gown. The heavy silk slid like water beneath her fingers. She could hardly believe Philip had designed it. Bereft of flounces or ruffles or other horrifying "improvements," the dress made her feel like a duchess. The cut was elegant: modest but sexy, too, like something Audrey Hepburn would have worn. She could almost hear Simon's gears turning as he watched her stroke the shimmering cloth. She hadn't dropped a single hint, just cooed over the fit and the style and the flow of the skirt around her legs. But she knew what he was thinking.

This man ought to be designing for Graves.

And maybe he would. Maybe, with Simon egging him on, Philip would revisit his old dream, his first dream. Lela certainly didn't intend for any other store to get their grubby paws on Philip's gowns. She smiled at her proprietary fervor. She wasn't losing a friend today, she was gaining an honorary brother. One more person to love. One more person to look out for.

At least, that's what she'd be getting if Bea ever dragged her butt up this aisle. They'd entered the vestibule together, but Bea had turned back with a harried exclamation that she'd forgotten something she simply had to have. Now poor Philip gnawed the side of his thumb and grew whiter by the second.

"She'll be here," Lela hissed, wanting him not to faint.

Philip's older sister jostled his elbow and tittered. Fortunately, no one could hear her over the organ. Philip's uncle Eustace, stone deaf and commensurately loud, was pumping away as if he meant to wake the very angels on their clouds.

And then, a miracle happened. Bea appeared at the entrance just as Uncle Eustace segued into an astonishingly lilting version of "Jerusalem." Ears ringing in the sudden hush, Lela pressed her hands together in front of her bosom. Bea looked so beautiful she barely saw the gorgeous gown. Behind the veil of Irish lace, her face glowed with happiness, cheeks pink, eyes bright. As everyone turned in the pews, a hum of admiration swept through the church. Lela's heart thumped with pride.

This was more exciting than getting the keys to Meilleurs Amis. This was the start of a whole new life.

BEA PAUSED AT the end of the pale pink runner and wished for just one moment that she had someone to give her away. If she'd been marrying anyone else, she imagined Philip would have done the deed. The elder Mr. Carmichael, as kind as his son, had offered to escort her, but she'd decided to walk alone. I give myself away, she thought, with all my heart and soul.

And so she rustled down the aisle in a froth of cream-colored satin, feeling ridiculously Cinderella-ish as she advanced toward her prince. The sight of him in his white tie and tails was enough to make her knees wobble—until she noticed his pallid face. She hadn't meant to scare him, but she'd forgotten Andrew's snowdrop bouquet, the one he'd sent in a special cold-pack box, along with a touching request for her forgiveness. Philip was a lucky man, he wrote, almost good enough to deserve her. She hadn't known the flirtatious American could be so humble. She wished now that she'd invited him, despite his not being on Philip's list of favorite people. Whatever else he'd done, Andrew had been a kind lover, one of her nicest. Maybe someday they'd find a way to be friends. For now, at the least, she would carry his flowers.

As soon as she was close enough, she shook them at Philip in explanation. "Couldn't find my bouquet."

Back in the first pew, Simon Graves uttered some expostulation she couldn't understand. When she looked at him, however, he merely beamed and shook his head.

Philip was not so calm. He pulled out his handkerchief to wipe his brow. Almost as one, the congregation laughed.

"Well," said the vicar, not to be outdone. "We *finally* come together in the presence of God."

The rest of the ceremony was no more typical. Philip, who'd never called her anything but Bea, stumbled over her proper name. His six-year-old nephew dropped the ring and had to chase it halfway across the church. And when her new husband treated her to what seemed like a perfectly nice nuptial kiss, Lela said in her best Bronx drawl, "C'mon, Phil. You can do betta than that."

He could, of course, and he did, bending her tango-style over his arm.

"I love you," he said, when at last he let her breathe.

"*Je t'aime pour toujours,*" she responded, the English not enough to bare her heart. "Forever, *mon amour.*"

"*Toujours,*" he agreed, and threw his head back on a laugh. It seemed a good way to start a marriage.

Slowly, with countless hugs and kisses and slaps on the back, the bridal party made its way outside. There, a surprise awaited: a gaggle of reporters with microphones at the ready.

"Damn," said Philip, shielding his eyes as a half-dozen flashbulbs exploded at once. "I thought we'd given them the slip."

"Is it true you and Simon Graves have buried the hatchet?" they called, and "How do you think your mother would feel about this marriage, Ms. Clouet?"

"Bastards," Philip muttered.

Béatrix couldn't be upset, not with his arm in hers and his kiss still tingling on her lips. She patted his lapel. "You know what Grandma Sophie would say. Better to be infamous than ignored."

Behind them, Simon snorted. "Better the love of your beloved than the admiration of the world."

They all gaped to hear the CEO wax so poetic. Lela and Bea exchanged glances, brows wagging with amusement.

"Well, it's true," he huffed as color washed his rugged cheeks.

Bea didn't say a word. She didn't have to. She knew as surely as if Simon had announced it that her friend would soon share all her joy and hope—and not just in spirit. Simon would make the home for her she'd never had. She reached between the men and squeezed Lela's hand.

No other present could have pleased her more.